THE HOUSEMAID

BOOKS BY FREIDA MCFADDEN

The Housemaid Series

The Housemaid

The Housemaid's Secret

"The Housemaid's Wedding: A Short Story"

The Housemaid Is Watching

Standalone Thrillers

Dear Debbie

The Intruder

The Tenant

The Crash

The Boyfriend

The Teacher

The Coworker

Ward D

Never Lie

The Inmate

Do You Remember?

Do Not Disturb

The Locked Door

Want to Know a Secret

One by One

The Wife Upstairs

The Perfect Son

The Ex

The Surrogate Mother

Brain Damage

Dead Med

Women's Fiction

The Devil Wears Scrubs

The Devil You Know

Baby City

Short Stories

"The Gift"

"The Widow's Husband's Secret Lie"

"Death Row"

THE HOUSEMAID

FREIDA McFADDEN

NEW YORK BOSTON

Grand Central Publishing
Hachette Book Group
1290 Avenue of the Americas, New York, NY 10104
grandcentralpublishing.com
twitter.com/grandcentralpub

Originally published by Bookouture, an imprint of Storyfire Ltd., in 2022
First Grand Central Publishing edition: August 2022

Grand Central Publishing is a division of Hachette Book Group, Inc. The Grand Central Publishing name and logo is a trademark of Hachette Book Group, Inc.

The publisher is not responsible for websites (or their content) that are not owned by the publisher.

The Hachette Speakers Bureau provides a wide range of authors for speaking events. To find out more, go to www.hachettespeakersbureau.com or call (866) 376-6591.

Library of Congress Control Number: 2022943661

ISBN: 9781538742570 (trade paperback)

Printed in the United States of America

LSC-H

10 9 8 7 6 5 4 3 2 1

PROLOGUE

If I leave this house, it will be in handcuffs.

I should have run for it while I had the chance. Now my shot is gone. Now that the police officers are in the house and they've discovered what's upstairs, there's no turning back.

They are about five seconds away from reading me my rights. I'm not sure why they haven't done it yet. Maybe they're hoping to trick me into telling them something I shouldn't.

Good luck with that.

The cop with the black hair threaded with gray is sitting on the sofa next to me. He shifts his stocky frame on the burnt-caramel Italian leather. I wonder what sort of sofa he has at home. It sure doesn't cost five figures like this one did. It's probably some tacky color like *orange*, covered in pet fur, and with more than one rip in the seams. I wonder if he's thinking about his sofa at home and wishing he had one like this.

Or more likely, he's thinking about the dead body in the attic upstairs.

"So let's go through this one more time," the cop says in his New York drawl. He told me his name earlier, but it flew out of my head. Police officers should wear bright red nametags. How else are you possibly supposed to remember their names in a high-stress situation? He's a detective, I think. "When did you find the body?"

I pause, wondering if this would be the right time to demand a lawyer. Aren't they supposed to offer me one? I am rusty on this protocol.

"About an hour ago," I answer.

"Why did you go up there in the first place?"

I press my lips together. "I told you. I heard a sound."

"And...?"

The officer leans forward, his eyes wide. He has a rough stubble on his chin, like he might've skipped shaving this morning. His tongue protrudes slightly from between his lips. I'm not stupid—I know exactly what he wants me to say.

I did it. I'm guilty. Take me away.

Instead, I lean back against the sofa. "That's it. That's everything I know."

Disappointment washes over the detective's face. He works his jaw as he thinks over the evidence that has been found so far in this house. He's wondering if he's got enough to snap those cuffs on my wrists yet. He isn't sure. If he were sure, he would have done it already.

"Hey, Connors!"

It's the voice of another officer. We break eye contact and I look up at the top of the staircase. The other, much younger cop is standing there, his long fingers clutching the top of the banister. His unlined face is pale.

"Connors," the younger officer says. "You gotta come up here—*now*. You gotta see what's up here." Even from the bottom of the stairs, I can see his Adam's apple bobbing. "You won't believe it."

PART I

THREE MONTHS EARLIER

ONE

MILLIE

"Tell me about yourself, Millie."

Nina Winchester leans forward on her caramel-colored leather sofa, her legs crossed to reveal just the slightest hint of her knees peeking out under her silky white skirt. I don't know much about labels, but it's obvious everything Nina Winchester is wearing is painfully expensive. Her cream blouse makes me long to reach out to feel the material, even though a move like that would mean I'd have no chance of getting hired.

To be fair, I have no chance of getting hired anyway.

"Well..." I begin, choosing my words carefully. Even after all the rejections, I still try. "I grew up in Brooklyn. I've had a lot of jobs doing housework for people, as you can see from my resume." My *carefully doctored* resume. "And I love children. And also..." I glance around the room, looking for a doggy chew toy or a cat litter box. "I love pets as well?"

The online ad for the housekeeper job didn't mention pets. But better to be safe. Who doesn't appreciate an animal lover?

"Brooklyn!" Mrs. Winchester beams at me. "I grew up in Brooklyn, too. We're practically neighbors!"

"We are!" I confirm, even though nothing could be further

from the truth. There are plenty of coveted neighborhoods in Brooklyn where you'll fork over an arm and a leg for a tiny townhouse. That's not where I grew up. Nina Winchester and I couldn't be more different, but if she'd like to believe we're neighbors, then I'm only too happy to go along with it.

Mrs. Winchester tucks a strand of shiny, golden-blond hair behind her ear. Her hair is chin-length, cut into a fashionable bob that de-emphasizes her double chin. She's in her late thirties, and with a different hairstyle and different clothing, she would be very ordinary-looking. But she has used her considerable wealth to make the most of what she's got. I can't say I don't respect that.

I have gone the exact opposite direction with my appearance. I may be over ten years younger than the woman sitting across from me, but I don't want her to feel at all threatened by me. So for my interview, I selected a long, chunky wool skirt that I bought at the thrift store and a polyester white blouse with puffy sleeves. My dirty-blond hair is pulled back into a severe bun behind my head. I even purchased a pair of oversized and unnecessary tortoiseshell glasses that sit perched on my nose. I look professional and utterly unattractive.

"So the job," she says. "It will be mostly cleaning and some light cooking if you're up for it. Are you a good cook, Millie?"

"Yes, I am." My ease in the kitchen is the only thing on my resume that isn't a lie. "I'm an excellent cook."

Her pale blue eyes light up. "That's wonderful! Honestly, we almost never have a good home-cooked meal." She titters. "Who has the time?"

I bite back any kind of judgmental response. Nina Winchester doesn't work, she only has one child who's in school all day, and she's hiring somebody to do all her cleaning for her. I even saw a man in her enormous front yard doing her gardening for her. How is it possible she doesn't have time to cook a meal for her small family?

I shouldn't judge her. I don't know anything about what her life is like. Just because she's rich, it doesn't mean she's spoiled.

But if I had to bet a hundred bucks either way, I'd bet Nina Winchester is spoiled rotten.

"And we'll need occasional help with Cecelia as well," Mrs. Winchester says. "Perhaps taking her to her afternoon lessons or playdates. You have a car, don't you?"

I almost laugh at her question. Yes, I do have a car—it's *all* I have right now. My ten-year-old Nissan is stinking up the street in front of her house, and it's where I am currently living. Everything I own is in the trunk of that car. I have spent the last month sleeping in the backseat.

After a month of living in your car, you realize the importance of some of the little things in life. A toilet. A sink. Being able to straighten your legs out while you're sleeping. I miss that last one most of all.

"Yes, I have a car," I confirm.

"Excellent!" Mrs. Winchester claps her hands together. "I'll provide you with a car seat for Cecelia, of course. She just needs a booster seat. She's not quite at the weight and height level to be without the booster yet. The Academy of Pediatrics recommends..."

While Nina Winchester drones on about the exact height and weight requirements for car seats, I take a moment to glance around the living room. The furnishing is all ultra-modern, with the largest flat-screen television I've ever seen, which I'm sure is high definition and has surround-sound speakers built into every nook and cranny of the room for optimal listening experience. In the corner of the room is what appears to be a working fireplace, the mantle littered with photographs of the Winchesters on trips to every corner of the world. When I glance up, the insanely high ceiling glows under the light of a sparkling chandelier.

"Don't you think so, Millie?" Mrs. Winchester is saying.

I blink at her. I attempt to rewind my memory and figure out what she had just asked me. But it's gone. "Yes?" I say.

Whatever I agreed to has made her very happy. "I'm *so* pleased you think so too."

"Absolutely," I say more firmly this time.

She uncrosses and re-crosses her somewhat stocky legs. "And of course," she adds, "there's the matter of reimbursement for you. You saw the offer in my advertisement, right? Is that acceptable to you?"

I swallow. The number in the advertisement is more than acceptable. If I were a cartoon character, dollar signs would have appeared in each of my eyeballs when I read that advertisement. But the money almost stopped me from applying for the job. Nobody offering that much money, living in a house like this one, would ever consider hiring me.

"Yes," I choke out. "It's fine."

She arches an eyebrow. "And you know it's a live-in position, right?"

Is she asking me if I'm okay with leaving the splendor of the backseat of my Nissan? "Right. I know."

"Fabulous!" She tugs at the hem of her skirt and rises to her feet. "Would you like the grand tour then? See what you're getting yourself into?"

I stand up as well. In her heels, Mrs. Winchester is only a few inches taller than I am in my flats, but it feels like she's much taller. "Sounds great!"

She guides me through the house in painstaking detail, to the point where I'm worried I got the ad wrong and maybe she's a realtor thinking I'm ready to buy. It *is* a beautiful house. If I had four or five million dollars burning a hole in my pocket, I would snap it up. In addition to the ground level containing the gigantic living room and the newly renovated kitchen, the second floor of the house features the Winchesters' master bedroom, her daughter Cecelia's room, Mr. Winchester's home office, and a guest bedroom that could be straight out of the best hotel in Manhattan. She pauses dramatically in front of the subsequent door.

"And here is..." She flings the door open. "Our home theater!"

It's a legit movie theater *right inside their home*—in addition to the oversized television downstairs. This room has several rows of stadium seating, facing a floor-to-ceiling monitor. There's even a popcorn machine in the corner of the room.

After a moment, I notice Mrs. Winchester is looking at me, waiting for a response.

"Wow!" I say with what I hope is appropriate enthusiasm.

"Isn't it marvelous?" She shivers with delight. "And we have a full library of movies to choose from. Of course, we also have all the usual channels as well as streaming services."

"Of course," I say.

After we leave the room, we come to a final door at the end of the hallway. Nina pauses, her hand lingering on the doorknob.

"Would this be my room?" I ask.

"Sort of..." She turns the doorknob, which creaks loudly. I can't help but notice the wood of this door is much thicker than any of the others. Behind the doorway, there's a dark stairwell. "Your room is upstairs. We have a finished attic as well."

This dark, narrow staircase is somewhat less glamorous than the rest of the house—and would it kill them to stick a lightbulb in here? But of course, I'm the hired help. I wouldn't expect her to spend as much money on my room as she would on the home theater.

At the top of the stairs is a little narrow hallway. Unlike on the first floor of the house, the ceiling is dangerously low here. I'm not tall by any means, but I almost feel like I need to stoop down.

"You have your own bathroom." She nods at a door on the left. "And this would be your room right here."

She flings open the last door. It's completely dark inside until she tugs on a string and the room lights up.

The room is tiny. There's no two ways about it. Not only that, but the ceiling is slanted with the roof of the house. The far side of the ceiling only comes about up to my waist. Instead of the huge king-size bed in the Winchesters' master bedroom with their armoire and chestnut vanity table, this room contains a small single cot, a half-height bookcase, and a small dresser, lit by two naked bulbs suspended from the ceiling.

This room is modest, but that's fine with me. If it were *too* nice, it would be a certainty I have no shot at this job. The fact that this room is kind of crappy means maybe her standards are low enough that I have a teeny, tiny chance.

But there's something else about this room. Something that's bothering me.

"Sorry it's small." Mrs. Winchester pulls a frown. "But you'll have a lot of privacy here."

I walk over to the single window. Like the room, it's small. Barely larger than my hand. And it overlooks the backyard. There's a landscaper down there—the same guy I saw out at the front—hacking at one of the hedges with an oversized set of clippers.

"So what do you think, Millie? Do you like it?"

I turn away from the window to look at Mrs. Winchester's smiling face. I still can't quite put my finger on what's bothering me. There's something about this room that's making a little ball of dread form in the pit of my stomach.

Maybe it's the window. It looks out on the back of the house. If I were in trouble and trying to get somebody's attention, nobody would be able to see me back here. I could scream and yell all I wanted, and nobody would hear.

But who am I kidding? I would be lucky to live in this room.

With my own bathroom and an actual bed where I could straighten my legs out all the way. That tiny cot looks so good compared to my car, I could cry.

"It's perfect," I say.

Mrs. Winchester seems ecstatic about my answer. She leads me back down the dark stairwell to the second floor of the house, and when I exit that stairwell, I let out a breath I didn't realize I was holding. There was something about that room that was very scary, but if I somehow manage to get this job, I'll get past it. Easily.

My shoulders finally relax and my lips are forming another question when I hear a voice from behind us:

"Mommy?"

I stop short and turn around to see a little girl standing behind us in the hallway. The girl has the same light blue eyes as Nina Winchester, except a few shades paler, and her hair is so blond that it's almost white. The girl is wearing a very pale blue dress trimmed in white lace. And she's staring at me like she can see right through me. Right through my *soul*.

Do you know those movies about the scary cult of, like, creepy kids who can read minds and worship the devil and live in the cornfields or something? Well, if they were casting for one of those movies, this girl would get the part. They wouldn't even have to audition her. They would take one look at her and be like, *Yes, you are creepy girl number three.*

"Cece!" Mrs. Winchester exclaims. "Are you back already from your ballet lesson?"

The girl nods slowly. "Bella's mom dropped me off."

Mrs. Winchester wraps her arms around the girl's skinny shoulders, but the girl's expression never changes and her pale blue eyes never leave my face. Is there something wrong with me that I am scared this nine-year-old girl is going to murder me?

"This is Millie," Mrs. Winchester tells her daughter. "Millie, this is my daughter, Cecelia."

Little Cecelia's eyes are two little pools of the ocean. "It's nice to meet you, Millie," she says politely.

I'd say there's at least a twenty-five percent chance she's going to murder me in my sleep if I get this job. But I still want it.

Mrs. Winchester pecks her daughter on the top of her blond head, and then the little girl scurries off to her bedroom. She doubtless has a creepy doll house in there where the dolls come to life at night. Maybe one of the dolls will be the one to kill me.

Okay, I'm being ridiculous. That little girl is probably extremely sweet. It's not her fault she's been dressed in a creepy Victorian ghost-child's outfit. And I love kids, in general. Not that I've interacted with them much over the last decade.

Once we get back down to the first floor, the tension leaves my body. Mrs. Winchester is nice and normal enough—for a lady this rich—and as she chatters about the house and her daughter and the job, I'm only vaguely listening. All I know is this will be a lovely place to work. I would give my right arm to get this job.

"Do you have any questions, Millie?" she asks me.

I shake my head. "No, Mrs. Winchester."

She clucks her tongue. "Please, call me Nina. If you're working here, I would feel so silly with you calling me *Mrs. Winchester*." She laughs. "Like I'm some sort of rich old lady."

"Thank you... Nina," I say.

Her face glows, although that could be the seaweed or cucumber peel or whatever rich people apply to their faces. Nina Winchester is the sort of woman who has regular spa treatments. "I have a good feeling about this, Millie. I really do."

It's hard not to get caught up in her enthusiasm. It's hard not to feel that glimmer of hope as she squeezes my rough palm in her baby smooth one. I want to believe that in the next few days, I'll get a call from Nina Winchester, offering me the opportunity to come work at her house and finally vacate Casa Nissan. I want to believe that so badly.

But whatever else I can say about Nina, she's no dummy. She's not going to hire a woman to work and live in her home and take care of her child without doing a simple background check. And once she does…

I swallow a lump in my throat.

Nina Winchester bids a warm goodbye to me at the front door. "Thank you so much for coming by, Millie." She reaches out to clasp my hand in hers one more time. "I promise you'll be hearing from me soon."

I won't. This will be the last time I set foot in that magnificent house. I should never have come here in the first place. I should have tried for a job I had a chance of getting instead of wasting both of our time here. Maybe something in the fast-food industry.

The landscaper who I saw from the window in the attic is back on the front lawn. He's still got those giant clippers and he's shaping one of the hedges right in front of the house. He's a big guy, wearing a T-shirt that shows off impressive muscles and just barely hides the tattoos on his upper arms. He adjusts his baseball cap and his dark, dark eyes lift briefly from the clippers to meet mine across the lawn.

I raise my hand in greeting. "Hi," I say.

The man stares at me. He doesn't say hello. He doesn't say "quit trampling my posies." He just stares at me.

"Nice to meet you too," I mutter under my breath.

I exit through the electronic metal gate that encircles the property and trudge back to my car/home. I look back one last time at the landscaper in the yard, and he is still watching me. There's something in his expression that sends a chill down my spine. And then he shakes his head, almost imperceptibly. Almost like he's trying to warn me.

But he doesn't say a word.

TWO

When you live in your car, you have to keep things simple.

You're not going to be hosting any major gatherings, for one thing. No wine and cheese parties, no poker nights. That's fine, because I don't have anyone I want to see. The bigger problem is where to take a shower. Three days after I was evicted from my studio, which was three weeks after I got fired from my job, I discovered a rest stop that had showers. I almost cried with joy when I saw it. Yes, the showers have very little privacy and smell faintly of human waste, but at that point, I was desperate to be clean.

Now I'm enjoying my lunch in the back seat of the car. I do have a hot plate that I can plug into the cigarette lighter for special occasions, but mostly I eat sandwiches. Lots and lots of sandwiches. I've got a cooler where I store the cold cuts and cheese, and I've got a loaf of white bread—ninety-nine cents at the supermarket. And then snacks, of course. Bags of chips. Crackers with peanut butter. Twinkies. The unhealthy options are endless.

Today I'm eating ham and American cheese, with a dollop

of mayonnaise. With every bite I take, I try not to think about how sick I am of sandwiches.

After I've forced down half my sandwich, my phone rings in my pocket. I have one of those prepaid flip phones that people only use if they're going to commit a crime or else they've traveled back fifteen years in the past. But I need a phone and this is all I can afford.

"Wilhelmina Calloway?" a woman's clipped voice says on the other line.

I wince at the use of my full name. Wilhelmina was my father's mother, who is long gone. I don't know what sort of psychopaths would name their child Wilhelmina, but I don't speak to my parents anymore (and likewise, they don't speak to me), so it's a little late to ask. Anyway, I've always just been Millie, and I try to correct people as quickly as I can. But I get the feeling that whoever is calling me isn't somebody I'm going to be on a first-name basis with anytime soon. "Yes...?"

"Ms. Calloway," the woman says. "This is Donna Stanton from Munch Burgers."

Oh right. Munch Burgers—the greasy fast-food joint that granted me an interview a few days ago. I would be flipping burgers or else manning the cash register. But if I worked hard, there was some opportunity for advancement. And better yet, an opportunity to have enough money to move out of my car.

Of course, the job I really would've loved was at the Winchester household. But it's been a whole week since I met with Nina Winchester. It's safe to say I didn't get my dream job.

"I just wanted to let you know," Ms. Stanton goes on, "that we have already filled the position at Munch Burgers. But we wish you luck with your job search."

The ham and American cheese in my stomach churn. I had read online that Munch Burgers didn't have very strict hiring practices. That even if I had a record, I might have a chance. This is the last interview I've managed to book, ever since Mrs.

Winchester failed to call me back—and I'm desperate. I can't eat one more sandwich in my car. I just *can't.*

"Ms. Stanton," I blurt out. "I'm just wondering if you might be able to hire me at any other location. I'm a really hard worker. I'm very reliable. I always..."

I stop talking. She's already hung up.

I clutch my sandwich in my right hand as I grip my phone in my left. This is hopeless. Nobody wants to hire me. Every potential employer looks at me in the exact same way. All I want is a fresh start. I'll work my butt off if I have to. I'll do whatever it takes.

I fight back tears, although I don't know why I'm bothering. Nobody will see me crying in the backseat of my Nissan. There isn't anybody who cares about me anymore. My parents wiped their hands of me more than ten years ago.

My phone rings again, startling me out of my pity party. I wipe my eyes with the back of my hand and click the green button to take the call. "Hello?" I croak.

"Hi? Is this Millie?"

The voice sounds vaguely familiar. I squeeze the phone to my ear, my heart leaping. "Yes..."

"This is Nina Winchester. You interviewed with me last week?"

"Oh." I bite down hard on my lower lip. Why is she calling back now? I assumed she had already hired somebody and decided not to inform me. "Yes, of course."

"So if you're interested, we would be delighted to offer you the job."

I feel a rush of blood to my head that makes me almost dizzy. *We would be delighted to offer you the job.* Is she serious? It was conceivable that Munch Burgers might hire me, but it seemed outright impossible that a woman like Nina Winchester might invite me into her home. To *live.*

Is it possible she didn't check my references? Didn't do a

simple background check? Maybe she's just so *busy*, she never got around to it. Maybe she's one of those women who prides herself on gut feelings.

"Millie? Are you there?"

I realize I've been completely silent on the other line. I'm that stunned. "Yes. I'm here."

"So are you interested in the position?"

"I am." I'm trying not to sound too ridiculously eager. "I definitely am. I would love to work for you."

"Work *with* me," Nina corrects me.

I let out a strangled laugh. "Right. Of course."

"So when can you start?"

"Um, when would you like me to start?"

"As soon as possible!" I'm jealous of Nina's easy laugh that sounds so different from my own. If only I could snap my fingers and trade places with her. "We have a ton of laundry that needs folding!"

I swallow. "How about tomorrow?"

"That would be wonderful! But don't you need time to get your stuff packed?"

I don't want to tell her that everything I own is already in the trunk of my car. "I'm a fast packer."

She laughs again. "I love your spirit, Millie. I can't wait for you to come work here."

As Nina and I exchange details about tomorrow, I wonder if she would feel the same way about me if she knew I spent the last ten years of my life in prison.

THREE

I arrive at the Winchester home the next morning, after Nina has already dropped Cecelia off at school. I park outside the metal gate surrounding their property. I've never been in a house that was protected by a gate before, much less lived there. But this swanky Long Island neighborhood seems to be all gated houses. Considering how low the crime rate is around here, it seems like overkill, but who am I to judge? Everything else being equal, if I had a choice between a house with a gate and a house with no gate, I'd pick the gate too.

The gate was open when I arrived last week, but today it's closed. Locked, apparently. I stand there a moment, my two duffel bags at my feet, trying to figure out how to get inside. There doesn't seem to be any sort of doorbell or buzzer. But that landscaper is on the property again, crouched in the dirt, a shovel in his hand.

"Excuse me!" I call out.

The man glances over his shoulder at me, then goes back to digging. Real nice.

"Excuse me!" I say again, loud enough that he can't ignore me.

This time, he slowly, *slowly* gets to his feet. He's in absolutely no hurry as he ambles across the giant front lawn to the entrance to the gate. He pulls off his thick rubber gloves and raises his eyebrows at me.

"Hi!" I say, trying to hide my annoyance with him. "My name is Millie Calloway, and it's my first day working here. I'm just trying to get inside because Mrs. Winchester is expecting me."

He doesn't say anything. From across the yard, I had only noticed how big he is—at least a head taller than me, with biceps the size of my thighs—but up close, I realize he's actually pretty hot. He looks to be in his mid-thirties with thick jet-black hair damp from exertion, olive skin, and rugged good looks. But his most striking feature is his eyes. His eyes are very black—so dark, I can't distinguish the pupil from the iris. Something about his gaze makes me take a step back.

"So, um, can you help me?" I ask.

The man finally opens his mouth. I expect him to tell me to get lost or to show him some ID, but instead, he lets loose with a string of rapid Italian. At least, I think it's Italian. I can't say I know a word of the language, but I saw an Italian movie with subtitles once, and it sort of sounded like this.

"Oh," I say when he finishes his monologue. "So, um… no English?"

"English?" he says in a voice so heavily accented, it's clear what the answer is. "No. No English."

Great. I clear my throat, trying to figure out the best way to express what I need to tell him. "So I…" I point to my chest. "I am working. For Mrs. Winchester." I point to the house. "And I need to get… inside." Now I point to the lock on the gate. "*Inside*."

He just frowns at me. Great.

I'm about ready to dig out my phone and call Nina when he

goes off to the side, hits some sort of switch, and the gates swing open, almost in slow motion.

Once the gates are open, I take a moment to gaze up at the house that will be my home for the foreseeable future. The house is two stories plus the attic, sprawling over what looks like about the length of a city block in Brooklyn. It's almost blindingly white —possibly freshly painted—and the architecture looks contemporary, but what do I know? I just know it looks like the people living here have more money than they know what to do with.

I start to pick up one of my bags, but before I can, the guy picks up both of them without even grunting and carries them to the front door for me. Those bags are very heavy—they contain literally everything I own aside from my car—so I'm grateful he volunteered to do the heavy lifting for me.

"*Gracias,*" I say.

He gives me a funny look. Hmm, that might have been Spanish. Oh well.

I point to my chest. "Millie," I say.

"Millie." He nods in understanding, then points to his own chest. "I am Enzo."

"Nice to meet you," I say awkwardly, even though he won't understand me. But God, if he lives here and has a job, he must have picked up a *little* English.

"*Piacere di conoscerti,*" he says.

I nod wordlessly. So much for making friends with the landscaping guy.

"Millie," he says again in his thick Italian accent. He looks like he has something to say, but he's struggling with the language. "You..."

He hisses a word in Italian, but as soon as we hear the front door start to unlock, Enzo hurries back to where he had been crouched in the front yard and makes himself very busy. I could just barely make out the word he said. *Pericolo.* Whatever that means. Maybe it means he wants a soft drink. *Peri cola—now with a twist of lime!*

"Millie!" Nina looks delighted to see me. So delighted that she throws her arms around me and squashes me in a hug. "I'm *so* glad you decided to take the job. I just felt like you and I had a *connection*. You know?"

That's what I thought. She got a "gut feeling" about me, so she didn't bother to do the research. Now I just have to make sure she never has any reason not to trust me. I have to be the perfect employee. "Yes, I know what you mean. I feel the same way."

"Well, come in!"

Nina grabs the crook of my elbow and leads me into the house, oblivious to the fact that I'm struggling with my two pieces of luggage. Not that I would have expected her to help me. It wouldn't have even occurred to her.

I can't help but notice when I walk inside that the house looks very different from the first time I was here. *Very* different. When I came for the interview, the Winchester house was immaculate—I could have eaten off any surface in the room. But now, the place looks like a pigsty. The coffee table in front of the sofa has six cups on it with varying amounts of different sticky liquids in them, about a dozen crumpled newspapers and magazines, and a dented pizza box. There's clothing and garbage strewn all over the living room and the dining table still has the remains of dinner last night.

"As you can see," Nina says, "you haven't arrived a moment too soon!"

So Nina Winchester is a slob—that's *her* secret. It's going to take me hours to get this place in any decent condition. Maybe days. But that's fine—I've been itching to do some good honest hard work. And I like that she needs me. If I can make myself invaluable to her, she's less likely to fire me if—or when—she finds out the truth.

"Let me just put my bags away," I tell her. "And then I'll get the entire place tidied up."

Nina lets out a happy sigh. "You are a miracle, Millie. Thank you *so* much. Also..." She grabs her purse off the kitchen counter and rifles around inside, finally pulling out the latest iPhone. "I got you this. I couldn't help but notice you were using a very outdated phone. If I need to reach you, I'd like you to have a reliable means of communication."

I hesitantly wrap my fingers around the brand-new iPhone. "Wow. This is really generous of you, but I can't afford a plan—"

She waves a hand. "I added you to our family plan. It cost almost nothing."

Almost nothing? I have a feeling her definition of those two words is very different from mine.

Before I can protest further, the sound of footsteps echoes on the stairs behind me. I turn around, and a man in a gray business suit is making his way down the stairwell. When he sees me standing in the living room, he stops short at the base of the stairs, as if shocked by my presence. His eyes widen further when he notices my luggage.

"Andy!" Nina calls out. "Come meet Millie!"

This must be Andrew Winchester. When I was googling the Winchester family, my eyes popped out a bit when I saw this man's net worth. After seeing all those dollar signs, the home theater and the gate surrounding the property made a bit more sense. He's a businessman, who took over his father's thriving company, and has doubled the profits since. But it's obvious from his surprised expression that he allows his wife to handle most of the household matters, and it's apparently flat out slipped her mind to tell him she's hired a live-in housekeeper.

"Hello..." Mr. Winchester steps into the living room, his brow furrowed. "Millie, is it? I'm sorry, I didn't realize..."

"Andy, I told you about her!" She tilts her head to the side. "I said we needed to hire somebody to help with cleaning and cooking and Cecelia. I'm sure I told you!"

"Yes, well." His face finally relaxes. "Welcome, Millie. We could certainly use the help."

Andrew Winchester holds his hand out for me to shake. It's hard not to notice he is an incredibly handsome man. Piercing brown eyes, a full head of hair the color of mahogany, and a sexy little cleft in his chin. It's also hard not to notice that he is several levels more attractive than his wife, even with her impeccable grooming, which strikes me as a bit strange. The man is filthy rich, after all. He could have any woman he wants. I respect him for not choosing a twenty-year-old supermodel to be his life partner.

I thrust my new phone into my jeans pocket and reach out to take his hand. "Nice to meet you, Mr. Winchester."

"Please." He smiles warmly at me. "Call me Andrew."

As he says the words, something flickers over Nina Winchester's face. Her lips twitch and her eyes narrow. I'm not exactly sure why though. She herself offered to let me call her by her first name. And it's not like Andrew Winchester is checking me out. His eyes are staying respectfully on mine and not dropping below the neck. Not that there's much to see—even though I didn't bother with the fake tortoiseshell glasses today, I'm wearing a modest blouse and comfortable blue jeans for my first day of work.

"Anyway," Nina snips, "don't you have to get to the office, Andy?"

"Oh yes." He straightens out his gray tie. "I've got a meeting at nine-thirty in the city. I better hurry."

Andrew gives Nina a lingering kiss on the lips and squeezes her shoulder. As far as I can see, they are quite happily married. And Andrew seems pretty down-to-earth for a man whose net worth has eight figures after the dollar sign. It's sweet how he blows her a kiss from the front door—this is a man who loves his wife.

"Your husband seems nice," I say to Nina as the door slams shut.

The dark, suspicious look returns to her eyes. "Do you think so?"

"Well, yes," I stammer. "I mean, he seems like... how long have you been married?"

Nina looks at me thoughtfully. But instead of answering my question, she says, "What happened to your glasses?"

"What?"

She lifts an eyebrow. "You were wearing a pair of glasses at your interview, weren't you?"

"Oh." I squirm, reluctant to admit that the eyeglasses were fake—my attempt to look more intelligent and serious, and yes, less attractive and threatening. "I... uh, I'm wearing my contacts."

"Are you?"

I don't know why I lied. I should've just said that I don't need the glasses that badly. Instead, I have now doubled down and invented contacts that I'm not actually wearing. I can feel Nina scrutinizing my pupils, searching for the lenses.

"Is... is that a problem?" I finally ask.

A muscle twitches under her right eye. For a moment, I'm scared she's going to tell me that I should get out. But then her face relaxes. "Of course not! I just thought those glasses were *so* cute on you. Very striking—you should wear them more often."

"Yes, well..." I grab the handle of one of my duffel bags with my shaking hand. "Maybe I should get my stuff upstairs so I can get started."

Nina claps her hands together. "Excellent idea!"

Once again, Nina doesn't offer to take either of my bags as we climb up the two flights of stairs to get to the attic. By halfway through the second flight, my arms feel like they're about ready to fall off, but Nina doesn't seem interested in pausing to give me a moment to readjust the straps. I gasp with relief when I'm able to drop the bags on the floor of my new room. Nina yanks on the cord to turn on the two lightbulbs that illuminate my tiny living space.

"I hope it's okay," Nina says. "I figure you'd rather have the privacy of being up here, as well as your own bathroom."

Maybe she feels guilty about the fact that their ginormous guestroom is lying empty while I am living in a room slightly larger than a broom closet. But that's fine. Anything larger than the backseat of my car is like a palace. I can't wait to sleep here tonight. I'm obscenely grateful.

"It's perfect," I say honestly.

In addition to the bed, dresser, and bookcase, I notice one other thing in the room that I didn't see the first time around. A little mini-fridge, about a foot tall. It's plugged into the wall and humming rhythmically. I crouch down and tug it open.

The mini-fridge has two small shelves. And on the top shelf, there are three tiny bottles of water.

"Good hydration is very important," Nina says earnestly.

"Yes..."

When she sees the perplexed expression on my face, she smiles. "Obviously, it's your fridge and you can put whatever you want in it. I thought I would give you a head start."

"Thank you." It's not that strange. Some people leave mints on a pillow. Nina leaves three tiny bottles of water.

"Anyway..." Nina wipes her hands on her thighs, even though her hands are spotless. "I'll let you get unpacked and then get started cleaning the house. I'll be preparing for my PTA meeting tomorrow."

"PTA?"

"Parent Teacher Association." She beams at me. "I'm the vice president."

"That's wonderful," I say, because it's what she wants to

hear. Nina is very easy to please. "I'll just unpack everything quickly and get right to work."

"Thank you so much." Her fingers briefly touch my bare arm—hers are warm and dry. "You're a lifesaver, Millie. I'm so glad you're here."

I rest my hand on the doorknob as Nina starts to leave my room. And that's when I notice it. What's been bothering me about this room from the moment I first walked in here. A sick feeling washes over me.

"Nina?"

"Hmm?"

"Why..." I clear my throat. "Why is the lock to this bedroom on the *outside* rather than the inside?"

Nina peers down at the doorknob, as if noticing it for the first time. "Oh! I'm so sorry about that. We used to use this room as a closet, so obviously we wanted it to lock from the outside. But then I converted it to a bedroom for the hired help, and I guess we never switched the lock."

If somebody wanted, they could easily lock me in here. And there's only that one window, looking out at the back of the house. This room could be a death trap.

But then again, why would anyone want to lock me in here?

"Could I have the key to the room?" I ask.

She shrugs. "I'm not even sure where it is."

"I'd like a copy."

Her light blue eyes narrow at me. "Why? What do you expect to be keeping in your room that you don't want us to know about?"

My mouth falls open. "I... Nothing, but..."

Nina throws her head back and laughs. "I'm just kidding. It's your room, Millie! If you want a key, I'll get you one. I promise."

Sometimes it feels like Nina has a split personality. She flips from hot to cold so rapidly. She claims she was joking, but I'm not so sure. It doesn't matter, though. I have no other prospects and this job is a blessing. I'm going to make it work. No matter what. I'm going to make Nina Winchester love me.

After Nina leaves my room, I close the door behind her. I'd like to lock it, but I can't. Obviously.

As I shut the door, I notice marks in the wood. Long thin lines running down the length of the door at about the level of my shoulder. I run my fingers over the indentations. They almost seem like...

Scratches. Like somebody was scraping at the door.

Trying to get out.

No, that's ridiculous. I'm being paranoid. Sometimes old wood gets scratched up. It doesn't mean anything ominous.

The room suddenly feels unbearably hot and stuffy. There's a small furnace in the corner of the room, which I'm sure keeps it comfortable in the winter, but there's nothing to cool it down in the warmer months. I'll have to buy a fan to prop up in front of the window. Even though it's way larger than my car, it's still a very small space—I'm not surprised they used it as a storage closet. I look around, opening the drawers to check their size. There's a little closet within the room, with just barely enough space to hang up my few dresses. The closet is empty except for a couple of hangers and a small blue bucket in the corner.

I attempt to wrench open the small window to get a bit of air. But it doesn't budge. I squint my eyes to investigate more closely. I run my finger along the frame of the window. It looks like it's been painted into place.

Even though I have a window, it doesn't open.

I could ask Nina about it, but I don't want it to seem like I'm complaining when I just started working here today. Maybe next week I could mention it. I don't think it's too much to hope for, to have one working window.

The landscaping guy, Enzo, is in the backyard now. He's running the lawnmower back there. He pauses for a moment to wipe sweat from his forehead with his muscular forearm, and then he looks up. He sees my face through the small window, and he shakes his head, just like he did the first time I met him. I remember the word he hissed at me in Italian before I went into the house. *Pericolo.*

I dig my brand-new cell phone out of my pocket. The screen jumps alive at my touch, filling with little icons for text messaging, calls, and the weather. These sorts of phones were not ubiquitous back at the start of my incarceration, and I haven't been able to afford one since I got out. But a couple of the girls had one at the halfway houses where I went when I first got out, so I sort of know how to use them. I know which icon brings up a browser.

I type into the browser window: *Translate pericolo.* The signal must be weak up here in the attic, because it takes a long time. Almost a minute has gone by when the translation of *pericolo* finally appears on the screen of my phone:

Danger.

FOUR

I spend the next seven hours cleaning.

Nina could not have made this house dirtier if she tried. Every room of the house is filthy. The pizza box on the coffee table still has two slices of pizza in it, and there is something sticky and foul-smelling spilled in the bottom of the box. It has leaked through and the box is fused to the coffee table. It takes an hour of soaking and thirty minutes of intense scrubbing to get it all clean.

The kitchen is the worst of it. In addition to whatever is in the garbage bin itself, there are two garbage bags in the kitchen, spilling over with their contents. One of the two bags has a rip in the bottom, and when I lift it to take it outside, all the garbage goes everywhere. And it smells beyond terrible. I gag but don't lose my lunch.

Dishes are piled high in the sink, and I wonder why Nina didn't just put them in their state-of-the-art dishwasher, until I open the dishwasher and notice that it is also packed to the brim with filthy dishes. That woman does *not* believe in scraping plates before putting them in the dishwasher. Or, apparently, *running* the dishwasher. Before I am done, I run three loads of dishes. I wash all the pans separately, most of which have food caked on them from days earlier.

By mid-afternoon, I've gotten the kitchen at least somewhat habitable again. I'm proud of myself. It's the first hard day's work I've done since I got fired from the bar (completely unfairly, but that's my life these days), and I feel great about it. All I want is to keep working here. And maybe to have a window in my room that opens.

"Who are you?"

A little voice startles me in the middle of putting away the last load of dishes. I whirl around—Cecelia is standing behind me, her pale blue eyes boring into me, wearing a white frilly dress that makes her look like a little doll. And by doll, I'm of course talking about that creepy talking doll in *The Twilight Zone* that murders people.

I didn't even see her come inside. And Nina is nowhere to be seen. Where did she even come from? If this is the part of the job where I find out Cecelia has actually been dead for ten years and is a ghost, I'm quitting.

Well, maybe not. But I might ask for a raise.

"Hi, Cecelia!" I say cheerfully. "I'm Millie. I'm going to be working around your house from now on—cleaning things up and watching you when your mom asks me to. I hope we can have fun together."

Cecelia blinks her pale eyes at me. "I'm hungry."

I have to remember that she is just a normal little girl who gets hungry and thirsty and cranky and uses the bathroom. "What would you like to eat?"

"I don't know."

"Well, what sorts of things do you like?"

"I don't know."

I grit my teeth. Cecelia has morphed from a creepy little girl to an annoying little girl. But we just met each other. I'm sure after a few weeks, we'll be best friends. "Okay, I'll just fix you a snack then."

She nods and climbs up on one of the stools set up around the kitchen island. Her eyes still feel like they're boring through me—like they can read all my secrets. I wish she would go in the living room and watch cartoons on her giant TV instead of just... watching me.

"So what do you like to watch on television?" I ask, hoping she'll take the hint.

She frowns like I offended her. "I prefer to read."

"That's great! What do you like to read?"

"Books."

"What kind of books?"

"The kind with words."

Oh, so that's how it's going to be, Cecelia. Fine, if she doesn't want to talk about books, I can change the subject. "Did you just come back from school?" I ask her.

She blinks at me. "Where else would I have come from?"

"But... how did you get home then?"

Cecelia lets out an exasperated huff. "Lucy's mom picked me up from ballet and brought me home."

I heard Nina upstairs about fifteen minutes ago, so I assume she's in the house. I wonder if I should let her know that Cecelia is home. Then again, I don't want to disturb her, and one of my jobs is to look after Cecelia.

Thank God, Cecelia seems to have lost interest in me and is now rifling around in her pale pink backpack. I find some Ritz crackers in the pantry as well as a jar of peanut butter. I spread the peanut butter over the crackers like my mother used to do. Repeating the same act that my mother used to do for me so many times makes me feel a little nostalgic. And sad. I never thought she would abandon me the way she did. *This is it, Millie. The last straw.*

After I've spread peanut butter on the crackers, I slice up a banana and put one slice on each. I love the combination of peanut butter and bananas.

"Ta-da!" I slide the plate onto the kitchen counter to present it to Cecelia. "Peanut butter and banana crackers!"

Her eyes widen. "Peanut butter and banana?"

"Trust me. It's really good."

"I'm allergic to peanut butter!" Cecelia's cheeks turn bright pink. "Peanut butter could kill me! Are you trying to kill me?"

My heart sinks. Nina never said anything about a peanut butter allergy. And they have peanut butter right in their pantry! If her daughter has a deadly peanut allergy, why would she keep it in the house?

"Mommy!" Cecelia shrieks as she runs toward the staircase. "The maid tried to hurt me with peanut butter! Help, Mommy!"

Oh God.

"Cecelia!" I hiss at her. "It was an accident! I didn't know you were allergic and—"

But Nina is already racing down the stairs. Despite the disarray of her house, she looks flawless right now in another one of her gleaming white skirt-and-blouse combinations. White is her color. Cecelia's too, apparently. They match the house.

"What's going on?" Nina cries when she reaches the bottom of the stairs.

I wince as Cecelia propels herself at her mother, wrapping her arms around Nina's bosom. "She tried to make me eat peanut butter, Mommy! I told her I was allergic, but she didn't listen."

Nina's pale skin flushes. "Millie, is this true?"

"I..." My throat feels completely dry. "I didn't know she was allergic. I swear."

Nina frowns. "I told you about her allergies, Millie. This is unacceptable."

She never told me. She never said a word about Cecelia being allergic to peanuts. I would bet my life on it. And even if she had, *why* would she leave a jar of peanut butter right in the pantry? It was right in front!

But she won't believe any of my excuses. In her head, I nearly killed her daughter. I see this job slipping out from under my fingers.

"I'm truly sorry." I speak around a lump in my throat. "I must've forgotten. I promise I'll never let it happen again."

Cecelia is sobbing now while Nina holds her close and gently strokes her blond hair. Eventually, the sobs subside, but Cecelia still clings to her mother. I feel a terrible stab of guilt. Deep down, I know you aren't supposed to feed kids before checking with the parents. I'm in the wrong here, and if Cecelia hadn't been so vigilant, something terrible could've happened.

Nina takes a deep breath. She shuts her eyes for a moment and opens them again. "Fine. But please be sure you don't forget anything so important ever again."

"I won't. I swear." I wring my fists together. "Do you want me to throw out the jar of peanut butter that was in the pantry?"

She's quiet for a moment. "No, better not. We might need it."

I want to throw up my hands. But it's her decision if she wants to keep life-threatening peanut butter in her home. All I know is that I will definitely never use it again.

"Also," Nina adds, "when will dinner be ready?"

Dinner? Was I supposed to be making dinner? Did Nina imagine another conversation between the two of us that we never had? But I'm not about to make excuses again after the debacle with the peanut butter. I'll find something in the fridge to prepare.

"Seven o'clock?" I say. Three hours should give me more than enough time.

She nods. “And you won’t put any peanut butter in the dinner, right?”

“No, of course not.”

“Please don’t forget again, Millie.”

“I won’t. And does anybody have any other allergies or... intolerances?”

Is she allergic to eggs? Bee stings? Too much homework? I need to know. I can’t risk being caught out again.

Nina shakes her head, just as Cecelia lifts her tear-streaked face off her mother’s chest long enough to glare at me. The two of us have not gotten off on the right foot. But I’ll find a way to fix it. I’ll make her brownies or something. Kids are easy. Adults are trickier, but I’m determined to win over Nina and Andrew as well.

FIVE

By 6:45, dinner is almost ready. There was some chicken breast in the fridge that was already marinated and somebody had printed instructions on the bag, so I just did what the instructions said and threw it in the oven. They must get their food from some sort of service with directions already on it.

The kitchen smells fantastic when the garage door slams. A minute later, Andrew Winchester is strolling into the room, his thumb in the knot of his tie to loosen it. I'm stirring some sauce on the stove top, and I do a bit of a double-take when I see him, having forgotten quite how handsome he is.

He grins at me—he's even more handsome when he smiles. "Millie, right?"

"That's right."

He inhales deeply. "Wow. That smells incredible."

My cheeks flush. "Thank you."

He looks around the kitchen in approval. "You got everything clean."

"That's my job."

He chuckles. "I suppose it is. Did you have a good first day?"

"I did." I'm not going to tell him about the peanut butter debacle. He doesn't need to know, although I suspect Nina will clue him in. I'm sure he won't appreciate me almost killing his daughter. "You have a beautiful home."

"Well, I have Nina to thank for that. She runs the household."

As if on cue, Nina arrives in the kitchen, wearing another of her white outfits—a different one than only a few hours ago. Once again, she looks impeccable. But while I was cleaning earlier, I took a few minutes to look at the photographs on their mantle. There's one of Nina and Andrew together from many years ago, and she looked so different then. Her hair wasn't as blond and she had on less makeup and more casual clothing—and she was at least fifty pounds thinner. I almost didn't recognize her—but Andrew looked exactly the same.

"Nina." Andrew's eyes light up at the sight of his wife. "You look beautiful—as usual."

He pulls her to him and kisses her deeply on the lips. She melts against him, grabbing his shoulders possessively. When they separate, she gazes up at him. "I missed you today."

"I missed you more."

"I missed *you* more."

Oh my God, how long are they going to debate who misses who more? I turn away, busying myself in the kitchen. It's awkward to be so close to this display of affection.

"So." Nina is the first to pull away. "Are you two getting to know each other?"

"Uh-huh," Andrew says. "And whatever Millie is making smells incredible, doesn't it?"

I glance behind me. Nina is watching me at the stove with that dark expression in her blue eyes. She doesn't like her husband complimenting me. I don't know what the problem is though—he's obviously nuts about her.

"It does," she agrees.

"Nina is hopeless in the kitchen," Andrew laughs, throwing an arm around her waist. "We would starve to death if it were all on her shoulders. My mother used to drop by with meals that she or her personal chef made. But since she and my father retired to Florida, we've been subsisting mostly on takeout. So you're a savior, Millie."

Nina gives a tight smile. He's just teasing her, but no woman wants to be compared unfavorably to another. He's an idiot if he doesn't know that. Then again, plenty of men are idiots.

"Dinner will be ready in about ten minutes," I say. "Why don't you go relax in the living room and I'll call you when it's ready?"

He raises his eyebrows. "Do you want to join us for dinner, Millie?"

The sound of Nina inhaling sharply fills the kitchen. Before she can say anything, I shake my head vigorously. "No, I'm just going to go up to my room and relax. Thank you for the invitation though."

"Really? Are you sure?"

Nina swats her husband in the arm. "Andy, she's been working all day. She doesn't want to have dinner with her *employers*. She just wants to go upstairs and text message her friends. Right, Millie?"

"Right," I say, even though I don't have any friends. At least, not on the outside.

Andrew doesn't seem concerned either way. He was just being polite, oblivious to the fact that Nina didn't want me at the dinner table. And that's just fine. I don't want to do anything to make her feel threatened. I just want to keep my head down and do my job.

SIX

I forgot how amazing it is to sleep with my legs straight.

Okay, this cot is nothing special. It's lumpy and the springs on the bed frame groan every time I move so much as a millimeter. But it is *so* much better than my car. And even more amazingly, if I need to use the bathroom during the night, it's right next to me! I don't have to drive around to find a rest stop and clutch my can of mace in my hand while emptying my bladder. I don't even need mace anymore.

It feels so good to sleep in a normal bed that within seconds of my head hitting the pillow, I pass out.

When I open my eyes again, it's still dark. I sit up in a panic, trying to remember where I am. All I know is I'm not in my car. It takes several seconds for the events of the last several days to come back to me. Nina offering me the job here. Moving out of my car. Falling asleep in an honest to goodness bed.

Gradually, my breathing slows.

I fumble on the dresser by my bed for the phone Nina bought me. The time is 3:46 in the morning. Not quite time to get up for the day. I shove the itchy covers off my legs and roll off the cot as my eyes adjust to the light from the moon filtering in through the tiny window. I'll hit the bathroom, then I'll try to fall back to sleep.

My feet creak against the bare floorboards of my tiny bedroom. I yawn, taking a second to stretch until my fingertips almost reach the lightbulbs on the ceiling. This room makes me feel like a giant.

I get to the door of my room and I grab the knob and...

It doesn't turn.

The panic that had drained from my body when I realized where I was now escalates once again. The door is locked. The Winchesters locked me in this room. *Nina* locked me in this room. But why? Is this all some kind of sick game? Were they looking for some ex-con to trap in here—someone nobody would miss? My fingers brush against the scratch marks on the door, wondering who the last poor woman trapped in here has been.

I knew this had to be too good to be true. Even with the spectacularly dirty kitchen, this seemed like a dream job. I knew Nina had to have done a background check. She probably locked me in here, thinking nobody would ever miss me.

I flashback to ten years ago, the first night when the door to my cell slammed shut, and I knew this would be my home for a long time to come. I swore to myself that if I ever got out, I would never let myself be trapped in any situation ever again. Yet it's less than a year after I got out, and here I am.

But I've got my phone. I can call 911.

I snatch up my phone from the dresser where I left it. I had a signal earlier today, but now there's nothing. No bars. No signal.

I'm stuck here. With only one tiny window that doesn't open, overlooking the backyard.

What am I going to do?

I reach for the doorknob one more time, wondering if I could somehow knock the door down. But this time, when I turn the knob sharply, it twists in my hand.

And the door pops open.

I stumble out into the hallway, breathing quickly. I stand there for a moment, as my heart rate slows to normal. I was never locked in the room after all. Nina didn't have some crazy plot to trap me in there. The door was just stuck.

But I can't seem to shake that uneasy feeling. That I should get out of here while I still can.

SEVEN

When I get downstairs in the morning, Nina is systematically destroying the kitchen.

She has pulled every pot and pan from the cabinet below the counter. She's ripped half the dishes from above the sink and several of them are lying broken on the kitchen floor. And now she is going through the refrigerator, haphazardly tossing food onto the floor. I watch in amazement as she takes an entire container of milk out of the refrigerator and hurls it onto the floor. Milk immediately started gushing out, forming a white river around the pots and pans and broken dishes.

"Nina?" I say tentatively.

Nina freezes, her hands curled around a bagel. She whips her head around to look at me. "Where is it?"

"Where... where is *what*?"

"My notes!" She lets out an anguished cry. "I left all my notes for the PTA meeting tonight on the kitchen counter! And now they're gone! What did you do with them?"

First of all, why would she think her notes were in the *refrigerator*? Second, I am certain I didn't throw out her notes. I mean, I'm ninety-nine percent certain. Is there some tiny chance that there was a little crumpled-up piece of paper on the counter that I assumed was garbage and threw away? Yes. I can't rule out the possibility. But I was pretty careful about not throwing away anything that wasn't garbage. To be fair, almost everything was garbage.

"I didn't do anything with them," I say.

Nina plants her fists on her hips. "So you're saying my notes just *walked away*?"

"No, I'm not saying that." I take a careful step toward her and my sneaker crunches on a broken plate. I make a note to myself to never come into the kitchen barefoot. "But maybe you left them somewhere else?"

"I did not!" she snaps at me. "I left them *right here*." She slams her palm on the kitchen counter loud enough that I jump. "Right on this counter. And now—gone! Vanished!"

All the commotion has gotten the attention of Andrew Winchester. He wanders into the kitchen, wearing a dark suit that makes him look even more handsome than he looked yesterday, if that was possible. He is clearly in the process of tying his tie, but his fingers freeze mid-knot when he sees the mess on the floor.

"Nina?"

Nina turns to look at her husband, her eyes brimming with tears. "Millie threw out my notes for the meeting tonight!"

I open my mouth to protest, but it's pointless. Nina is certain I threw out her notes, and it's entirely possible I did. I mean, if they were so important, why would she just leave them lying on the kitchen counter? The way the kitchen looked yesterday, it could have been condemned.

"That's terrible." Andrew opens his arms and she flies into them. "But don't you have some of your notes saved on the computer?"

Nina sniffles into his expensive suit. She's probably getting snot all over it, but Andrew doesn't seem to mind. "Some of them. But I'll have to redo a lot of it."

And then she turns to look at me accusingly.

I'm done trying to assert my innocence. If she is sure that I threw out her notes, the best thing to do is just apologize. "I'm so sorry, Nina," I say. "If there's anything I can do..."

Nina's eyes lower onto the disaster on the kitchen floor. "You can clean up this disgusting mess you left in my kitchen while I fix this problem."

With those words, she stomps out of the kitchen. Her footsteps disappear up the stairs as I contemplate how I'm going to clean up all these broken dishes, now intermingled with spilled milk and about twenty grapes rolling around the floor. I stepped on one of them, and it's all over the bottom of my sneaker.

Andrew lingers behind in the kitchen, shaking his head. Now that Nina has left, I feel like I should say something. "Listen," I say, "I wasn't the one who—"

"I know," he says before I can get out my protest of innocence. "Nina is... high strung. But she has a good heart."

"Yeah..."

He pulls off his dark jacket and starts rolling up the sleeves of his crisp white dress shirt. "Let me help you get this cleaned up."

"You don't have to do that."

"It'll be faster if we work together."

He goes into the closet by the kitchen and pulls out the mop —I'm shocked he knew exactly where it was. Actually, he knows his way around the closet of cleaning supplies very well. And now I get it. Nina has done things like this before. He's gotten used to cleaning up her messes.

But still, I work here now. This isn't his job.

"I'll clean it up." I put my hand on the mop he's holding and tug it away from him. "You're all dressed up, and this is what I'm here for."

For a moment, he holds onto the mop. Then he allows me to take it from him. "Okay, thanks, Millie. I appreciate your hard work."

At least somebody does.

As I get to work cleaning the kitchen, I think back to the photograph on the mantle of Andrew and Nina when they were first together, before they were married, before they had Cecelia. They look so young and happy together. It's obvious Andrew is still crazy about Nina, but something has changed. I can sense it. Nina isn't the person she used to be.

But it doesn't matter. It's none of my business.

EIGHT

Nina must have thrown half the contents of the refrigerator on the kitchen floor, so I have to make a run to the grocery store today. Since apparently, I'm also going to be cooking for them, I select some raw meat and seasoning that I can use to throw together a few meals. Nina loaded her credit card onto my phone. Everything I buy will be automatically charged to their account.

In prison, the food options were not too exciting. The menu rotated between chicken, hamburgers, hotdogs, lasagna, burritos, and a mysterious fish patty that always made me gag. There would be vegetables on the side that would be cooked to the point of disintegration. I used to fantasize about what I would eat when I got out, but on my budget, the options weren't much better. I could only buy what was on sale, and once I was living in my car, I was even more restricted.

It's different shopping for the Winchesters. I go straight for the finest cuts of steak—I'll look up on YouTube how to cook them. I sometimes used to cook steak for my father, but that was a long time ago. If I buy expensive ingredients, they'll come out good no matter what I do.

When I get back to the Winchester house, I've got four overflowing bags of groceries in the trunk of my car. Nina and Andrew's cars take up the two spots in the garage, and she instructed me not to park in the driveway, so I have to leave my car on the street. As I'm fumbling to get the bags out of the trunk, the landscaper Enzo emerges from the house next to ours with some sort of scary gardening device in his right hand.

Enzo notices me struggling, and after a moment of hesitation, he jogs over to my car. He frowns at me. "I do it," he says in his heavily accented English.

I start to take one of the bags, but then he scoops all four of them up in his massive arms, and he carries them to the front door. He nods at the door, waiting patiently for me to unlock it. I do it as quickly as possible, given that he's carrying about eighty pounds' worth of groceries in his arms. He stomps his boots on the welcome mat, then carries the groceries the rest of the way into the kitchen and deposits them on the kitchen counter.

"*Gracias*," I say.

His lips twitch. "No. *Grazie*."

"*Grazie*," I repeat.

He lingers in the kitchen for a moment, his brows knitted together. I notice again that Enzo is handsome, in a dark and terrifying sort of way. He's got tattoos on his upper arms, partially obscured by his T-shirt—I can make out the name "Antonia" inscribed in a heart on his right biceps. Those muscular arms could kill me without him even breaking a sweat if he got it in his head to do so. But I don't get a sense that this man wants to hurt me at all. If anything, he seems concerned about me.

I remember what he mumbled to me before Nina interrupted us the other day. *Pericolo. Danger.* What was he trying to tell me? Does he think I'm in danger here?

Maybe I should download a translator app on my phone. He could type in what he wants to tell me and—

A noise from upstairs interrupts my thoughts. Enzo sucks in a breath. "I go," he says, turning on his heel and striding back toward the door.

"But..." I hurry after him, but he's much faster than me. He's out the front door before I've even cleared the kitchen.

I stand in the living room for a moment, torn between putting away the groceries and going after him. But then the decision is made for me when Nina comes down the stairs to the living room, wearing a white pants suit. I don't think I've ever seen her wear anything besides white—it does complement her hair, but the effort of keeping it clean would drive me crazy. Of course, I'm going to be the one taking care of the laundry from now on. I make a note to myself to buy more bleach next time I'm at the grocery store.

Nina sees me standing there and her eyebrows shoot up to her hairline. "Millie?"

I force a smile. "Yes?"

"I heard voices down here. Were you having company?"

"No. Nothing like that."

"You may not invite strangers into our home." She frowns at me. "If you want to have any guests over, I expect you to ask permission and give us at least two days' notice. And I would ask you to keep them in your room."

"It was just that landscaper guy," I explain. "He was helping me carry groceries into the house. That's all."

I had expected the explanation would satisfy Nina, but instead, her eyes darken. A muscle twitches under her right eye. "The landscaper? Enzo? He was *here*?"

"Um." I rub the back of my neck. "Is that his name? I don't know. He just carried the groceries in."

Nina studies my face as if trying to detect a lie. "I don't

want him inside this house again. He's filthy from working outside. I work so hard to keep this house clean."

I don't know what to say to that. Enzo wiped his boots off when he came into the house and he didn't track in any dirt. And nothing is comparable to the mess I saw when I first walked into this house yesterday.

"Do you understand me, Millie?" she presses me.

"Yes," I say quickly. "I understand."

Her eyes flick over me in a way that makes me very uncomfortable. I shift between my feet. "By the way, how come you never wear your glasses?"

My fingers fly to my face. Why did I wear those stupid glasses the first day? I should never have worn them, and when she asked me about them yesterday, I shouldn't have lied. "Um..."

She arches an eyebrow. "I was up in the bathroom in the attic and I didn't see any contact lens solution. I didn't mean to snoop, but if you're going to be driving around with my child at some point, I expect you to have good vision."

"Right..." I wipe my sweaty hands on my jeans. I should just come clean. "The thing is, I don't really..." I clear my throat. "I don't actually need glasses. The ones I was wearing at my interview were more... sort of, decorative. You know?"

She licks her lips. "I see. So you lied to me."

"I wasn't lying. It was a fashion statement."

"Yes." Her blue eyes are like ice. "But then later I asked you about it and you said you had on contacts. Didn't you?"

"Oh." I wring my hands together. "Well, I guess... Yes, I was lying that time. I guess I felt embarrassed about the glasses... I'm really sorry."

The corners of her lips tug down. "Please don't lie to me ever again."

"I won't. I'm so sorry."

She stares at me for a moment, her eyes unreadable. Then

she glances around the living room, her eyes sweeping over every surface. “And please clean up this room. I’m not paying you to flirt with the landscaper.”

With those words, Nina strides out the front door, slamming it behind her.

NINE

Nina is at her PTA meeting tonight—the one I *ruined* by throwing out her notes. She is grabbing a bite to eat with some of the other parents, so I've been tasked with making dinner for Andrew and Cecelia.

The house is so much quieter when Nina isn't here. I'm not sure why, but she just has an energy that fills the entire space. Right now I'm alone in the kitchen, searing a filet mignon in the frying pan before sticking it in the oven, and it's heavenly silent in the Winchester household. It's nice. This job would be so great if not for my boss.

Andrew has incredible timing—he comes home just as I'm taking the steaks out of the oven and letting them rest on the kitchen counter. He peeks into the kitchen. "Smells great —again."

"Thanks." I add a little bit more salt to the mashed potatoes, which are already drenched in butter and cream. "Can you tell Cecelia to come down? I called her twice but..." Actually, I called up to her three times. She has not yet answered me.

Andrew nods. "Gotcha."

Shortly after Andrew disappears into the dining room and

calls her name, I hear her quick footsteps on the staircase. So that's how it's going to be.

I put together two plates containing the steak, mashed potatoes, and a side of broccoli. The portions are smaller on Cecelia's plate, and I am not going to enforce whether she eats the broccoli or not. If her father wants her to eat it, he can make her do it. But I would be remiss if I didn't provide vegetables. When I was growing up, my mother always made sure to have a serving of vegetables on a dinner plate.

I'm sure she's still wondering where she went wrong with raising me.

Cecelia is wearing another of her overly fancy dresses in an impractical pale color. I've never seen her wear normal kid clothing, and it just seems wrong. You can't play in the dresses Cecelia wears—they're too uncomfortable and they show every speck of dirt. She sits down at one of the chairs at the dining table, takes the napkin I laid out, and places it down on her lap daintily. For a moment, I'm a bit charmed. Then she opens her mouth.

"Why did you give me water?" She crinkles her nose at the glass of filtered water I put at her place setting. "I *hate* water. Get me apple juice."

If I had spoken to somebody like that when I was a child, my mother would have smacked my hand and told me to say "please." But Cecelia isn't my child, and I haven't managed to endear myself to her yet in the time I've been here. So I smile politely, take the water away, and bring her a glass of apple juice.

When I place the new glass in front of her, she carefully examines it. She holds it up to the light, narrowing her eyes. "This glass is dirty. Get me another one."

"It's not dirty," I protest. "It just came out of the dishwasher."

"It's *smudged*." She makes a face. "I don't want it. Give me another one."

I take a deep, calming breath. I'm not going to fight with this little girl. If she wants a new glass for her apple juice, I'll get her a new glass.

As I'm fetching Cecelia her new glass, Andrew comes out to the dining table. He's removed his tie and unbuttoned the top button on his white dress shirt. Just the tiniest hint of chest hair peeks out. And I have to look away.

Men are something I am still learning how to navigate in my post-incarceration life. And by "learning," I of course mean that I am completely avoiding it. At my last job waitressing at that bar—my only job since I got out—customers would inevitably ask me out. I always said no. There just isn't room in my messed-up life right now for something like that. And of course, the men who asked me were men I wouldn't have ever wanted to go out with.

I went to prison when I was seventeen. I wasn't a virgin, but my only experiences included clumsy high school sex. Over my time in jail, I would sometimes feel the tug around attractive male guards. Sometimes the tug was almost painful. And one of the things I looked forward to when I got out was the possibility of having a relationship with a man. Or even just feeling a man's lips against mine. I want it. Of course I do.

But not now. Someday.

Still, when I look at a man like Andrew Winchester, I think about the fact that I haven't even *touched* a man in over a decade—not like that, anyway. He's not anything like those creeps at the seedy bar where I used to wait tables. When I do eventually put myself back out there, he's the sort of man I'm looking for. Except obviously not married.

An idea occurs to me: if I ever want to release a little tension, Enzo might be a good candidate. No, he doesn't speak English. But if it's just one night, it shouldn't matter. He looks like he would know what to do without having to say much. And unlike Andrew, he doesn't wear a wedding ring—although I can't help but wonder about this Antonia person, whose name is tattooed on his arm.

I wrench myself from my fantasies about the sexy landscaper as I return to the kitchen to retrieve the two plates of food. Andrew's eyes light up when he sees the juicy steak, seared to perfection. I am really proud of how it came out.

"This looks incredible, Millie!" he says.

"Thanks," I say.

I look over at Cecelia, who has the opposite response. "Yuck! This is steak." Stating the obvious, I guess.

"Steak is good, Cece," Andrew tells her. "You should try it."

Cecelia looks at her father then back down at her plate. She prods her steak gingerly with her fork, as if she's anxious it might leap off the plate and into her mouth. She has a pained expression on her face.

"Cece..." Andrew says.

I look between Cecelia and Andrew, not sure what to do. It hits me now that I probably shouldn't have made steak for a nine-year-old girl. I just assumed she had to have highbrow taste, living in a place like this.

"Um," I say. "Should I...?"

Andrew pushes back his chair and grabs Cecelia's plate from the table. "Okay, I'll make you some chicken nuggets."

I follow Andrew back into the kitchen, apologizing profusely. He just laughs. "Don't worry about it. Cecelia is obsessed with chicken, and especially chicken nuggets. We could be dining at the fanciest restaurant in Long Island, and she'll order chicken nuggets."

My shoulders relax a bit. "You don't have to do this. I can make her chicken nuggets."

Andrew lays her plate down on the kitchen counter and

wags a finger at me. "Oh, but I do. If you're going to work here, you need a tutorial."

"Okay..."

He wrenches the freezer open and pulls out a giant family pack of chicken nuggets. "See, these are the nuggets Cecelia likes. Don't get any other brands. Anything else is unacceptable." He fumbles with the Ziploc seal on the bag and removes one of the frozen nuggets. "Also, they must be dinosaur-shaped. Dinosaur—got that?"

I can't suppress a smile. "Got it."

"Also"—he holds up the chicken nugget—"you have to first examine the nugget for any deformities. Missing head, missing leg, or missing tail. If the dinosaur nugget has any of these critical defects, it *will* be rejected." Now he pulls a plate from the cabinet above the microwave. He lays five perfect nuggets on the plate. "She likes to have five nuggets. You put it in the microwave for exactly ninety seconds. Any less, it's frozen. Any more, it's overcooked. It's a very tenuous balance."

I nod solemnly. "I understand."

As the chicken nuggets rotate in the microwave, he glances around the kitchen, which is at least twice as large as the apartment I was evicted from. "I can't even tell you how much money we spent renovating this kitchen, and Cecelia won't eat anything that doesn't come out of the microwave."

The words "spoiled brat" are at the tip of my tongue, but I don't say them. "She knows what she likes."

"She sure does." The microwave beeps and he pulls out the plate of piping hot chicken nuggets. "How about you? Have you eaten yet?"

"I'll just bring some food up to my room."

He raises an eyebrow. "You don't want to join us?"

Part of me would like to join him. There's something very engaging about Andrew Winchester, and I can't help but want to get to know him better. But at the same time, it would be a mistake. If Nina walked in and saw the two of us laughing it up at the dining table, she wouldn't like it. I also have a feeling that Cecelia won't make the evening pleasant.

"I'd rather just eat in my room," I say.

He looks like he's going to protest, but then he thinks better of it. "Sorry," he says. "We've never had live-in help before, so I'm not sure about the etiquette."

"Me either," I admit. "But I don't think Nina would like it if she saw me eating with you."

I hold my breath, wondering if I've overstepped by stating the obvious. But Andrew just nods. "You're probably right."

"Anyway." I lift my chin to look at his eyes. "Thank you for the tutorial on the chicken nuggets."

He grins at me. "Any time."

Andrew takes the plate of chicken back into the dining room. When he's gone, I gobble up the food from Cecelia's rejected plate while standing over the kitchen sink, then return to my bedroom.

TEN

A week later, I come down to the living room and find Nina holding a full garbage bag. My first thought is: Oh God, what now?

In only a week of living with the Winchesters, I feel like I've been here for years. No, *centuries*. Nina's moods are wildly unpredictable. At one moment, she's hugging me and telling me how much she appreciates having me here. In the next, she's berating me for not completing some task she never even told me about. She's flighty, to say the least. And Cecelia is a total brat, who clearly resents my presence here. If I had any other options, I would quit.

But I don't, so I don't.

The only member of the family who isn't completely intolerable is Andrew. He is not around much, but my few interactions with him have been... uneventful. And at this point, I'm thrilled with *uneventful*. Truthfully, I feel sorry for Andrew sometimes. It can't be easy being married to Nina.

I hover at the entrance to the living room, trying to figure out what Nina could possibly be doing with a garbage bag. Does she want me to sort the garbage from now on, alphabetically and by color and odor? Have I purchased some sort of unacceptable garbage bag and now I need to re-bag the garbage? I can't even begin to guess.

"Millie!" she calls out.

My stomach clenches. I have a feeling I'm about to figure out what she wants me to do with the garbage. "Yes?"

She waves me over to her—I try to walk over like I'm not being led to my execution. It's not easy.

"Is there something wrong?" I ask.

Nina picks up the heavy garbage bag and drops it on her gorgeous leather sofa. I grimace, wanting to warn her not to get garbage all over the expensive leather material.

"I just went through my closet," she says. "And unfortunately, a few of my dresses have gotten a *tad* too small. So I've collected them in this bag. Would you be a dear and take this to a donation bin?"

Is that it? That's not so bad. "Of course. No problem."

"Actually..." Nina takes a step back, her eyes raking over me. "What size are you?"

"Um, six?"

Her face lights up. "Oh, that's perfect! These dresses are all size six or eight."

Six or eight? Nina looks like she's at least a size fourteen. She must not have cleared out her closet in a while. "Oh..."

"You should take them," she says. "You don't have any nice clothes."

I flinch at her statement, although she's right. I don't have any nice clothing. "I'm not sure if I should..."

"Of course you should!" She thrusts the bag in my direction. "They would look amazing on you. I insist!"

I accept the bag from her and nudge it open. There's a little white dress on top and I pull it out. It looks incredibly expensive and the material is so soft, I want to bathe in it. She's right. This would look amazing on me—it would look amazing on anyone.

If I do decide to get out there and start dating again, it would be nice to have some decent clothing. Even if it is all white.

"Okay," I agree. "Thank you so much. This is so generous of you."

"You're very welcome! I hope you enjoy them!"

"And if you ever decide you want it back, just let me know."

When she throws back her head and laughs, her double chin wobbles. "I don't think I'm going to drop any dress sizes anytime soon. Especially since Andy and I are having a baby."

My mouth falls open. "You're pregnant?"

I'm not sure if Nina being pregnant is a good or bad thing. Although that would explain her moodiness. But she shakes her head. "Not yet. We've been trying for a bit, but no luck. But we're both really eager to have a baby, and we've got an appointment with a specialist soon. So I would guess in the next year or so, there will be another little one in the house."

I'm not sure how to respond. "Um... congratulations?"

"Thank you." She beams at me. "Anyway, please enjoy the clothes, Millie. Also, I have something else for you." She fishes around in her white purse and pulls out a key. "You wanted a key to your room, didn't you?"

"Thank you." After that first night, when I woke up in terror thinking I was locked in the room, I haven't given that much thought to the lock on the door. I have noticed the door sticks a bit, but nobody is sneaking up to my room and locking me in there—not that the key would help if I were inside. But I pocket the key. It might be good to lock the door when I leave the room. Nina seems like somebody who might snoop. Also, this seems like a good time to bring up another of my concerns. "One other thing. The window in the room doesn't open. It seems like it's painted shut."

"Is it?" Nina sounds like she finds this to be a particularly uninteresting piece of information.

"It's a fire hazard, probably."

She looks down at her nails and frowns at one where the white paint is chipped. "I don't think so."

"Well, I'm not sure, but… I mean, the room should have a window that opens, shouldn't it? It does get awfully stuffy up there."

Nina doesn't seem eager to help me, but I hate the idea of the only window in the room being painted shut.

"I'll have somebody take a look at it then," she says in a way that makes me think she is absolutely never going to get somebody to take a look at it and I will never have a window that opens. She glances down at the garbage bag. "Millie, I'm happy to give you my clothes but please don't leave that garbage bag lying around our living room. It's bad manners."

"Oh, sorry," I mumble.

And then she sighs like she just doesn't know what to do with me.

ELEVEN

"Millie!" Nina's voice sounds frantic on the other line. "I need you to pick up Cecelia from school!"

I've got a pile of laundry balanced in my arms, and my cell phone is between my shoulder and my ear. I always pick up immediately when Nina calls, no matter what I'm doing. Because if I don't, she will call over and over (and over) until I do.

"Sure, no problem," I say.

"Oh, thank you!" Nina gushes. "You're *such* a dear! Just grab her from the Winter Academy at 2:45! You're the best, Millie!"

Before I can ask any other questions, like where I'm supposed to meet Cecelia or the address of the Winter Academy, Nina has hung up. As I remove the phone wedged under my ear, I feel a jolt of panic when I see the time. I've got less than fifteen minutes to figure out where this school is and retrieve my employer's daughter. Laundry is going to have to wait.

I type the name of the school into Google as I sprint down

the stairs. Nothing comes up. The closest school by that name is in Wisconsin, and even though Nina makes some odd requests, I doubt she expects me to pick her daughter up in Wisconsin in fifteen minutes. I call Nina back, but naturally, she doesn't pick up. Neither does Andy when I try him.

Great.

While I pace across the kitchen, trying to figure out what to do next, I notice a piece of paper stuck to the refrigerator with a magnet. It's a school holiday schedule. From the *Windsor* Academy.

She said Winter. Winter Academy. I'm sure of it. Didn't she?

I don't have time to wonder if Nina told me the wrong name or if she doesn't know the name of the school her daughter attends, where she is also vice president of the PTA. Thankfully, there's an address on the flier, so I know exactly where to go. And I've only got ten minutes to get there.

The Winchesters live in a town that boasts some of the best public schools in the country but Cecelia goes to private school, because of course she does. The Windsor Academy is a huge elegant structure with lots of ivory columns, dark brown bricks, and ivy running along the walls that makes me feel like I'm picking Cecelia up at Hogwarts or something unreal like that. One other thing I wish Nina had warned me about was the parking situation at pick-up time. It is an absolute nightmare. I have to drive around for several minutes searching for a spot, and I finally squeeze in between a Mercedes and a Rolls-Royce. I'm scared somebody might tow my dented Nissan just on principle.

Given how little time I had to get to the school, I'm huffing and puffing as I sprint to the entrance. And naturally, there are five separate entrances. Which one will Cecelia be coming out of? There's no indication where I should go. I try calling Nina again, but once more, the call goes to voicemail. Where *is* she? It's none of my business, but the woman doesn't have a job and I do all the chores. What could she be doing with herself?

After questioning several irritable parents, I ascertain that Cecelia will be coming out of the very last entrance on the right side of the school. But just because I am determined not to screw this up, I approach two immaculately dressed women chatting by the door and ask, "Is this the exit for the fourth graders?"

"Yes, it is." The thinner of the two women—a brunette with the most perfectly shaped eyebrows I've ever seen—looks me up and down. "Who are you looking for?"

I squirm under her gaze. "Cecelia Winchester."

The two women exchange knowing looks. "You must be the new maid Nina hired," the shorter woman—a redhead—says.

"Housekeeper," I correct her, although I don't know why. Nina can call me whatever she wants.

The brunette snickers at my comment, but doesn't say anything about it. "So how is it so far working there?"

She's digging for dirt. Good luck with that—I'm not going to give her any. "It's great."

The women exchange looks again. "So Nina isn't driving you crazy?" the redhead asks me.

"What do you mean?" I say carefully. I don't want to gossip with these harpies, but at the same time, I'm curious about Nina.

"Nina is just a bit... high strung," the brunette says.

"Nina is nuts," the redhead pipes up. "*Literally*."

I suck in a breath. "What?"

The brunette elbows the redhead hard enough to make her gasp. "Nothing. She's just joking around."

At that moment, the doors to the school swing open and children pour out. If there were any chance to get more information out of these two women, the chance is gone as they both move in the direction of their own fourth graders. But I can't stop thinking about what they said.

I spot Cecelia's pale blond hair near the entrance. Even though most of the other kids are wearing jeans and T-shirts, she's wearing another lacy dress, this one a pale sea green. She sticks out like a sore thumb. I have no problem keeping her in my sight as I move toward her.

"Cecelia!" I wave my arm frantically as I get closer. "I'm here to pick you up!"

Cecelia looks at me like she would much rather get into the back of the van of some bearded homeless man than go home with me. She shakes her head and turns away from me.

"Cecelia!" I say, more sharply. "Come on. Your mom said I should pick you up."

She turns back to look at me, and her eyes say she thinks I'm a moron. "No, she didn't. Sophia's mother is picking me up and taking me to karate."

Before I can protest, a woman in her forties wearing yoga pants and a pullover comes over and rests her hand on Cecelia's shoulder. "Ready for karate, girls?"

I blink up at the woman. She does not appear to be a kidnapper. But there's obviously been some misunderstanding. Nina called me and told me to pick up Cecelia. She was very clear about it. Well, except for the part where she told me the wrong school. But other than that, she was very clear.

"Excuse me," I say to the woman. "I work for the Winchesters and Nina asked me to pick up Cecelia today."

The woman arches an eyebrow and places a recently manicured hand on her hip. "I don't think so. I pick up Cecelia every single Wednesday and take the girls to karate. Nina didn't mention a change in plans. Maybe *you* got it wrong."

"I didn't," I say, but my voice wavers.

The woman reaches into her Gucci purse and whips out her phone. "Let's clear this up with Nina, shall we?"

I watch as the woman presses a button on her phone. She taps her long fingernails against her purse as she waits for Nina to pick up. "Hello, Nina? It's Rachel." She pauses. "Yes, well, there's a *girl* here saying you told her to pick up Cecelia, but I explained to her that I take Cecelia to karate every Wednesday." Another long pause as the woman, Rachel, nods. "Right, that's exactly what I told her. I'm so glad I checked." After another pause, Rachel laughs. "I know *exactly* what you mean. It's *so* hard to find somebody good."

It's not hard to imagine Nina's end of the conversation.

"Well," Rachel says. "Just as I thought. Nina says you got it mixed up. So I'm going to go ahead and take Cecelia to karate."

And then to put the icing on the cake, Cecelia sticks her tongue out at me. But on the plus side, I don't have to drive home with her.

I take out my own phone, checking for a message from Nina, retracting her request that I pick up Cecelia. There's nothing. I shoot off a text to her:

A woman named Rachel just spoke with you and said you asked her to bring Cecelia to karate. So I'll go home then?

Nina's reply comes a second later:

Yes. Why on earth did you think I wanted you to pick up Cecelia?

Because you asked me to! My jaw twitches, but I can't let it get to me. This is just how Nina is. And there are plenty of good things about working for her. (Or *with* her—ha!) She's just a little flighty. A little eccentric.

Nina is nuts. Literally.

I can't help but think back to what that nosy redhead said to me. What did she mean by that? Is Nina more than just an eccentric and demanding boss? Is there something else going on with her?

Maybe it's better if I don't know.

TWELVE

Even though I had resigned myself to minding my own business about Nina's mental health history, I can't help but wonder. I work for this woman. I *live with* this woman.

And there's something else strange about Nina. Like this morning as I'm cleaning the master bathroom, I can't help but think nobody with good mental health could leave the bathroom in this sort of disorder—the towels on the floor, the toothpaste hugging the basin of the sink. I know depression can sometimes make people unmotivated to clean up. But Nina motivates herself enough to get out and about every day, wherever she goes.

The worst thing was finding a used tampon on the floor a few days ago. A used, bloody tampon. I wanted to throw up.

While I'm scrubbing the toothpaste and the globs of makeup adhered to the sink, my eyes stray to the medicine cabinet. If Nina's actually "nuts," she's probably on medication, right? But I can't look in the medicine cabinet. That would be a massive violation of trust.

But then again, it's not like anyone would know if I took a look. Just a quick look.

I look out at the bedroom. Nobody is in there. I peek around the corner just to make absolutely sure. I'm alone. I go back into the bathroom and after a moment of hesitation, I nudge the medicine cabinet open.

Wow, there are a *lot* of medications in here.

I pick up one of the orange pill bottles. The name on it is Nina Winchester. I read off the name of the medication: haloperidol. Whatever that is.

I start to pick up a second pill bottle when a voice floats down the hallway: "Millie? Are you in there?"

Oh no.

I hastily stuff the bottle back in the cabinet and slam it shut. My heart is racing, and a cold sweat breaks out on my palms. I plaster a smile on my face just in time for Nina to burst into the bedroom, wearing a white sleeveless blouse and white jeans. She stops short when she sees me in the bathroom.

"What are you doing?" she asks me.

"I'm cleaning the bathroom." I'm not looking at your medications, that's for sure.

Nina squints at me, and for a moment, I'm certain she's going to accuse me of going through the medicine cabinet. And I'm a horrible liar, so she'll almost certainly know the truth. But then her eyes fall on the sink.

"How do you clean the sink?" she asks.

"Um." I lift the spray bottle in my hand. "I use this sink cleaner."

"Is it *organic*?"

"I..." I look at the bottle I picked up at the grocery store last week. "No. It isn't."

Nina's face falls. "I really prefer organic cleaning products, Millie. They don't have as many chemicals. You know what I mean?"

"Right..." I don't say what I'm thinking, which is I can't believe a woman who is taking that many medications is concerned about a few chemicals in a cleaning product. I mean, yes, it's in her sink, but she's not *ingesting* it. It's not going into her bloodstream.

"I just feel like..." She frowns. "You aren't doing a good job getting the sink clean. Can I watch how you're doing it? I'd like to see what you're doing wrong."

She wants to watch me clean her sink? "Okay..."

I spray more of the product in her sink and scrub at the porcelain until the toothpaste residue vanishes. I glance over at Nina, who is nodding thoughtfully.

"That's fine," she says. "I guess the real question is how are you cleaning the sink when I'm *not* watching you."

"Um, the same?"

"Hmm. I highly doubt that." She rolls her eyes. "Anyway, I don't have time to supervise your cleaning all day. Try to make sure to do a thorough job this time."

"Right," I mutter. "Okay, I will."

Nina wanders out of the bedroom to go to the spa, or a luncheon with her friends, or whatever the hell she does to fill her time, because she doesn't have a job. I look back at the sink, which is now spotless. I get seized by the irrepressible urge to dunk her toothbrush in the toilet.

I don't dunk her toothbrush in the toilet. But I do take out my phone and punch in the word "haloperidol."

Several hits fill the screen. Haloperidol is an antipsychotic medication, used to treat schizophrenia, bipolar disorder, delirium, agitation, and acute psychosis.

And that's just *one* of at least a dozen pill bottles. God knows what else is in there. Part of me is burning with shame that I looked in the first place. And part of me is scared at what else I might find.

THIRTEEN

I'm busy vacuuming the living room when the shadow goes by the window.

I wander over to the window, and sure enough, Enzo is working in the backyard today. As far as I can tell, he alternates houses from day to day, doing various gardening and landscaping tasks. Right now, he is digging at the flower bed in the front yard.

I grab an empty glass from the kitchen and fill it up with cold water. Then I head outside.

I'm not entirely sure what I hope to accomplish here. But ever since those two women talked about Nina being crazy ("literally"), I can't stop thinking about it. And then I found that antipsychotic medication in her medicine cabinet. Far be it from me to judge Nina for having psychological problems—I met my fair share of women struggling with mental illness in prison—but it would be helpful information for me to know. Maybe I could even help her if I understood her better.

I remember how on my first day, Enzo seemed to be warning me about something. Nina is out of the house, Andrew is at work, and Cecelia is at school, so this seems like a perfect time to interrogate him. The only tiny complication is that he hardly speaks a word of English.

But it can't hurt. And I'm sure he's thirsty and will appreciate the water.

When I get outside, Enzo is busy digging a hole in the ground. He seems intensely focused on his task, even after I clear my throat loudly. Twice. Finally, I wave my hand and say, "*Hola*!"

That may have been Spanish again.

Enzo looks up from the hole he was digging. There's an amused expression on his lips. "*Ciao*," he says.

"*Ciao*," I correct myself, vowing to get it right next time.

He has a vee of sweat on his T-shirt, which is sticking to his skin and emphasizing every single muscle. And they're not bodybuilder's muscles—they are the firm muscles of a man who does manual labor for a living.

So I'm staring. So sue me.

I clear my throat again. "I brought you... um, water. How do you say...?"

"*Acqua*," he says.

I nod vigorously. "Yes. That."

See? We're doing it. We're communicating. This is going great.

Enzo strides over to me and gratefully takes the water glass. He drains half of it in what looks like a single gulp. He lets out a sigh and wipes his lips with the back of his hand. "*Grazie*."

"You're welcome." I smile up at him. "So, um, have you worked for the Winchesters for a long time?" He looks at me blankly. "I mean, have you... Do you work here... many years?"

He takes another swig from the water glass. He's emptied nearly three-quarters of it. When it's gone, he's going to go back to work—I don't have much time. "*Tre anni*," he says finally. Then adds in his heavily accented English, "Three year."

"And, uh…" I squeeze my hands together. "Nina Winchester… Do you…"

He frowns at me. But it's not a blank look, like he doesn't understand me. He looks like he's waiting to hear what I'm going to say. Maybe he understands English better than he can speak it.

"Do you…" I start again. "Do you think that Nina is… I mean, do you like her?"

Enzo narrows his eyes at me. He takes another long drink from the water glass, then shoves it back into my hand. Without another word, he goes back to the hole he was digging, picks up his shovel, and gets back to work.

I open my mouth to try again, but then I shut it. When I first came here, Enzo was trying to warn me about something, but Nina opened the door before he could say anything. And obviously, he's changed his mind. Whatever Enzo knows or thinks, he isn't going to tell me. At least not now.

FOURTEEN

I've been living with the Winchesters for about three weeks when I have my first parole officer meeting. I waited to schedule it for my day off. I don't want them to know where I'm going.

I'm down to monthly meetings with my officer, Pam, a stocky middle-aged woman with a strong jaw. Right after I got out, I was living in housing subsidized by the prison, but after Pam helped me get that waitressing job, I moved out and got my own place. Then after I lost the waitressing job, I never exactly told Pam about it. Also, I never told her about my eviction. At our last meeting a little over a month ago, I lied through my teeth.

Lying to a parole officer is a violation of parole. Not having a residence and living out of your car is also a violation of parole. I don't like to lie, but I didn't want to have my parole revoked and go right back to prison to serve the last five years of my sentence. I couldn't let that happen.

But things have turned around. I can be honest with Pam today. Well, almost.

Even though it's a breezy spring day, Pam's small office is like a hundred degrees. Half the year, her office is a sauna, and the other half of the year it's freezing. There's no in-between. She's got the small window wrenched open, and there's a fan blowing the dozens of papers around her desk. She has to keep her hands on them to keep them from blowing away.

"Millie." She smiles at me when I come in. She's a nice person and genuinely seems like she wants to help me, which made me feel all the worse about how I lied to her. "Good to see you! How is it going?"

I settle down into one of the wooden chairs in front of her desk. "Great!" That's a bit of a lie. But it's going fine. Good enough. "Nothing to report."

Pam rifles through the papers on her desk. "I got your message about the address change. You're working for a family in Long Island as a housekeeper?"

"That's right."

"You didn't like the job at Charlie's?"

I chew on my lip. "Not really."

This is one of the things I lied to her about. Telling her that I quit the job at Charlie's. When the reality is that they fired me. But it was *completely* unfair.

At least I was lucky enough that they quietly fired me and didn't get the police involved. That was part of the deal—I go quietly and they don't involve the cops. I didn't have much of a choice. If they had gone to the police about what happened, I would've been right back in prison.

So I didn't tell Pam I got fired, because if I did, she would have called them to find out why. And then when I lost my apartment, I couldn't tell her about that either.

But it's fine now. I have a new job and a place to live. I'm not in danger of being locked up again. At my last appointment with Pam, I was sitting on the edge of my seat, but I feel okay this time.

"I'm proud of you, Millie," Pam says. "Sometimes it's hard

for people to adjust when they have been incarcerated since they were teenagers, but you've done great."

"Thank you." No, she definitely doesn't need to know about that month when I was living in my car.

"So how is the new job?" she asks. "How are they treating you?"

"Um..." I rub my knees. "It's fine. The woman I work for is a bit... eccentric. But I'm just cleaning. It's not a big deal."

Another thing that's a slight lie. I don't want to tell her that Nina Winchester has been making me increasingly uncomfortable. I searched online to see if she herself had any kind of record. Nothing popped up, but I didn't pay for the actual background check. Anyway, Nina is rich enough to keep her nose clean.

"Well, that's great," Pam says. "And how is your social life?"

That's not technically an area a parole officer is supposed to be asking about, but Pam and I have become friendly, so I don't mind the question. "Nonexistent."

She throws back her head and laughs so that I can see a shiny filling in the back of her mouth. "I understand if you don't feel ready to date yet. But you should try to make some friends, Millie."

"Yeah," I say, even though I don't mean it.

"And when you do start dating," she says, "don't just settle for anyone. Don't date a jerk just because you're an ex-con. You deserve someone who treats you right."

"Mmm..."

For a moment, I allow myself to think about the possibility of dating a man in the future. I close my eyes, trying to imagine what he might look like. Unbidden, the image of Andrew Winchester fills my head, with his easy charm and handsome smile.

My eyes fly open. Oh no. No way. I can't even *think* it.

"Also," Pam adds, "you're beautiful. You shouldn't settle."

I almost laugh out loud. I've been doing everything I can to look as unattractive as I possibly can. I wear baggy clothing, I always keep my hair in a bun or a ponytail, and I haven't put on even one scrap of makeup. But Nina still looks at me like I'm some kind of vamp.

"I'm just not ready to think about that yet," I say.

"That's fine," Pam says. "But remember, having a job and shelter is important, but human connections are even more important."

She might be right, but I'm just not ready for that right now, I have to focus on keeping my nose clean. The last thing I want is to end up back in prison. That's all that matters.

* * *

I have trouble sleeping at night.

When you're in prison, you're always sleeping with one eye open. You don't want things to be going on around you without you knowing about it. And now that I'm out, the instinct hasn't left me. When I first got an actual bed, I was able to sleep really well for a while, but now my old insomnia has come back full force. Especially because my bedroom is so unbearably stuffy.

My first paycheck has been deposited in my bank account, and the next chance I have, I'm going to go out and buy myself a television for my bedroom. If I turn on the television, I might be able to drift off to sleep with it on. The sound will mimic the noise at night in the prison.

Up until now, I've been hesitant to use the Winchesters' television. Not the huge home theater, obviously, but their "normal" TV in the living room. It doesn't seem like it should be a big deal, considering Nina and Andrew go to bed early. They have a very specific routine every night. Nina goes upstairs to put Cecelia to bed at precisely 8:30. I can hear her reading a bedtime story, then she sings to her. Every night she sings the same song: "Somewhere Over the Rainbow" from *The Wizard of Oz*. Nina doesn't sound like she has any vocal training, but there's something strangely, hauntingly beautiful about the way she sings to Cecelia.

After Cecelia goes to sleep, Nina reads or watches television in the bedroom. Andrew follows upstairs not long after. If I come downstairs after ten o'clock, the first floor is completely empty.

So this particular night I decided to take advantage.

This is why I'm sprawled out on the sofa, watching an episode of *Family Feud*. It's nearly one in the morning, so the high energy level of the contestants seems almost bizarre. Steve Harvey is joking around with them, and despite how tired I am, I laugh out loud when one of the contestants gets up to demonstrate his tap-dancing skills. I used to watch the show when I was a kid, and I always imagined going on it myself; I'm not sure who I would've invited to go with me. My parents, me—that's three. Who else could I have invited?

"Is that *Family Feud*?"

I jerk my head up. Even though it's the middle of the night, Andrew Winchester is somehow standing behind me, as wide awake as the people on the television screen.

Damn. I knew I should have stayed in my room.

"Oh!" I say. "I, uh... I'm sorry. I didn't mean to..."

He arches an eyebrow. "What are you sorry for? You live here, too. You have every right to watch the television."

I grab a pillow from the couch to conceal my flimsy gym shorts that I've been sleeping in. Also, I'm not wearing a bra. "I was going to buy a set for my room."

"It's fine to use our monitor, Millie. You probably won't get much reception up there anyway." The whites of his eyes glow in the light of the television. "I'll be out of your hair in a minute. I'm just grabbing a glass of water."

I sit on the couch, clutching the pillow to my chest, debating if I should go upstairs. I'm never going to fall asleep now because my heart is racing. He said he was just getting some water, so maybe I can stay. I watch him shuffle into the kitchen and I hear the tap running.

He comes back into the living room, sipping from his water glass. That's when I notice he's only got on a white undershirt and boxers. But at least he's not shirtless.

"How come you poured water from the sink?" I can't help but ask him.

He plops down next to me on the sofa, even though I wish he wouldn't. "What do you mean?"

It would be rude to jump off the sofa, so I just scoot down as far as I can. The last thing I need is for Nina to see the two of us getting cozy together on the sofa in our underwear. "Like, you didn't use the water filter in the refrigerator."

He laughs. "I don't know. I've always just gotten water from the sink. Like, is it poison?"

"I don't know. I think it has chemicals in it."

He runs a hand through his dark hair until it sticks up a bit. "I'm hungry for some reason. Any leftovers from dinner in the fridge?"

"No, sorry."

"Hmm." He rubs his stomach. "Would it be really bad manners if I eat some peanut butter right out of the jar?"

I cringe at the mention of peanut butter. "As long as you're not eating in front of Cecelia."

He tilts his head. "Why?"

"You know. Because she's allergic." They really don't seem very respectful of Cecelia's deadly peanut allergy in this household.

Even more surprising, Andrew laughs. "No, she's not."

"Yes, she is. She told me she is. The first day I was here."

"Um, I think I would know if my daughter were allergic to

peanuts." He snorts. "Anyway, do you think we would keep a big jar of it in the pantry if she were allergic?"

That was exactly what I thought when Cecelia told me about her allergy. Was she just making it up to torture me? I wouldn't put it past her. Then again, Nina also said Cecelia had a peanut allergy. What's going on here? But Andrew makes the most valid point: the fact that there's a big jar of peanut butter in the pantry indicates nobody here has a deadly peanut allergy.

"Blueberries," Andrew says.

I frown. "I don't think there are any blueberries in the refrigerator."

"No." He nods at the television screen, where *Family Feud* has entered the second round. "They surveyed a hundred people and asked them to name a fruit you can fit in your mouth whole."

The contestant on the screen answers blueberries, and it's the number one answer. Andrew pumps his fist. "See? I knew it. I would be great on this show."

"The top answer is always easy to get," I say. "The tricky part is getting the more obscure answers."

"Okay, smarty pants." He grins at me. "Name a fruit you can fit in your mouth whole."

"Um..." I tap a finger against my chin. "A grape."

Sure enough, the next contestant answers "grape" and is correct.

"I stand corrected," he says. "You're good at this, too. Okay, what about a strawberry?"

"It's probably up there," I say, "even though you wouldn't really want to put a whole strawberry in your mouth because it has the stem and all that."

The contestants manage to name strawberries and cherries, but they get stuck on the last answer. Andrew is cracking up when one of them says a peach.

"A peach!" he cries. "Who could fit a peach in their mouth? You'd have to unhinge your jaw!"

I giggle. "Better than a watermelon."

"That's probably the answer! I bet anything."

The final answer on the board turns out to be a plum. Andrew shakes his head. "I don't know about that. I'd like to see a picture of the contestants who said they could fit a plum in their mouth whole."

"That should be part of the show," I say. "You get to hear from the hundred people surveyed and get the rationale behind their answers."

"You should write to *Family Feud* and suggest that," he says soberly. "You could revolutionize the whole show."

I giggle again. When I first met Andrew, I assumed he was a stuffy rich guy. But he's not like that at all. Nina is certifiable, but Andrew is *nice*. He's completely down-to-earth, and he's funny. And it seems like he's a really good dad to Cecelia.

The truth is, I feel a bit sorry for him sometimes.

I shouldn't think that. Nina is my boss. She gives me paychecks and a place to live. My loyalty is to her. But at the same time, she's *awful*. She's a slob, she's constantly telling me conflicting information, and she can be incredibly cruel. Even Enzo, who's got to be two hundred pounds of solid muscle, seems afraid of her.

Of course, I might not feel that way if Andrew wasn't so incredibly attractive. Even though I have sat as far away from him as I possibly can without falling off the side of the couch, I can't help but think about the fact that he is wearing his underwear right now. He's in his freaking boxers. And his undershirt material is thin enough that I can see the outline of some very sexy muscles. He could do a lot better than Nina.

I wonder if he knows it.

Just as I'm starting to relax and feel glad that Andrew

joined me down here, a screechy voice breaks into my thoughts: "Gosh, what's the big joke you're laughing about down here?"

I whip my head around. Nina is standing at the foot of the stairs, staring at us. When she's in her heels, I can hear her coming a mile away, but she's surprisingly light-footed in her bare feet. She's wearing a white nightgown that falls to her ankles, and her arms are folded across her chest.

"Hey, Nina." Andrew yawns and climbs off the sofa. "What are you doing up?"

Nina is glaring at us. I don't know how he isn't panicking right now. I'm one second away from peeing in my pants. But he seems totally cavalier about the fact that his wife just caught the two of us alone in the living room at one in the morning, both of us *in our underwear*. Not that we were *doing* anything, but still.

"I could ask you the same thing," Nina retorts. "You two seem to be having a lot of fun. What's the joke?"

Andrew lifts a shoulder. "I came down to get some water and Millie was here watching television. I got distracted by *Family Feud*."

"Millie." Nina turns her attention to me. "Why don't you get a television for your own room? This is the family room."

"I'm sorry," I say quickly. "I'm going to buy a television next chance I get."

"Hey." Andrew raises his eyebrows. "What's so wrong with Millie watching a little television down here if nobody's around?"

"Well, you're around."

"And she wasn't bothering me."

"Don't you have a meeting first thing in the morning?" Nina's eyes bore into him. "Should you really be awake watching television at one in the morning?"

He sucks in a breath. I hold my own breath, hoping for a

minute that he's going to stand up to her. But then his shoulders sag. "You're right, Nina. I better turn in."

Nina stands there, her arms folded across her ample chest, watching Andrew trudge up the stairs, like he's a child she's sending up without supper. It's unsettling to see the extent of her jealousy.

I get up from the couch as well and shut off the television. Nina is still lingering at the base of the stairs. Her eyes rake over my gym shorts and tank top. My lack of a bra. Again, it strikes me how bad this looks. But I thought I would be all alone down here.

"Millie," Nina says, "in the future, I expect you to wear appropriate attire around the house."

"I'm so sorry," I say for the second time. "I didn't think anyone would be awake."

"Really?" She snorts. "Would you just wander around any stranger's house in the middle of the night because you assume they won't be around?"

I don't know what to say to that. This is not a stranger's house. I *live* here, albeit up in the attic. "No..."

"Please stay up in the attic after bedtime," she says. "The rest of the house is for my family. Do you understand?"

"I understand."

She shakes her head. "Honestly, I'm not even sure how much we need a maid. Maybe this was a mistake..."

Oh no. Is she firing me at one in the morning because I was watching television in her living room? This is bad. And there's no chance Nina is going to give me a good recommendation for another job. She seems more like the sort of person who would call every potential employer to tell them how much she hated me.

I've got to fix this.

I dig my fingernails into the palm of my hand. "Listen,

Nina," I begin. "Nothing was going on between me and Andrew..."

She throws her head back and laughs. It's a disturbing sound, something almost between a laugh and a cry. "Is that what you think I'm worried about? Andrew and I are soulmates. We have a child together and soon we'll have another baby together. You think I'm scared that my husband would risk everything in his life for some trampy servant living in the attic?"

I swallow. I may have just made things much worse. "No, he wouldn't."

"Damn straight he wouldn't." She looks me in the eyes. "And don't ever forget it."

I stand there, not sure what to say. Finally, she jerks her head in the direction of the coffee table, "Clean up that mess—right now."

With those words, she turns on her heel and goes back upstairs.

There isn't really a mess. It's just the water glass Andrew left behind. My cheeks burn with humiliation as I walk over to the coffee table and snatch up the glass. The bedroom door slams upstairs, and I look down at the glass in my hand.

Before I can stop myself, I hurl it to the ground.

It smashes spectacularly on the floor. Glass goes everywhere. I take a step back, and a shard digs into the pad of my foot.

Wow, that was extremely stupid.

I blink down at the mess I made on the ground. I've got to get it cleaned up, and moreover, I've got to find some shoes so I don't get any more glass in my feet. I take a deep breath, trying to slow down my breathing. I'll get the glass cleaned up and it will be fine. Nina will never know.

But I'll have to be more careful in the future.

FIFTEEN

This Saturday afternoon, Nina is throwing a small PTA gathering in her backyard. They're meeting up to plan something called "field day" in which the kids play in a field for a few hours, and somehow it takes months of planning to prepare for it. Nina has been talking about it nonstop lately. And she has texted me no less than a dozen times to remind me to pick up the hors d'oeuvres.

I'm starting to get stressed because, as usual, the entire house was a mess when I woke up this morning. I don't know how this house gets so messy. Is Nina's medication treating some sort of disorder where she gets up in the middle of the night and makes a mess in the house? Is that a thing?

I don't know how the bathrooms get so bad overnight, for example. When I come into her bathroom to clean in the morning, there are usually at least three or four towels strewn on the floor, sopping wet. There's usually toothpaste caked into the sink that I have to scrub to get free. Nina has some sort of aversion to throwing her clothes in the laundry basket, so it takes me a good ten minutes to gather her bra, underwear, pants, pantyhose, etc. Thank God Andrew is better at getting his clothing in the laundry basket. Then there's the stuff that needs to be dry cleaned, of which there is a lot. Nina doesn't distinguish between the two, and God forbid I make the wrong decision about what goes in the laundry machine and what needs to be run to the dry cleaner. That would be a hanging offense.

The other thing is the food wrappers. I find candy wrappers stuffed into nearly every crevice in her bedroom and bathroom. I suppose that explains why Nina is fifty pounds heavier than she was in the photographs of when she and Andrew first met.

By the time I have cleaned the house top to bottom, dropped off the dry cleaning, and completed the laundry and the ironing, I'm running very short on time. The women are going to arrive within the hour, and I'm still not done with all the tasks Nina assigned me, including picking up the hors d'oeuvres. She's not going to understand if I try to explain that to her. Considering she nearly fired me last week when she caught me watching *Family Feud* with Andrew, I can't afford to make any mistakes. I've got to make sure this afternoon is perfect.

Then I get to the backyard. The Winchesters' backyard is one of the most beautiful sights in the neighborhood. Enzo has done his job well—the hedges are trimmed so precisely, it's like he used a ruler. Flowers dot the edges of the yard, adding a pop of color. And the grass is so lush and green, I'm half tempted to lie down in it, waving my arms around to make grass angels.

But apparently, they don't spend much time out here, because all the patio furniture has a thick layer of dust on it. Everything has a thick layer of dust on it.

Oh God, I do *not* have time to get everything done.

"Millie? Are you okay?"

Andrew is standing behind me, dressed casually for a change, in a blue polo shirt and khaki slacks. Somehow, he looks even better than he does in an expensive suit.

"I'm fine," I mumble. I shouldn't even be talking to him.

"You look like you're about to cry," he points out.

I wipe my eyes self-consciously with the back of my hand. "I'm fine. There's just a lot to do for this PTA meeting."

"Aw, that's not worth crying over." His brow crinkles. "These PTA women are never going to be satisfied no matter what you do. They're all awful."

That does *not* make me feel any better.

"Look, maybe I have a..." He digs around in his pocket and pulls out a crumpled tissue. "I can't believe I have a tissue in my pocket, but here."

I manage a smile as I accept the tissue. As I dab my nose, I catch a whiff of Andrew's aftershave.

"Now," he says, "what can I do to help?"

I shake my head. "It's fine. I can handle it."

"You're crying." He props one of his feet up on the dirty chair. "Seriously, I'm not completely useless. Just tell me what you need me to do." When I hesitate, he adds, "Look, we both want to make Nina happy, right? This is how you make her happy. She's not going to be happy if I let you screw this up."

"Fine," I grumble. "It would be incredibly helpful if you could pick up the hors d'oeuvres."

"Done."

It feels like a giant weight has been lifted from my shoulders. It was going to take me twenty minutes to get to the store to pick up the hors d'oeuvres and twenty minutes to get back. That would've left me only fifteen minutes to clean this filthy patio furniture. Could you imagine that Nina sat in one of these chairs in one of her white outfits?

"Thank you," I say. "I really, really appreciate it. Really."

He grins at me. "Really?"

"Really, really."

Cecelia bursts into the backyard that moment, wearing a light pink dress with white trim. Like her mother, she doesn't have so much as a hair out of place. "Daddy," she says.

He turns his gaze on Cecelia. "What's up, Cece?"

"The computer isn't working," she says. "I can't do my homework. Can you fix it?"

"I absolutely can." He rests a hand on her shoulder. "But first we are going on a little road trip and it's going to be super fun."

She looks at him dubiously.

He ignores her skepticism. "Go put on your shoes."

It would have taken me half the day to convince Cecelia to put on her shoes, but she obediently goes back into the house to do what he says. Cecelia is nice enough, as long as I'm not in charge of her.

"You're good with her," I comment.

"Thanks."

"She looks a lot like you."

Andrew shakes his head. "Not really. She looks like Nina."

"She does," I insist. "She has Nina's coloring and hair, but she has your nose."

He toys with the hem of his polo shirt. "Cecelia isn't my biological daughter. So any resemblance between the two of us is, you know, coincidental."

Wow, I can't stop putting my foot in my mouth. "Oh. I didn't realize..."

"It's not a big deal." His brown eyes are trained on the back door, waiting for Cecelia to return. "I met Nina when Cecelia was a baby, so I'm the only father she's ever known. I think of her as my daughter. It's the same difference."

"Of course." My opinion of Andrew Winchester goes up a few notches. Not only did he not go for some kind of supermodel, but he married a woman who already had a child and raised that child as his own. "Like I said, you're good with her."

"I think kids are great... I wish we had a dozen of them."

Andrew looks like he wants to say something else, but then he presses his lips shut. I remember what Nina told me weeks ago about how they were trying to get pregnant. I remember the bloody tampon I found on the bathroom floor. I wonder if they've had any success since then. Based on the sad look in Andrew's eyes, I suspect the answer is no.

But I'm sure Nina will be able to get pregnant if that's what they want. After all, they have all the resources in the world. Either way, it's none of my business.

SIXTEEN

It's safe to say I hate every single woman at this PTA meeting.

There are four of them total, including Nina. I've memorized their names. Jillianne (Jilly-anne), Patrice, and Suzanne (not to be confused with Jillianne). The reason I have memorized their names is because Nina will not let me leave the backyard. She's been making me stand in the corner, constantly at attention in case they need something.

At least the hors d'oeuvres are a success. And Nina has no idea Andrew picked them up for me.

"I'm just not happy with the field day menu." Suzanne taps her pen against her chin. I've heard Nina refer to Suzanne before as her "best friend," but as far as I can tell, Nina isn't close with any of her so-called friends. "I feel like there needs to be more than one gluten-free option."

"I agree," Jillianne says. "And even though there is a vegan option, it's not vegan *and* gluten-free. So what are people who are both vegan and gluten-free supposed to eat?"

I don't know? Grass? I've honestly never seen women more obsessed with gluten. Every time I brought out an hors d'oeuvre, each of them questioned me about the amount of gluten in it. As if I have any idea. I don't even know what gluten is.

It's a sweltering hot day today, and I would give anything to be back in the house, under the air conditioner. Hell, I would give anything to have a drink of the pink sparkling lemonade the women are sharing. I keep wiping sweat from my forehead every time they're not looking at me. I'm afraid I may have pit stains.

"This blueberry goat's cheese flatbread should have been heated up," Patrice comments as she chews on the morsel in her mouth. "They're barely lukewarm."

"I know," Nina says regretfully. "I asked my maid to take care of it, but you know how it is. It is *so* hard to find good help."

My mouth falls open. She never asked me any such thing. Also, does she realize I'm standing *right here*?

"Oh, it truly is." Jillianne nods sympathetically. "You just can't hire anyone good anymore. The work ethic in this country is so horrible. You wonder why people like that can't find better jobs, right? It's laziness, pure and simple."

"Or else you get someone foreign," Suzanne adds. "And they barely speak the language. Like Enzo."

"At least he's nice to look at!" Patrice laughs.

The rest of them hoot and giggle, although Nina is oddly silent. I suppose she doesn't have to ogle the hot landscaper when she's married to Andrew—I can't blame her on that one. She also seems to have some sort of strange grudge against Enzo.

I'm itching to say something after the way they've been bad mouthing me behind my… Well, not behind my back because I'm standing *right here*, as I mentioned. But I've got to show them that I'm not a lazy American. I have worked my butt off in this job and never complained once.

"Nina." I clear my throat. "Do you want me to heat up the hors d'oeuvres?"

Nina turns to look at me, her eyes flashing in a way that

makes me take a step back. "Millie," she says calmly, "we're having a *conversation* here. Please don't interrupt. It's so rude."

"Oh, I—"

"Also," she adds, "I'd thank you not to refer to me as *Nina* —I'm not your drinking buddy." She snickers at the other women. "It's *Mrs. Winchester*. Don't make me remind you again."

I stare at her, flabbergasted. On the very first day I met her, she instructed me to call her Nina. I've been calling her that the entire time I've been working here, and she's never said a word about it. Now she's acting like I'm taking liberties.

The worst part is the other women are acting like Nina is a hero for telling me off. Patrice launches into some story about how her cleaning woman had the gall to tell her about how her dog died. "I don't want to be mean," Patrice says, "but what do I care if Juanita's dog died? She was going on and on about it. Honestly."

"We definitely do need the help though." Nina pops one of the unacceptable hors d'oeuvres into her mouth. I've been watching her and she's eaten about half of them while the other women are eating like birds. "Especially when Andrew and I have another baby."

The other women let out gasps of excitement. "Nina, are you pregnant?" Suzanne cries.

"I knew you were eating like five times as much as the rest of us for a reason!" Jillianne says triumphantly.

Nina shoots her a look—I have to stifle a laugh. "I'm not pregnant *yet*. But Andy and I are seeing this fertility specialist who is supposed to be *amazing*. Trust me, I'll have a baby by the end of the year."

"That is so great." Patrice puts a hand on Nina's shoulder. "I know you guys have been wanting a baby for a long time. And Andrew is *such* a great dad."

Nina nods, and for a moment, her eyes look a bit moist. She

clears her throat. "Excuse me for a moment, ladies. I'll be right back."

Nina dashes into the house, and I'm not sure if I'm supposed to follow her. She's probably going to the bathroom or something. Of course, maybe now that's one of my responsibilities—following Nina into the bathroom so that I can pat her hands dry for her or flush the toilet or God only knows what.

As soon as Nina is gone, the other women burst into quiet laughter. "Oh my God!" Jillianne snickers. "That was so awkward! I can't believe I said that to her. I really thought she was pregnant! I mean, doesn't she look pregnant?"

"She is getting like a house," Patrice agrees. "She seriously needs to hire a nutritionist and a personal trainer. And did anyone else notice her roots showing?"

The other women nod in agreement. Even though I'm not participating in this conversation, I also noticed Nina's roots. On the day I interviewed with her, her hair looked so immaculate. Now she's got a good centimeter of darker roots showing. I'm surprised she let it get that bad.

"Like, I would be embarrassed to walk around like that," Patrice says. "How does she expect to keep that hottie husband of hers?"

"Especially since I heard they have an airtight prenup," Suzanne adds. "If they were to get a divorce, she'd get practically nothing. Not even child support, because you know he never adopted Cecelia."

"A prenup!" Patrice bursts out. "What is wrong with Nina? Why would she sign something like that? She better do whatever she can to keep him happy."

"Well, I'm not going to be the one to tell her she needs to go on a diet!" Jillianne speaks up. "God, I don't want to send her back to that mental institution. You know Nina isn't all there."

I stifle a gasp. I had been hoping when those other women at the school were hinting that Nina was crazy, she was just *suburban* crazy. Like that she saw a therapist and popped a few sedatives every now and then. But it sounds like Nina is a level above that. If these gossipy shrews are to be believed, she's been in a *psychiatric institution*. She has a serious illness.

I feel a jab of guilt for getting so frustrated with her when she tells me the wrong information or her mood changes on a dime. It isn't her fault. Nina has serious issues going on. Everything makes a little more sense now.

"I'll tell you one thing." Patrice drops her voice several notches. She's doing it so I can't hear, which means she has no idea how loud she is. "If I were Nina, the last thing I would do would be to hire a pretty, young maid to live in my house. She must be out of her mind with jealousy."

I look away, trying not to let on that I can hear every word she says. I have done everything I can to keep Nina from feeling jealous. I don't want her to get even the slightest idea that I am interested in her husband. I don't want her to know that I think he's attractive or for her to think that there's any chance something could happen between the two of us.

I mean, yes, if Andrew were single, I'd be interested. But he's not. I'm staying far away from that man. Nina has nothing to worry about.

SEVENTEEN

Today Andrew and Nina have an appointment with that fertility specialist.

They've both been nervous and excited about the appointment all week. I heard snatches of their conversation during dinner. Apparently, Nina got a bunch of fertility tests and they're going to be discussing the results today. Nina thinks they're going to be doing IVF, which is expensive, but they've got money to burn.

As much as Nina gets on my nerves sometimes, it's sweet how the two of them are planning for the new baby. Yesterday, they were talking about how they were going to turn the guestroom into a nursery. I'm not sure who is more excited—Nina or Andrew. For their sakes, I hope they get pregnant soon.

While they're at the appointment, I'm supposed to be watching Cecelia. Watching a nine-year-old girl shouldn't be difficult. But Cecelia seems determined to make it so. After a friend's mother dropped her off after God knows what lesson she had today (karate, ballet, piano, soccer, gymnastics—I've completely lost track), she kicks one of her shoes off in one direction, the second in another, and then throws her backpack in yet a third direction. Luckily, it's too warm for a coat, or else she would have to find a fourth place to abandon her coat.

"Cecelia," I say patiently. "Can you please put your shoes in the shoe rack?"

"Later," she says absently, as she plops down on the sofa, smoothing out the fabric of her pale yellow dress. She grabs the remote and flicks on the television to an obnoxiously loud cartoon. An orange and a pear appear to be arguing on the screen. "I'm hungry."

I take a deep, calming breath. "What would you like to eat?"

I assume she's going to come up with something ridiculous that I need to make her, just to get me to sweat. So I'm surprised when she says, "How about a bologna sandwich?"

I'm so relieved by the fact that we have all the makings of a bologna sandwich in the house that I don't even insist that she say please. If Nina wants her daughter to be a brat, that's her prerogative. It's not my job to discipline her.

I head to the kitchen and grab some bread and a pack of beef bologna from the overflowing fridge. I don't know whether Cecelia likes mayonnaise on her sandwich, and furthermore, I'm sure I'll put too much or too little on it. So I decide to just give her the bottle of mayonnaise and she can portion it out herself to the exact perfect amount. Ha, I've outsmarted you, Cecelia!

I return to the living room and place the sandwich and mayonnaise on the coffee table for Cecelia. She looks down at the sandwich, crinkling her brow. She picks it up tentatively and then her face fills with disgust.

"Ew!" she cries. "I don't want that."

I swear to God, I'm going to strangle this girl with my bare hands. "You said you wanted a bologna sandwich. I made you a bologna sandwich."

"I didn't say I wanted a bologna sandwich," she whines. "I said I wanted an *abalone* sandwich!"

I stare at her, open-mouthed. "An abalone sandwich? What is *that*?"

Cecelia grunts in frustration and throws the sandwich on the ground. The bread and meat separate, landing in three separate piles on the carpet. The only positive is that I didn't use any mayonnaise, so at least I don't have to clean up mayonnaise.

Okay, I've had enough of this girl. Maybe it's not my place, but she's old enough to know not to throw food on the floor. And especially if there's going to be a baby in the house sometime soon, she needs to learn to act like a child her age.

"Cecelia," I say through my teeth.

She lifts her slightly pointed chin. "*What*?"

I'm not sure what would've happened between me and Cecelia, but our showdown gets interrupted by the front door unlocking. That must be Andrew and Nina, back from their appointment. I turn away from Cecelia and plaster a smile on my face. I'm sure Nina will be bursting with excitement over this visit.

Except when they come into the living room, neither of them are smiling.

That's an understatement. Nina's blond hair is in disarray and her white blouse is wrinkled. Her eyes are bloodshot and puffy. Andrew doesn't look so great either. His tie is half undone, like he started to pull it off and then got distracted during the process. And actually, his eyes look bloodshot, too.

I squeeze my hands together. "Everything okay?"

I should have just kept my mouth shut. That would have been the smart thing to do. Because now Nina directs her gaze at me and her pale skin turns bright red. "For God's sake, Millie," she snaps at me. "Why do you have to be so *nosy*? This is none of your goddamn business."

I swallow. "I'm so sorry, Nina."

Her eyes drift down to the mess on the floor. Cecelia's shoes. The bread and bologna near the coffee table. And sometime in the last minute, Cecelia has scurried out of the living room and is nowhere to be seen. Nina's face contorts. "Is this really what I have to come home to? This *mess*? What am I paying you for anyway? Maybe you should start looking for another job."

My throat constricts. "I... I was going to clean that up..."

"Don't do any work on *my* account." She shoots Andrew a withering look. "I'm going to go lie down. I have a pounding headache."

Nina stomps up the staircase, her heels like bullets on each step, punctuated by the door to their bedroom slamming shut. Obviously, something did not go well at that appointment. There's no point in trying to talk to her right now.

Andrew sinks onto the leather sofa and drops his head back. "Well, that sucked."

I bite down on my lip and sit beside him, even though I sense I probably shouldn't. "Are you okay?"

He rubs his eyes with his fingertips. "Not really."

"Do... do you want to talk about it?"

"Not really." He squeezes his eyes shut for a moment. He lets out a sigh. "It's not going to happen for us. Nina is not going to get pregnant."

My first reaction is surprise. Not that I know much about it, but I can't quite believe that Nina and Andrew aren't able to pay their way out of this dilemma. I swear I saw on the news that a sixty-year-old woman got pregnant.

But I can't say that to Andrew. They just saw one of the leading fertility specialists. There's nothing I know that this person doesn't. If he said Nina won't get pregnant, that's that. There's not going to be a baby. "I'm so sorry, Andrew."

"Yeah..." He rakes a hand through his hair. "I'm trying to be okay with this, but I can't say I'm not disappointed. I mean, I love Cecelia like she's my own, but... I wanted... I mean, I always dreamed of..."

It's the deepest conversation we've ever had. It's kind of nice that he's opening up to me. "I understand," I murmur. "It must be so hard... for both of you."

He looks down at his lap. "I need to be strong for Nina. She's devastated about this."

"Is there anything I can do?"

He's quiet for a moment, running his finger along a crease in the leather of the sofa. "There's this show Nina wants to see in the city—she keeps mentioning it. *Showdown.* I know it would give her a lift if we got tickets. If you could ask her for some dates and book orchestra seats, that would be great."

"Done," I say. I can't stand Nina for lots of reasons, but I can't imagine what it must be like to get this news—my heart goes out to her.

He rubs his bloodshot eyes again. "Thanks, Millie. I honestly don't know what we would do without you. I'm sorry about the way Nina treats you sometimes. She's just a little temperamental, but she really does like you and appreciates your help."

I'm not entirely sure that's true, but I'm not going to argue with him. I'm going to have to keep working here until I've saved up a reasonable amount of money. And I'm just going to have to do my best to make Nina happy.

EIGHTEEN

That night, I wake up to the sound of shouting.

The attic is incredibly well insulated, so I can't hear anything being said. But there are loud voices coming from below my room. A male voice and a female voice. Andrew and Nina.

Then I hear a crash.

Instinctively, I roll out of bed. Maybe it's none of my business, but something is going on down there. I have to at least make sure everything is okay.

I put my hand on the doorknob to my room, and it doesn't turn. Most of the time, I'm used to the fact that the door sticks. But every once in a while, I get a jab of panic. But then the knob shifts under my hand. And I'm out.

I descend the creaky steps to the second floor. Now that I'm out of the attic, the shouting is much louder. It's coming from the master bedroom. Nina's voice, yelling at Andrew. She sounds almost hysterical.

"It's not fair!" she cries. "I did everything I could and—"

"Nina," he says. "It's not your fault."

"It *is* my fault! If you were with a younger woman, you could have a baby like you want! It's *my* fault!"

"Nina..."

"You'd be better off without me!"

"Come on, don't say that..."

"It's true!" But she doesn't sound sad. She sounds angry. "You wish I were gone!"

"Nina, stop it!"

There's another loud crash from inside the room. Followed by a third crash. I take a step back, torn between knocking on the door to make sure everything is okay and wanting to scurry back to my room and hide. I stand there several seconds, paralyzed by my indecision. Then the door is yanked open.

Nina is standing there in the same lily-white nightgown she was wearing the night she caught me and Andrew in the living room. But now I notice a streak of crimson on the pale material, starting at the side of her hip and running down the length of the skirt.

"Millie." Her eyes bore into me. "What are you doing here?"

I look down at her hands and see the same crimson is all over her right palm. "I..."

"Are you spying on us?" She arches an eyebrow. "Are you listening to our conversation?"

"No!" I take a step back. "I just heard a crash and I was worried that... I wanted to make sure everything is okay."

She notices my gaze directed at what I'm almost sure is a blood stain on her gown. She looks almost amused by it. "I just cut my hand a bit. Nothing to worry about. I don't need *your* help."

But what was going on in there? Is that really why there's blood all over her nightgown? And where is Andrew?

What if she killed him? What if he's lying dead in the

middle of the bedroom? Or worse, what if he's bleeding to death right now, and I have a chance to save him? I can't just walk away. I may have done some bad things in my life, but I'm not going to let Nina get away with murder.

"Where's Andrew?" I say.

Pink circles form on her cheeks. "*Excuse* me?"

"I just…" I shift between my bare feet. "I heard a crash. Is he okay?"

Nina stares at me. "How dare you! What are you accusing me of?"

It occurs to me that Andrew is a big, strong man. If Nina made short work of him, what chance would I stand against her? But I can't move. I have to make sure he's okay.

"Go back to your room," she orders me.

I swallow a lump in my throat. "No."

"Go back to your room or else you're fired."

She means it. I can see it in her eyes. But I can't move. I start to protest again, but then I hear something. Something that makes my shoulders sag with relief:

The sound of the faucet turning on in the master bedroom.

Andrew is okay. He's just in the bathroom.

Thank God.

"Happy?" Her light blue eyes are like ice, but there's something else there. A twinge of amusement. She likes scaring me. "My husband is alive and well."

I bow my head. "Okay, I just wanted to… I'm sorry I bothered you."

I turn around and trudge down the hallway. I can feel Nina's eyes on my back. When I'm almost at the stairwell, her voice rings out behind me.

"Millie?"

I turn around. Her white dress glows in the moonlight filtering into the hallway, like she's an angel. Except for the blood. And now I can also see a tiny pool of crimson forming on the floor, under her injured right hand. "Yes?"

"Stay up in the attic at night." She blinks at me. "Do you understand?"

She doesn't have to tell me a second time. I never want to come out of the attic again.

NINETEEN

The next morning, Nina has morphed back into the more pleasant version of herself, having seemingly forgotten last night. I would think it was all a terrifying dream except for the bandage wrapped around her right hand. The white gauze is dotted with crimson.

Although she's not being directly weird with me, Nina *is* more frazzled than usual this morning. When she goes to drive Cecelia to school, her tires screech against the pavement. When she returns, she just stands in the middle of the living room for a moment, staring at the walls, until I finally come out of the kitchen and ask if she's all right.

"I'm fine." She tugs at the collar of her white blouse, which is wrinkled even though I am certain I ironed it. "Would you be so kind as to make me some breakfast, Millie? The usual?"

"Of course," I say.

"The usual" for Nina is three eggs, scrambled in a lot of butter and Parmesan cheese, four slices of bacon, and an English muffin, also buttered. I can't help but think of the comments the other PTA woman made about Nina's weight while she was in the other room, although I respect that she doesn't scrutinize every calorie that goes in her mouth the way they do. Nina isn't gluten-free or vegan. As far as I can tell, she eats whatever she wants and then some. She even has late-night snacks, as evidenced by the dirty plates she leaves behind on the counter for me to wash in the morning. Not one of those plates has ever made it into the dishwasher.

I serve the plate of food to her at the dining table with a glass of orange juice on the side. She scrutinizes the food, and I'm worried I've got the version of Nina that's going to tell me that everything on this plate is cooked poorly, or else claim that she flat out never asked me for breakfast in the first place. But instead, she smiles sweetly at me. "Thank you, Millie."

"You're welcome." I hesitate, hovering over her. "By the way, Andrew asked me if I would get you two tickets to *Showdown* on Broadway."

Her eyes light up. "He's *so* thoughtful. Yes, that would be lovely."

"What are some days that work for you?"

She scoops some eggs into her mouth and chews thoughtfully. "I'm free a week from Sunday, if you can swing it."

"Sure. And I can watch Cecelia, of course."

She scoops more eggs into her mouth. Some of it misses her lips and falls onto her white blouse. She doesn't seem to even notice it's there and continues shoveling food into her mouth.

"Thank you again, Millie." She winks at me. "I really don't know what we would do without you."

She likes to tell me that. Or that she's going to fire me. One or the other.

But I suppose it's not her fault. Nina definitely has emotional problems like her friends said. I can't stop thinking about her alleged stay in a psychiatric hospital. They don't lock you up for nothing. Something bad must've happened, and part of me is dying to know what it is. But it's not like I could ask her. And my attempts to get the story out of Enzo have been fruitless.

Nina has nearly cleaned her entire plate, having devoured the eggs, bacon, and English muffin in less than five minutes, when Andrew jogs downstairs. I had been a little worried about him after last night, even though I heard the water running. Not that it was a likely scenario, but maybe, I don't know, Nina had the faucet on some sort of automatic timer just to make it seem like he was in the bathroom, alive and well. Like I said, it didn't seem likely, but it also didn't seem *impossible*. In any case, it's a relief to find him intact. My breath catches a bit at the sight of his dark gray suit paired with a light blue dress shirt.

Just before Andrew enters the dining room, Nina pushes her plate of food away. She stands up and smooths out her blond hair, which lacks its usual shine, and the dark roots are even more visible than before.

"Hello, Andy." She offers him a dazzling smile. "How are you this morning?"

He starts to answer her, but then his eyes dart down to the bit of egg still clinging to her blouse. One side of his lips quirks up. "Nina, you have a little egg on you."

"Oh!" Her cheeks turn pink as she dabs at the egg on her blouse. But it's been sitting there several minutes, and a stain still mars the delicate white fabric. "Sorry about that!"

"It's okay—you still look beautiful." He grabs her shoulders and pulls her in for a kiss. I watch her melt against him and ignore the twinge of jealousy in my chest. "I've got to run to the office, but I'll see you tonight."

"I'll walk you out, darling."

Nina is so freaking lucky. She's got everything. Yes, she did have a stay at a mental institution, but at least she wasn't in prison. And here she is, with an incredible house, tons of money, and a husband who is kind, funny, wealthy, considerate, and... well, absolutely gorgeous.

I close my eyes for a moment and think about what it would be like to live in Nina's shoes. To be the woman in charge of this household. To have the expensive clothing and the shoes and the fancy car. To have a maid I could boss around—force her to cook for me and clean for me and live in a tiny hole in the attic while I had the big bedroom with the king-size bed and zillion-count sheets. And most of all, to have a husband like Andrew. To have him press his lips against mine the way he did to hers. To feel his body heat against my chest...

Oh my God, I *must* stop thinking about this. *Now*. In my defense, it's been a really long time for me. I spent ten years in prison, fantasizing about some perfect guy I would meet when I got out, who would save me from everything. And now...

Well, it could happen. It's possible.

I climb the stairs and get to work making the beds and cleaning the bedrooms. I've just finished up and am returning downstairs when the doorbell rings. I hurry over to answer it, and I'm surprised to see Enzo at the door, clutching a giant cardboard box in his arms.

"*Ciao*," I say, remembering the greeting he taught me.

Amusement flickers over his face. "*Ciao*. This... for you."

I understand immediately what must've happened. Sometimes delivery people don't realize they can enter through the gate, so they dump heavy packages outside the gate, and I have to heave them into the house. Enzo must have seen the delivery man leave the package, and now he's kindly carried it in for me.

"*Grazie*," I say.

He raises his eyebrows at me. "You want I..."

It takes me a second to realize what he is asking. "Oh... yes, just put it on the dining table."

I point to the dining table and he carries the package over there. I remember Nina freaked out that time when Enzo came into the house, but she's not here and that box looks too heavy for me to lift. After he rests it on the table, I glance at the return address: Evelyn Winchester. Probably somebody in Andrew's family.

"*Grazie*," I say again.

Enzo nods. He's wearing a white T-shirt and jeans—he looks *good*. He's always out somewhere in the neighborhood, working up a sweat in the yard, and a lot of the rich women in this neighborhood love to ogle him. Truthfully, I prefer Andrew's looks, and of course, there's the language barrier. But maybe having a little fun with Enzo would be good for me. It would relieve a little of that pent-up energy, and maybe I would stop having wholly inappropriate fantasies about my boss's husband.

I'm not quite sure how to broach the subject, given he doesn't seem to speak any English. But I'm pretty sure the language of love is universal.

"Water?" I offer him, while I'm trying to figure out exactly how to go about this.

He nods. "*Si*."

I run to the kitchen and grab a glass from the cabinet. I fill it halfway with water, then I bring it out to him. He takes it gratefully. "*Grazie*."

His biceps bulge as he drinks from the glass. He has a *really* good body. I wonder what he's like in bed. Probably fantastic.

I wring my hands together as he drinks from the glass of water. "So, um... are you... busy?"

He lowers the glass and looks at me blankly. "Eh?"

"Um." I clear my throat. "Like, do you have much... work?"

"Work." He nods at a word he understands. Seriously, I don't get it. He's been working here three years, and he really doesn't understand any English? "*Si. Molto occupato*."

"Oh."

This isn't going well. Maybe I should just get right to the point.

"Listen." I take a step toward him. "I just thought maybe you want to take... a little break?"

His dark eyes study my face. He does have pretty eyes. "I... no understand."

I can do this—language of love, all that. "A break." I reach out, place my hand on his chest, and raise an eyebrow suggestively. "You know."

I had expected at this point, he would grin at me, scoop me off my feet, and carry me up to the attic, where he would ravish me for hours. What I did not expect is the way his eyes darken. He leaps away from me like my hand is on fire and lets loose with a string of rapid, angry Italian. I have no idea what he's saying, aside from the fact that he's not saying "hello" or "thank you."

"I... I'm so sorry," I say helplessly.

"*Sei pazzo*!" he yells at me. He rakes a hand through his black hair. "*Che cavolo*!"

This is so freaking embarrassing. I want to crawl under the table. I mean, I thought there was a chance he might reject me, but not quite so vehemently. "I... I didn't mean to..."

He looks up to the stairwell almost fearfully and then back at my face. "I... I go. Now."

"Right." I nod at him. "Of course. I... I'm so sorry. I was just being friendly. I didn't mean to..."

He gives me a look like he knows what I just said was bullshit. I guess some stuff *is* universal.

"I'm sorry," I say for the third time as he strides toward the door. "And... thank you for the package. *Grazie*."

He pauses at the door, turning so his dark eyes meet mine. "You... you get out, Millie," he says in his broken English. "It's..." He presses his lips together, then manages to get out the word he said to me the first day we met, this time in English: "Dangerous."

He looks back up at the stairwell again, a troubled expression on his face. Then he shakes his head, and before I can stop him to try to figure out what he means, he's hurried out the front door.

TWENTY

God, that was humiliating.

I'm still reeling from the mortification of Enzo rejecting me while I'm waiting for Cecelia to finish her tap-dancing class. My head is throbbing, and the tapping of little feet in unison coming from the dance classroom isn't helping matters at all. I look around the room, wondering if anyone else finds it as annoying as I do. No? Just me?

The woman in the seat next to mine finally gives me a sympathetic look. Based on her naturally smooth skin, with no signs of a facelift or Botox, I'd estimate her to be about my age, which makes me think she's not picking up her own kid, either. She's one of the *servants*, like me.

"Advil?" she asks. She must have a sixth sense to notice my discomfort. Either that or my sighs are giving her the message.

I hesitate, then nod. A painkiller won't get rid of the humiliation of the hot Italian landscaper turning me down, but it will ease my headache at least.

She reaches into her big black purse and takes out a bottle of Advil. She raises her eyebrows at me, then I put out my hand and she shakes two little red pills into my palm. I throw them back into my mouth and swallow them dry. I wonder how long it'll take them to kick in.

"I'm Amanda, by the way," she tells me. "I'm your official tap-dancing waiting-room drug dealer."

I laugh, despite myself. "Who are you here to pick up?"

She flicks her brown ponytail off her shoulder. "The Bernstein twins. You should see them tap dance in unison. It's something to behold—speaking of pounding headaches. How about you?"

"Cecelia Winchester."

Amanda lets out a low whistle. "You work for the Winchesters? Good luck with that."

I squeeze my knees. "What do you mean?"

She lifts a shoulder. "Nina Winchester. You know. She's..." She makes the universal "cuckoo" sign with her index finger. "Right?"

"How do you know?"

"Oh, *everyone* knows." She shoots me a look. "Also, I get the feeling Nina is the jealous type. And her husband is *really* hot—don't you think?"

I avert my eyes. "He's okay, I guess."

Amanda starts digging around in her purse as I lick my lips. This is the opportunity I've been waiting for. Somebody I can pump for information about Nina.

"So," I say, "why do people say Nina is crazy?"

She looks up, and for a moment I'm scared she's going to be offended by my obvious digging. But she just grins. "You know she was locked up in a loony bin, right? Everyone talks about it."

I wince at her use of the term "loony bin." I'm sure she has some equally colorful terms for the place where I spent the last decade of my life. But I need to hear this. My heart speeds up, beating in sync with the tapping of little feet in the other room. "I did hear something about that..."

Amanda clucks. "Cecelia was a baby then. Poor thing—if the police had arrived a second later..."

"What?"

She drops her voice a notch, looking around the room. "You know what she did, don't you?"

I shake my head wordlessly.

"It was horrible..." Amanda sucks in a breath. "She tried to drown Cecelia in the bathtub."

I clasp a hand over my mouth. "She... *what?*"

She nods solemnly. "Nina drugged her, threw her in the tub with running water, then took a bunch of pills herself."

I open my mouth but no words come out. I have been expecting some story like, I don't know, she got into a fight with some other mother at ballet practice over the best color for tutus and then had a meltdown when they couldn't agree. Or maybe her favorite manicurist decided to retire and she couldn't take it. This is entirely different. The woman tried to murder her own child. I can't think of anything more horrible than that.

"Andrew Winchester was apparently in the city at his office," she says. "But he got worried when he couldn't get through to her. Thank God he called the police when he did."

My headache has escalated, despite the Advil. I'm truly about to throw up. Nina tried to kill her daughter. She tried to kill herself. God, no wonder she's on an antipsychotic.

It doesn't make any sense to me. Whatever else I can say about Nina, she clearly loves Cecelia very much. You can't fake that sort of thing. Yet I believe Amanda—I've certainly heard this rumor from enough people. It doesn't seem possible that everybody in town has got it wrong.

Nina really did try to kill her daughter.

Then again, I don't know the context. I've heard about postpartum depression, and how it can make your mind go to dark places. Maybe she didn't have any idea what she was doing. It's not like they're saying she *plotted* to kill her daughter. If that were true, she would be in prison right now. Forever.

Still. As much as I worried about Nina's mental status, I never truly believed she had the capacity for real violence. She's capable of much more than I thought.

For the first time since Enzo rejected me, I think back to the panic in his eyes as he hurried toward the front door. *You get out, Millie. It's... dangerous.* He's scared for me. He's scared of Nina Winchester. If only he spoke English. If he did, I have a feeling I might have moved out by now.

But really, what can I do? The Winchesters are paying me well, but not well enough to strike out on my own without at least a few more paychecks under my belt. If I quit, they'll never give me a decent recommendation. I'll have to go back to searching through the want ads, faced with rejection after rejection when they find out about my prison record.

I just have to hang in there a little longer. And do my best not to piss off Nina Winchester. My life might depend on it.

TWENTY-ONE

By dinner time tonight, the cardboard box Enzo brought into the house is still sitting on the dining table. In the interest of setting the table, I try to move it, but it is *very* heavy—Enzo made it seem lighter than it was by the way he effortlessly carried it into the room. I'm scared if I try to move it, I'll accidentally drop it. Odds are good there's some priceless Ming vase inside, or something equally fragile and expensive.

I study the return address on the box again. Evelyn Winchester—I wonder who that is. The handwriting is big and loopy. I give it a tentative shove and something rattles inside.

"Early Christmas present?"

I look up from the package—Andrew is home. He must have come in from the garage entrance, and he's smiling crookedly at me, his tie loose around his neck. I'm glad he seems to be in better spirits than yesterday. I really thought he was going to lose it after that doctor's appointment. And then that terrible argument last night, where I was half-convinced Nina had murdered him. Of course, now that I know why she was institutionalized, it doesn't seem nearly as far-fetched.

"It's June," I remind him.

He clucks his tongue. "It's never too early for Christmas." He rounds the side of the table to examine the return address on the package. He is only a few inches away from me, and I can smell his aftershave. It smells... nice. Expensive.

Stop it, Millie. Stop smelling your boss.

"It's from my mother," he notes.

I grin up at him. "Your mother still sends you care packages?"

He laughs. "She used to, actually. Especially in the past, when Nina was... sick."

Sick. That's a nice euphemism for what Nina did. I just can't wrap my head around it.

"It's probably something for Cece," he remarks. "My mother loves to spoil her. She always says since Cece only has one grandmother, it's her duty to spoil her."

"What about Nina's parents?"

He pauses, his hands on the box. "Nina's parents are gone. Since she was young. I never met them."

Nina tried to kill herself. Tried to kill her own daughter. And now it turns out she's also left a couple of dead parents in her wake. I just hope the maid isn't next.

No. I need to stop thinking this way. It's more likely Nina's parents died of cancer or heart disease. Whatever was wrong with Nina, they obviously felt she was ready to rejoin society. I should give her the benefit of the doubt.

"Anyway"—Andrew straightens up—"let me get this open."

He dashes into the kitchen and returns a minute later with a box cutter. He slices open the top and pulls up the flaps. I'm pretty curious at this point. I've been staring at this box all day, wondering what's inside. I'm sure whatever it is, it's something insanely expensive. I raise my eyebrows as Andrew stares into the box, the color draining from his face.

"Andrew?" I frown. "Are you okay?"

He doesn't answer. Instead, he sinks into one of the chairs

and presses his fingertips into his temples. I hurry over to comfort him, but I can't help but stop to take a look inside the box.

And then I understand why he looks so upset.

The box is filled with baby stuff. Little white baby blankets, rattles, dolls. There's a little pile of tiny white onesies.

Nina had been blabbing to anyone who would listen that they were expecting a baby soon. Surely, she mentioned it to Andrew's mother, who decided to send supplies. Unfortunately, she jumped the gun.

Andrew has a glazed look in his eyes. "Are you okay?" I ask again.

He blinks like he forgot I was in the room with him. He manages a watery smile. "I'm okay. Really. I just... I didn't need to see that."

I slide into the chair next to his. "Maybe that doctor was wrong?"

Although part of me wonders why he would even *want* to have a child with Nina. Especially after what she almost did to Cecelia. How could he trust her with a baby after she did something like that?

He rubs his face. "It's fine. Nina is older than me and then she had some... issues when we first married and I didn't feel comfortable trying to have a baby then. So we waited and now..."

I look at him in surprise. "Nina is older than you?"

"A little." He shrugs. "You don't think about age when you're in love. And I loved her." It doesn't escape me that he used the past tense to refer to his feelings for his wife. He notices it too because his face turns red. "I mean, I *love* her. I love Nina. And whatever happens, we've got each other."

He says the words with conviction, but then when he looks over at the box again, a really sad expression comes over his face. No matter what he says, he's not happy about the fact that he and Nina won't have another child together. It's weighing on him.

"I… I'll put the box in the basement," he mumbles. "Maybe somebody in the neighborhood will have a baby and we can give it to them. Or else we'll just… We can donate it. I'm sure it will go to good use."

I am seized by the irrepressible urge to wrap my arms around him. In spite of his financial success, I feel sorry for Andrew. He's a really good guy and he deserves to be happy. And I'm beginning to wonder if Nina—with all her issues and wild mood swings—is capable of making him happy. Or if he's just stuck with her out of obligation.

"If you ever want to talk about it," I say softly, "I'm here."

His eyes meet mine. "Thanks, Millie."

I put my hand on his—a gesture meant to comfort him. He turns his hand and gives my hand a squeeze. At the touch of his palm against mine, a sensation shoots through me like a lightning bolt. It's something I've never felt before. I look up at Andrew's brown eyes, and I can tell he feels it, too. For a moment, the two of us just stare at each other, drawn together by some invisible, indescribable connection. Then his face turns red.

"I better go." He tugs his hand away from mine. "I should… I mean, I've got to…"

"Right…"

He jumps up from the table and darts out of the dining room. But just before he disappears up the stairs, he gives me one last long lingering look.

TWENTY-TWO

I spend the next week avoiding Andrew Winchester.

I can't even deny anymore that I have feelings for him. Not just feelings. I have a very serious crush on this man. I think about him all the time. I even dream about him kissing me.

And he might have feelings for me, too, even though he claims he loves Nina. But the key point is I don't want to lose this job. You don't keep jobs by sleeping with your married boss. So I do my best to stuff all my feelings away. Andrew is at work most of the day anyway. It's easy enough to stay out of his way.

Tonight, as I'm putting plates of food out for dinner, preparing to dash off before Andrew comes into the room, Nina wanders into the dining area. She bobs her head in approval at the salmon with a side of wild rice. And of course, chicken nuggets for Cecelia.

"That smells wonderful, Millie," she remarks.

"Thanks." I hover near the kitchen, ready to call it quits for the evening—our usual routine. "Will that be all?"

"Just one thing." She pats her blond hair. "Were you able to book those tickets for *Showdown*?"

"Yes!" I snatched up the last two orchestra seats for *Show-*

down this Sunday night—I was so proud of myself. They cost a small fortune, but the Winchesters can afford it. "You are in the sixth row from the stage. You could practically touch the actors."

"Wonderful!" Nina claps her hands together. "And you booked the hotel room?"

"At The Plaza."

Since it's a bit of a drive into the city, Nina and Andrew will be staying overnight at The Plaza hotel. Cecelia is going to be staying at a friend's house, and I'll get the whole damn house to myself. I can walk around naked if I want. (I'm not planning to walk around naked. But it's nice to know I could.)

"It will be so lovely," Nina sighs. "Andy and I *really* need this."

I bite my tongue. I'm not going to comment on the state of Nina and Andrew's relationship, especially since the door slams at that moment, which means Andrew is home. Suffice to say, ever since that doctor's visit and their subsequent fight, they seem to have been somewhat distant from each other. Not that I'm paying attention, but it's hard not to notice the awkward politeness they have around each other. And Nina herself seems off her game. Like right now, her white blouse is buttoned wrong. She missed a button, and the whole thing is lopsided. I'm itching to tell her, but she'll scream at me if I do, so I keep my mouth shut.

"I hope you have a wonderful time," I say.

"We will!" She beams at me. "I can hardly wait all week!"

I frown. "All week? The show is in three days."

Andrew strides into the kitchen dining room, pulling off his tie. He stops short when he sees me, but he stifles a reaction. And I stifle my own reaction to how handsome he looks in that suit.

"Three days?" Nina repeats. "Millie, I asked you to book the tickets for a week from Sunday! I distinctly remember."

"Yes..." I shake my head. "But you told me that over a week ago. So I booked them for *this* Sunday."

Nina's cheeks turn pink. "So you admit I told you to book it for a week from Sunday and you still booked for *this* Sunday?"

"No, what I'm saying is—"

"I can't believe you could be so careless." She folds her arms across her chest. "I can't make the show this Sunday. I have to drive Cecelia to her summer camp in Massachusetts Sunday and I'm spending the night out there."

What? I could've sworn she told me to book it for this coming Sunday, and that Cecelia would be staying at a friend's house. There's no way I got this messed up. "Maybe somebody else could take her? I mean, the tickets are nonrefundable."

Nina looks affronted. "I'm not letting somebody else take my daughter to summer camp when I'm not going to see her for two weeks!"

Why not? That's no worse than trying to kill her. But I can't say that.

"I can't believe how badly you screwed this up, Millie." She shakes her head. "The cost of these tickets and the hotel room is coming right out of your paycheck."

My mouth falls open. The cost of those tickets and a hotel room at The Plaza are more than my paycheck. Hell, it's more than *three* paychecks. I'm trying to save up so I can get the hell out of here. I blink back tears at the thought of not getting paid for the foreseeable future.

"Nina," Andrew breaks in. "Don't get upset about this. Look, I'm sure there's a way to refund the tickets. I'll call the credit card company and I'll take care of it."

Nina shoots me a seething look. "Fine. But if we can't get the money back, I expect you to pay for it. Do you understand?"

I nod wordlessly, and then I dash off to the kitchen before she can catch me crying.

TWENTY-THREE

On Sunday afternoon, I get two pieces of good news:

First, Andrew managed to refund the tickets and I won't have to work for free.

Second, Cecelia is going to be gone for two whole weeks.

I'm not sure which of these revelations I'm happier about. I'm glad I don't have to shell out money for the tickets. But I'm even happier that I don't have to wait on Cecelia anymore. The apple doesn't fall far from the tree with that one.

Cecelia has packed enough luggage to last her at least one year. I swear to God, it's like she's put everything she owns in those bags, and then if there was any space left, she filled it with *rocks*. That's how it feels as I'm carrying the bags out to Nina's Lexus.

"Please be careful with that, Millie." Nina watches me fretfully as I summon superhuman strength to lift the bags into her trunk. My palms are bright red from where I was holding the straps. "Please don't break anything."

What could Cecelia possibly be carrying to camp that's so fragile? Don't they mostly just bring clothing and books and bug spray? But far be it from me to question her. "Sorry."

When I get back in the house to retrieve the last of Cecelia's bags, I catch Andrew jogging down the stairs. He catches me about to lift the monstrous piece of luggage and his eyes widen.

"Hey," he says. "I'll carry that for you. That looks really heavy."

"I'm fine," I insist, only because Nina is coming out of the garage.

"Yes, she's got it, Andy." Nina wags a finger. "You need to be careful about your bad back."

He shoots her a look. "My back is fine. Anyway, I want to say goodbye to Cece."

Nina pulls a face. "Are you sure you won't come with us?"

"I wish I could," he says. "But I can't miss an entire day of work tomorrow. I've got meetings in the afternoon."

She sniffs. "You always put work first."

He grimaces. I don't blame him for being hurt by her comment—as far as I can tell, it's completely untrue. Despite being a successful businessman, Andrew is home every single night for dinner. He does occasionally go to work on the weekends, but he's also attended two dance recitals this month, one piano recital, a fourth-grade graduation ceremony, a karate demonstration, and one night they were gone for hours for some sort of art show at the day school.

"I'm sorry," he says anyway.

She sniffs again and turns her head. Andrew reaches out to touch her arm, but she jerks it away and dashes to the kitchen to get her purse.

Instead, he heaves the last piece of luggage into his arms and goes out to the garage to dump it in the trunk and say goodbye to Cecelia, who is sitting in Nina's snow-colored Lexus, wearing a lacy white dress that is wildly inappropriate for summer camp. Not that I would ever say anything.

Two whole weeks without that little monster. I want to jump with joy. But instead, I turn my lips down. "It will be sad without Cecelia here this month," I say as Nina comes back out of the kitchen.

"Really?" she says dryly. "I thought you couldn't stand her."

My jaw drops open. I mean, yes, she's right that Cecelia and I have not hit it off. But I didn't realize she knew I felt that way. If she knows that, does she realize I'm not a big fan of Nina herself either?

Nina smooths down her white blouse and goes back out to the garage. As soon as she leaves the room, it's like all the tension has been sucked out of me. I always feel on edge when Nina is around. It's like she's dissecting everything I do.

Andrew emerges from the garage, wiping his hands on his jeans. I love how he wears a T-shirt and jeans on the weekends. I love the way his hair gets tousled when he's doing physical activity. I love the way he smiles and winks at me.

I wonder if he feels the same way I do about Nina leaving.

"So," he says, "now that Nina is gone, I have a confession to make."

"Oh?"

A confession? *I'm madly in love with you. I'm going to leave Nina so we can run off together to Aruba.*

Nah, not too likely.

"I couldn't get a refund on those show tickets." He hangs his head. "I didn't want Nina to give you a hard time over it. Or try to *charge* you, for Christ's sake. I'm sure she was the one who told you the wrong date."

I nod slowly. "Yes, she did, but... Well, anyway, thank you. I appreciate it."

"So... I mean, you should take the tickets. Go to the city tonight and see the show with a friend. And you can stay at The Plaza hotel room overnight."

I almost gasp. "That's so *generous*."

The right side of his lips quirks up. "Well, we've got the tickets. Why should they go to waste? Enjoy it."

"Yeah..." I toy with the hem of my T-shirt, thinking. I can't imagine what Nina would say if she found out. And I have to admit, just the thought of going gives me anxiety. "I appreciate the gesture, but I'll pass on the show."

"Really? This is supposed to be the best show of the decade! You don't like going to shows on Broadway?"

He has no idea about my life—what I've been doing for the last decade. "I've never even been to a show on Broadway."

"Then you need to go! I insist!"

"Right, but..." I take a deep breath. "The truth is, I don't have anyone to go with. And I don't feel like going alone. So like I said, I'll pass."

Andrew stares at me for a moment, rubbing his finger against the slight stubble on his jaw. Finally, he says, "I'll go with you."

I raise my eyebrows. "Are you sure that's a good idea?"

He hesitates. "I know Nina has jealousy issues, but that's no reason to let these expensive tickets go to waste. And it's a crime you've never seen a show on Broadway before. It'll be fun."

Yes, it will be fun. That's what I'm worried about, damn it.

I imagine my evening unfolding. Driving out to Manhattan in Andrew's BMW, sitting in the orchestra for one of the hottest shows on Broadway, then maybe grabbing a bite to eat at one of the nearby restaurants and enjoying a glass of Prosecco. Having a conversation with Andrew where we don't have to worry about Nina showing up and glowering at us.

It sounds wonderful.

"Sure," I say. "Let's do it."

Andrew's face lights up. "Awesome. I'll go change and let's meet down here in about an hour, okay?"

"You got it."

As I climb the stairs to the attic, I get a dark, heavy sensation in the pit of my stomach. As much as I'm looking forward to tonight, I have a bad feeling about it. I have a feeling that if I go to the show tonight, something terrible will happen. I already have a totally inappropriate crush on Andrew. It seems like spending the entire night with him, just the two of us, is tempting fate.

But that's ridiculous. We're just going to go to Manhattan to enjoy a show. We are two adults, and we are completely in control of our own actions. This will be fine.

TWENTY-FOUR

I can't go to a Broadway show in jeans and a T-shirt—that's for sure. I checked online, and officially there's no dress code, but it just feels wrong. Anyway, Andrew said he was going to change, so I need to wear something nice.

The problem is, I don't own anything nice.

Well, technically I do. I have that bag of clothing Nina gave me. I hung up the outfits so they wouldn't get damaged but I have yet to wear any of them. For the most part, they're all fancy dresses, and it's not like I've had many occasions to dress up while cleaning the Winchester house. I don't really want to put on a ballgown to do my vacuuming.

But tonight is an occasion to dress up for. Maybe the only such occasion I'll have for a long time.

The biggest problem is that all of the dresses are so blindingly *white*. Obviously, it's Nina's favorite color. White is *not* my favorite color. I don't even think I have a favorite color (anything but orange). But I never liked wearing white because it gets dirty so easily. I'll have to be especially careful tonight. And I won't be wearing all white, because I don't have any white shoes. All I've got are some black pumps, so that's what I'm wearing.

I look through the dresses, trying to figure out which one would be most appropriate for tonight. They're all beautiful, and also extremely *sexy*. I select a form-fitting cocktail dress that falls just above my knees with a lace halter neckline. I had assumed since Nina is quite a bit heavier than I am, it would be loose on me. But she must have purchased it many years ago—it fits me so perfectly, I couldn't have found something better if I'd bought it specifically for myself.

I take it easy with the makeup. Just a few dabs of lipstick, a tiny bit of eyeliner, and that's it. Whatever else happens tonight, I'm going to behave myself. The last thing I want is any trouble.

And I have no doubt that if Nina suspects a whiff of anything between me and her husband, she'll make it her mission to destroy me.

Andrew is already in the living room when I descend the stairs. He's wearing a gray suit jacket and a matching tie, and he's taken the time to shower and shave off that stubble on his chin. He looks... God, he looks incredible. Devastatingly handsome. So handsome, I want to grab him by the lapels. But the most amazing thing is the way his eyes fly open when he catches sight of me, and he inhales audibly.

And then for a few moments, the two of us are just staring at each other.

"Jesus, Millie." His hand is shaking a bit as he adjusts his tie. "You look..."

He doesn't complete his thought, which is probably a good thing. Because he's not looking at me in a way you're supposed to be looking at a woman who is not your wife.

I open my mouth, wondering if I should ask him if this is a bad idea. If maybe we should call off the whole thing. But I can't quite make myself say that.

Andrew manages to rip his eyes away from me and looks

down at his watch. "We better get going. Parking can be a pain around Broadway."

"Yes, of course. Let's go."

There's no turning back now.

I feel almost like a celebrity when I'm sliding into the cool leather seat of Andrew's BMW. This car is nothing like my Nissan. Andrew climbs into the driver seat and that's when I notice my skirt is riding up my thighs. When I put on the dress, it came nearly down to my knees, but sitting down, it's somehow mid-thigh. I tug at it but the second I let go, it rides back up.

Fortunately, Andrew's eyes are on the road as we exit the gate surrounding the property. He is a good, faithful husband. Just because he looked like he was nearly going to pass out when he saw me in this dress, that doesn't mean he's not going to be able to control himself.

"I'm so excited about this," I comment as he makes his way to the Long Island Expressway. "I can't believe I'm going to see *Showdown*."

He nods. "I've heard it's incredible."

"I even listened to some of the songs on my phone while I was getting dressed," I admit.

He laughs. "You said we're in the sixth row, right?"

"That's right." Not only are we going to see the hottest show on Broadway, but we're so close, we can almost touch the actors. If they enunciate too much, we will be showered in their saliva. And weirdly, I'm excited about that. "But, listen..."

He raises his eyebrows.

"I feel bad you're not going with Nina." I tug at the hem of my skirt, which seems like it's on a *mission* to show off my underwear. "She was the one who wanted these tickets."

He waves a hand. "Don't worry about it. In the time we've been married, Nina has seen more Broadway shows than I can count. This is special to you. You're really going to enjoy it. I'm sure she would want you to enjoy it."

"Hmm." I'm not so sure about that.

"Trust me. It's fine."

He slows to a stop at a red light. As his fingers drum against the steering wheel, I notice his eyes stray from the windshield. After a moment, I realize where he's looking.

He's looking at my legs.

I lift my eyes, and he realizes he's been caught. His cheeks color and he looks away.

I cross my legs and shift in my seat. Nina would definitely not be happy if she knew about any of this, but there's no chance she's going to find out. And anyway, we're not doing anything wrong. So what if Andrew looked at my legs? Looking isn't a crime.

TWENTY-FIVE

It's a beautiful June evening. I brought a wrap with me, but it's so warm out, I end up leaving it in Andrew's car, so I've got nothing besides my white dress and my purse that doesn't match as we wait in line to be allowed into the theater.

I gasp when I see the inside of the theater. I don't think I've ever seen anything like this in my lifetime. The orchestra alone contains rows and rows of seats, but then when I lift my head, there are two sets of seats stretching up all the way to the ceiling above. And up in the front is a red curtain that is lit from below with tantalizing yellow light.

When I finally tear my eyes away from the sight in front of me, I noticed Andrew has an amused look on his face. "What?" I say.

"It's just cute," he says. "The look on your face. I'm so used to it, but I love seeing it through your eyes."

"It's just so big," I say self-consciously.

An usher comes to hand us playbills and lead us to our seats. And then comes the really amazing part—he keeps leading us closer and closer and closer. And when we finally get to our seats, I can't believe how close we are to the stage. If I wanted, I could grab the actors by their ankles. Not that I would because that would definitely violate my parole, but it might be possible.

As I sit next to Andrew in one of the best seats of the hottest show in town in this amazing theater, I don't feel like a girl who just got out of prison, who doesn't have a penny to her name, who is working a job she hates. I feel *special.* Like maybe I deserve to be here.

I gaze at Andrew's profile. This is all because of him. He could have been a jerk about the whole thing and charged me for the tickets, or gone with a friend of his. He would have had every right to do so. But he didn't. He took me here tonight. And I'll never forget it.

"Thank you," I blurt out.

He rotates his head to look at me. His lips curl. He's so handsome when he smiles. "My pleasure."

Over the music playing and the commotion of people finding their seats, I just barely hear a buzzing sound coming from my purse. It's my phone. I take it out and discover a message from Nina on the screen:

Don't forget to put out the trash.

I grit my teeth. If anything can bring your fantasies of being more than a maid to a screeching halt, it's a message from your employer telling you to lug the garbage to the curb. Nina always reminds me about trash day, every single week, even though I've never once forgotten. But the absolute worst part is that when I see her text, I realize that I *have* forgotten to take the garbage to the curb. I usually do it after dinner, and the change in the schedule threw me off.

It's fine though. I just have to remember to do it tonight when we get back. After Andrew's BMW turns back into a pumpkin.

"You okay?"

Andrew's eyebrows are knitted together as he watches me read the text. My warm feelings for him evaporate slightly. Andrew isn't a guy I'm dating who is spoiling me with a Broadway show. He's my employer. He's married. He only brought me here because he feels sorry for me for being so uncultured.

And I can't let myself forget it.

The show is absolutely amazing.

I am literally at the edge of my seat in the sixth row, my mouth hanging open. I can tell why this show is one of the most popular on Broadway. The musical numbers are so catchy, the dance numbers are so elaborate, and the actor playing the lead is dreamy.

Although I can't help but think he's not quite as handsome as Andrew.

After three standing ovations, the show is finally over and the audience starts to filter toward the exits. Andrew leisurely rises from his seat and stretches out a kink in his back. "So how about some dinner?"

I slide the playbill into my purse. It's risky to save it, but I'm desperate to hold onto the memory of this magical experience. "Sounds good. Do you have a place in mind?"

"There's an amazing French restaurant a couple of blocks away. Do you like French food?"

"I've never had French food before," I admit. "Although I like the fries."

He laughs. "I think you'll enjoy it. My treat, of course. What do you say?"

I say that Nina wouldn't enjoy finding out that her husband took me to a Broadway show and then treated me to an expensive French dinner. But what the hell. We're already here, and it's not like the meal would make her *more* mad than the show alone. May as well go for broke. "Sounds good."

In my old life, before I worked for the Winchesters, I never could have gone into a French restaurant like the one where Andrew takes me. There's a menu posted on the door, and I only glance at a few of the prices, but any appetizer would wipe me out for several weeks. But standing next to Andrew, wearing Nina's white dress, I fit in here. Nobody is going to ask me to leave, anyway.

I'm sure as we walk into the restaurant, everybody thinks we're a couple. I saw our reflection in the glass outside the restaurant, and we look *good* together. If I'm honest, we look better as a couple than he and Nina do. Nobody notices that he has a wedding band and I don't. What they might notice is the way he gently places a hand on the small of my back to lead me to our table, then pulls out a chair for me.

"You're such a gentleman," I remark.

He chuckles. "Thank my mother. That's the way I was raised."

"Well, she raised you right."

He beams at me. "She'd be very glad to hear that."

Of course, it makes me think about Cecelia. That spoiled little brat who seemed to get off on ordering me around. Then again, Cecelia has been through a lot. Her mother tried to murder her, after all.

When the waiter comes to take our drink orders, Andrew orders a glass of red wine, so I do the same. I don't even look at the prices. It's just going to make me sick, and he already said he's paying.

"I have no idea what to order." None of the names of dishes sound familiar; the whole menu is in French. "Do you understand this menu?"

"*Oui*," Andrew says.

I raise my eyebrows. "Do you speak French?"

"*Oui, mademoiselle.*" He winks at me. "I'm fluent, actually. I spent my junior year of college studying in Paris."

"Wow." Not only did I not spend any time studying French in college, I never went to college at all. My high school diploma is a GED.

"Do you want me to read the menu to you in English?"

My cheeks grow warm. "You don't have to do that. Just pick out some things you think I'd like."

He looks pleased by that answer. "Okay, I can do that."

The waiter arrives with a bottle of wine and two glasses. I watch as he uncorks the bottle and pours us both heaping glasses. Andrew gestures for him to leave the bottle. I grab my glass and take a long sip.

Oh God, that's really good. So much better than what I get for five bucks at the local liquor store.

"How about you?" he says. "Do you speak any other languages?"

I shake my head. "I'm lucky I speak English."

Andrew doesn't smile at my joke. "You shouldn't put yourself down, Millie. You've been working for us for months, and you have a great work ethic and you're obviously smart. I don't even know why you would want this job, although we're lucky to have you. Don't you have any other career aspirations?"

I play with my napkin, avoiding his eyes. He doesn't know anything about me. If he did, he would understand. "I don't want to talk about it."

He hesitates for a moment, then he nods, respecting my request. "Well, either way, I'm glad you came out tonight."

I lift my eyes and his brown ones are staring at me across the table. "Me too."

He looks like he's about to say something more, but then his phone starts ringing. He pulls it out of his pocket and looks at the screen while I take another sip of wine. It's so good, I want to guzzle it. But that wouldn't be a good idea.

"It's Nina." Maybe it's my imagination, but he has a pained expression on his face. "I better take this."

I can't hear what Nina is saying, but her shaky voice is audible across the table. She sounds upset. He holds the phone about a centimeter from his ear, wincing with each word.

"Nina," he says. "Look, it's... yeah, I won't... Nina, just relax." He purses his lips. "I can't talk to you about this right now. I'll see you when you get home tomorrow, okay?"

Andrew jabs at a button on his phone to end the call, then he slams the phone on the table next to him. Finally, he picks up his wine glass and drains about half the contents.

"Everything okay?" I ask.

"Yeah." He presses his fingertips into his temples. "I just... I love Nina, but sometimes I can't figure out how my marriage got this way. Where ninety percent of our interactions are her yelling at me."

I don't know what to say to that. "I... I'm sorry. If it makes you feel better, that describes ninety percent of my interactions with her also."

His lips twitch. "Well, we've got that in common."

"So... she used to be different?"

"Completely different." He grabs his wine and drains the rest of it. "When we met, she was a single mom working two jobs. I admired her so much. She had a hard life, and her strength was what drew me to her. And now... She doesn't do anything except complain. She doesn't have any interest in working. She spoils Cecelia. And the worst part is..."

"What?"

He picks up the bottle of wine and fills up his glass again. He runs his finger along the rim. "Nothing. Never mind. I shouldn't..." He looks around the restaurant. "Where is our waiter?"

I'm dying to know what Andrew was about to confess to me. But then our waiter rushes over, eager for the giant tip he will almost certainly get from this meal, and it looks like the moment has passed.

Andrew orders for the both of us, as he said he would. I don't even ask him what he has ordered, because I want it to be a surprise and I'm sure it will be incredible. I'm also impressed with his French accent. I've always wished I could speak another language. It's probably too late for me though.

"I hope you like what I ordered," he says, almost shyly.

"I'm sure I will." I smile at him. "You have great taste. I mean, look at your house. Or did Nina pick out everything?"

He takes another sip from his fresh glass of wine. "No, I own the house and most of the design was done before we were married. Before we even met, actually."

"Really? Most men who work in the city prefer to have a bachelor pad before they settle down."

He snorts. "No, I was never interested in that. I was ready to get married. In fact, right before Nina, I was engaged to somebody else..."

Right before Nina? What does that mean? Is he saying that Nina broke up his engagement?

"Anyway," he says, "all I wanted was to settle down, buy a house, have a few kids..."

At that last statement, his lips turn down. Even though he hasn't mentioned it, I'm sure he's still smarting from learning that Nina wouldn't be able to have any more children.

"I'm sorry about the..." I swish my wine around in the glass. "You know, fertility issues. That must be hard on both of you."

"Yeah..." He looks up from his wine glass and blurts out: "We haven't had sex since that doctor's visit."

I nearly topple my glass on the table. At that moment, the waiter arrives back at our table with our appetizer. It's little circles of bread topped with a pink spread. But I can hardly focus on it after Andrew's confession.

"*Mousse de saumon canapés*," he says as the waiter leaves us. "Basically, smoked salmon mousse on a baguette."

I just stare at him.

"I'm sorry." He sighs. "I should never have said that. It was in really bad taste."

"Um..."

"Let's just..." He gestures down at the little slices of baguette on the table. "Let's enjoy dinner. Please forget I said that. Me and Nina... we're fine. Every couple goes through a dry spell."

"Of course."

But forgetting what he said about Nina is an exercise in futility.

TWENTY-SIX

We end up having a great time at dinner. We don't discuss Nina again, and the conversation flows easily, especially after we get to our second bottle of wine. I can't remember the last time I've had such a nice evening. I feel sad when it's coming to an end.

"Thank you so much for this," I tell him as he pays the check. I'm afraid to even look at it. Just the wine alone probably cost a small fortune.

"No, thank *you*." His face is almost glowing. "I had a great time. I haven't had this much fun in..." He clears his throat. "Anyway, it was really fun. Just what I needed."

He stands up after signing the check, and sways on his feet. We drank a *lot* of wine tonight. Which wouldn't be the greatest idea under the best circumstances, but I just remembered he's got to drive us back to Long Island. On the highway.

Andrew must realize what I'm thinking. He holds onto the table to steady himself. "I shouldn't be driving," he acknowledges.

"No," I say. "Probably not."

He rubs his face. "We still have that reservation at The Plaza. What do you think?"

Well, it doesn't take a genius to know this is a huge mistake. We're both drunk, his wife is out of town, and he apparently hasn't had sex in a while. And I haven't had sex in a much, much longer while. I should say no. This can't end well.

"I don't think it's a great idea," I mumble.

Andrew lays a hand on his chest. "I'll be a perfect gentleman. I swear. It's a suite. There are two beds."

"I know, but..."

"You don't trust me?"

I don't trust *me*. That's the bigger problem.

"Well, I can't drive us back to the island tonight." He looks down at his Rolex. "I'll tell you what. I'll get us two separate rooms at The Plaza."

"Oh my God, that will cost a fortune!"

He waves a hand. "Nah, I'll get a deal because I host clients there sometimes. It's fine."

Andrew is definitely too drunk to drive, and I probably am too, even if I wasn't terrified to get behind the wheel of his expensive car. I suppose we could get a taxi back to the island, but he hasn't suggested the idea. "All right, as long as we have separate rooms."

He hails a taxi to get us over to The Plaza hotel. As we slide into the backseat of the yellow cab, my white dress again rides up my thigh. What is wrong with the stupid dress? I'm trying so hard to be good, but this dress won't let me. I grab at the hem to pull it down again, but before I can, I notice Andrew taking another look. And this time when I catch him, he grins at me.

"What?" he says. Boy, he must be really drunk.

"You're looking at my legs!"

"So?" His grin widens. "You have great legs. And there's no harm in looking."

I smack him in the arm and he holds his shoulder, pretending to be wounded. "We're getting separate rooms. Don't forget that."

But his brown eyes meet mine across the backseat of the taxi. And for a moment, I'm having trouble breathing. Andrew wants to be faithful to Nina. I'm sure of it. But she's in a different state, he's drunk, and the two of them have been having problems—maybe for a long time. As far as I can see, she's been horrible to him the whole time I've been working there. He deserves so much better.

"What are *you* looking at?" he says in a low voice.

I swallow a lump in my throat. "Nothing."

"You look beautiful tonight, Millie," he breathes. "I'm not sure if I told you that. But you should know."

"Andrew..."

"I just..." His Adam's apple bobs. "Lately, I've just felt so..."

Before he can get any more words out, the cab jerks us to the right. I never put on my seatbelt and I find my body thrust against his. He catches me before I bash my head against the window. His body presses against me, his breath on my neck.

"Millie," he whispers.

And then he kisses me.

And God help me, I kiss him back.

TWENTY-SEVEN

Needless to say, we don't get two separate rooms at The Plaza.

So yes, I slept with my married boss.

After he kissed me in the taxi, there was no going back. We were basically ripping each other's clothing off at that point. It was all we could do to keep our hands off each other while Andrew was checking us into our room. We made out in the elevator like a couple of teenagers.

And then when we got to the room, there was no chance of trying to be good or trying to slow things down for the sake of his marriage. I don't know when the last time he had sex was, but for me, it's been so long, I was afraid he was going to have to clear away cobwebs. There was no way I wasn't doing this. I even had a few condoms in my purse from when I thought things might happen with Enzo.

And it was good. No, more than good. It was freaking amazing. Just what I needed.

The sun has just come up in the giant picture window overlooking the city. I'm lying in my decadent Plaza hotel queen-size bed, and Andrew is asleep next to me, softly blowing air through his lips with each breath. I think about what he did last night and shiver deliciously. Part of me wants to wake him up and see if he might want to go again. But the more realistic part of me knows it will never—can never—happen again.

I mean, Andrew is married. I'm his maid. Last night, he was drunk. It was a one-time thing.

But for a moment, I watch his handsome profile as he sleeps and allow myself to fantasize. Maybe he'll wake up and decide he's had enough of Nina and her bullshit. He'll decide he loves me and he wants me to live with him in his gorgeous gated home. And then I can give him the baby he so badly wants, which Nina will never be able to do. I remember those obnoxious women at the PTA meeting, saying that Andrew and Nina have an airtight prenup. He could leave her and it wouldn't even cost him that much money, although I'm sure he'll be generous with her.

It's stupid. It will never happen. If he knew the truth about me, he'd run a mile. But I can daydream.

Andrew groans and rubs the balls of his hands over his eyes. He rolls his head to the side and cracks his eyes open. I take it as a plus that he doesn't look horrified when he sees me lying there. "Hey," he says in a hoarse voice.

"Hey."

He rubs his eyes again. "How are you doing? Are you okay?"

Aside from the sinking feeling in my chest, I'm great. "I'm okay. Are you okay?"

He tries to sit up in bed and fails. His head drops against the pillow. "I think I'm hungover. Christ, how much did we drink?"

He drank far more than I did. But I am more of a lightweight, so it hit me just as hard. "Two bottles of wine."

"I..." His brow scrunches up. "Are *we* okay?"

"We're fine." I manage a smile. "Completely fine. I promise."

He tries a second time to sit up, wincing at the pain in his head. But this time he makes it. "I'm so sorry. I shouldn't have…"

I flinch at his apology. "Don't worry about it." My voice sounds clipped and I clear my throat. "I'll go take a shower. We should probably head back home."

"Yeah…" He heaves a sigh. "You won't say anything to Nina, right? I mean, we were both really drunk and…"

Of course. That's all he cares about. "I won't."

"Thanks. Thanks so much."

I'm naked under the blankets, but I don't want him to see me that way. I grab one of the sheets from the bed and wrap it around myself as I climb out of the bed and stumble in the direction of the bathroom. I can feel Andrew's eyes on me, but I don't turn to look at him. It's humiliating.

"Millie?"

I still can't look. "What?"

"I'm not sorry," he says. "I had a great time with you last night, and I'm not sorry for any part of it. And I hope you're not either."

I venture a look at him. He is still in bed, the covers up to his waist, revealing his bare, muscular chest. "No, I'm not sorry at all."

"But…" He heaves a sigh. "It can't happen again. You know that, right?"

I nod. "Yes, I understand."

A troubled expression comes over his face. He runs a hand through his dark hair to smooth it out. "I wish things could be different."

"I know."

"I wish I'd met you back when…"

He doesn't have to complete his sentence. I know what he's thinking. If only we had met back when he was still single. He could have walked into the bar where I was waiting tables, our eyes would have met, and when he asked me for my number, I would have given it to him. But that's not the situation. He's married. He's a father. Nothing more can happen between the two of us.

"I know," I say again.

He keeps his eyes on me, and for a moment, I wonder if he's going to ask if he can join me in the shower. After all, we've already desecrated this hotel room. What's one more time? But he behaves himself. He turns away from me, pulls up the covers, and I go take my cold shower.

TWENTY-EIGHT

We hardly talk during the drive back to the Island—Andrew turns on the radio and we listen to the DJ's mindless chatter. It occurs to me that he mentioned a meeting later in the city, so he's going to have to turn right back around soon after we get home. But the journey is not entirely for me. He is still wearing the same clothing he was wearing yesterday, and I'm sure he wants to change into a new suit before showing up at his meeting.

"Almost back," he mumbles, when we exit the Long Island Expressway. He's got on a pair of sunglasses, making his expression impossible to read.

"Great."

My dress is riding up yet again—this damn dress is what caused all our problems. I tug at it, and even with his shades on, I can't help but notice Andrew is looking again. I raise my eyebrows at him and he smiles sheepishly. "One more for the road."

As we're driving down a residential block, he swerves to get around a garbage truck. And that's when a horrible thought occurs to me.

"Andrew," I hiss. "I never put out the garbage last night!"

"Oh..."

He doesn't seem to quite be understanding the gravity of the situation. "Nina specifically texted me to put out the trash last night. I never did it because I wasn't home. I've never forgotten before. If she finds out..."

He pulls off his sunglasses, revealing slightly bloodshot eyes. "Shit. Do you still have time to do it?"

I watch the garbage truck, which is traveling in the opposite direction of his house. "I doubt it. I think it's too late. They come really early."

"You could just say you forgot, right?"

"You think Nina will buy that?"

"Shit," he says again. He taps on the steering wheel. "Okay, I'll take care of it. Don't worry."

The only way to take care of it is to lug all the trash down to the dump personally. I'm not even sure where the dump is, but the trunk of my Nissan is tiny, and it will take me several trips, wherever it is. So I truly hope Andrew means it when he says he'll take care of it.

When we get back to the house, Andrew presses the button in his car that makes the gate doors swing open automatically. Enzo is working in our yard, and he jerks his head up when he sees the BMW making its way down the driveway. It's unusual to see the BMW arriving home at this hour—it would make more sense for it to be leaving—so his surprise is warranted.

I should have ducked down, but it's too late. Enzo pauses in the middle of his yard work, and his dark eyes meet mine. And he shakes his head, just like he did that first day.

Damn it.

Andrew notices him too, but he just raises his hand and waves like there's nothing strange about him arriving home at 9:30 in the morning with a woman who is not his wife. Before pulling into the garage, he throws the car into the park.

"Let me see if Enzo can take care of the trash," he says.

I want to beg him not to ask, but before I can get my mouth open, he's leaped out of the car, leaving the door slightly ajar. Enzo takes a step back like he does not want to have this conversation.

"*Ciao*, Enzo." Andrew flashes the landscaper a broad smile. God, he looks handsome when he smiles. I close my eyes for a moment, shivering as I remember his hands all over my body last night. "I need your help."

Enzo doesn't say a word. He just stares at him.

"We have a problem with the garbage." Andrew gestures at the four stuffed trash bags at the side of the house. "We forgot to put them out last night for the garbagemen. Do you think you could bring them out to the dump for us in your truck? I'll give you fifty bucks."

Enzo looks over at the garbage bags, then back at Andrew. He doesn't say anything.

"Garbage..." Andrew repeats. "To... dump. Garbage dump. *Capisci*?"

Enzo shakes his head.

Andrew grits his teeth and takes out his wallet from his back pocket. "Get rid of the garbage for us. I'll give you..." He digs around in his wallet. "One hundred dollars." He fans out the bills in Enzo's face. "Get rid of garbage. You have a truck. Take it to the garbage dump."

Finally, Enzo says, "No. I busy."

"Right, but this is *our* yard and..." Andrew lets out a sigh and goes back into his wallet. "Two hundred dollars. One trip to the garbage dump. Help me out. Please."

At first, I think for sure Enzo is going to refuse again. But he reaches out and takes the bills from Andrew's hand. Then he goes to the side of the house and grabs the garbage bags. He manages to get all of them in one trip as the muscles in his biceps bulge under his white T-shirt.

"Right," Andrew says. "To the dump."

Enzo just stares at him for a moment, then walks right past him with the garbage bags. Without another word, he throws them into his truck and takes off. So I guess he got the message.

Andrew strides back over to the car and slides back into the driver's seat. "Well, that's taken care of. But sheesh, what an asshole."

"I didn't think he understood you."

"Yeah, right." He rolls his eyes at me. "He understands more than he lets on. He was just holding out for more money."

I agree that Enzo did not seem to want to take out the garbage, but I don't think it was because he wanted more money.

"I don't like that guy," Andrew grumbles. "He works on all the houses in the neighborhood, but he spends a third of his time in our yard. He's *always* out there. I don't even know what the hell he's doing half the time."

"You do have the biggest house on the block," I point out. "And the biggest lawn."

"Right, but..." Andrew stares at Enzo's truck, disappearing down the street. "I don't know. I told Nina to get rid of him and hire somebody else, but she says everybody uses him and he's apparently 'the best.'"

Of course, Enzo isn't my favorite person ever since he not-so-subtly rejected me, but that's not why he makes me so uncomfortable. I can't forget the way he hissed the Italian word for "danger" at me on my first day here. The way he seems scared to defy Nina, even though he's large enough to crush her with one hand. Does Andrew have any clue how wary Enzo is of his wife?

Well, I'm not going to be the one to tell him.

TWENTY-NINE

Nina comes home from dropping Cecelia off at camp at around two in the afternoon. She's carrying four large shopping bags from an impromptu spree during the drive home, which she dumps unceremoniously on the living room floor.

"I found the *cutest* little shop," she tells me. "I just couldn't help myself!"

"Great," I say with forced enthusiasm.

Nina's cheeks are flushed, there are sweat stains under her armpits, and her blond hair is frizzy. She still hasn't taken care of her roots, and the mascara on her right eye is caked in the corner. When I look her over, I genuinely can't figure out what Andrew sees in her.

"Take those bags upstairs for me, would you, Millie?" She plops down on the leather sofa and takes out her phone. "Thanks so much."

I pick up one of the bags and, holy crap, it's heavy. What kind of shop did she go to? A dumbbell store? This is going to end up being two trips—I don't have big guns like Enzo. "Kind of heavy," I comment.

"Really?" She laughs. "I didn't think so. Maybe it's time to start going to the gym, Millie. You're getting a little soft."

My cheeks burn. *I'm* getting soft? Nina doesn't look like she has an ounce of muscle on her. She never works out, as far as I can tell. I've never seen her even wear sneakers.

As I slowly and painfully make my way to the stairs with two of the shopping bags, Nina calls out to me again, "Oh, by the way, Millie?"

I clench my teeth. "Yes?"

Nina rotates on the couch to look up at me. "I called the house line last night. How come nobody answered?"

I freeze. My arms tremble under the weight of the shopping bags. "What?"

"I dialed the house phone number last night," she says slower this time. "At around eleven o'clock. Answering the house phone is one of your responsibilities. But you and Andrew both didn't pick up."

"Um." I put down the shopping bags for a moment and rub my chin, like I'm thinking about it. "I may have already been asleep by then and the phone isn't loud enough in my room to wake me up. Maybe Andrew went out?"

She arches an eyebrow. "Andrew went out at eleven o'clock on a Sunday night? With whom?"

I lift my shoulders. "I have no idea. Did you try his cell?"

I know she didn't. I was with Andrew at eleven o'clock. We were in bed together.

"I didn't," she says, but doesn't offer any further explanation.

I clear my throat. "Well, as I said, I was in my room at that point. I have no idea what he was doing."

"Hmm." Her pale blue eyes darken as she stares at me across the living room. "Maybe you're right. I'll have to ask him."

I nod, relieved she isn't questioning me further. She doesn't know what happened. She doesn't know we drove into the city together, saw the show she was meant to see with him, and then spent the night together at The Plaza. God only knows what she would do to me if she knew.

But she doesn't know.

I grab the shopping bags and heave them the rest of the way up the steps. I deposit them in the master bedroom, then rub my arms, which seem to have gone numb during the journey. My eyes are drawn to the master bathroom, which I cleaned this morning—although since Nina was out of town, it was unusually clean already. I slip inside the room. The bathroom is nearly as large as my room upstairs, with a full-size porcelain bathtub. The tub is higher than most tubs, the rim at the level of my knees.

I frown down at the bathtub, imagining what must've happened all those years ago. Little Cecelia, taking a bath in the tub, as it slowly fills up with water. Then Nina grabs her daughter, forcing her under the water, watching her gasp for air...

I close my eyes and turn away from the tub. I can't think about this. But I can never forget how emotionally fragile Nina is. She can never know what happened between me and Andrew last night. It would destroy her. And then she would destroy me.

So I reach into my pocket and pull out my phone. I punch in a message to Andrew's cell number:

Just a warning: Nina called the house last night.

He'll know what to do. He always does.

THIRTY

The house is quieter with Cecelia gone.

Even though she stayed up in her room a lot, there was a certain energy she brought. With her gone, it seems like silence has descended over the Winchester household. And to my surprise, Nina seems more cheerful. Thank God, she hasn't brought up the phone call on the night we went away.

Andrew and I have been meticulously avoiding each other, which is difficult when we live in the same house. If we pass each other, we both avert our eyes. Hopefully, we can get past it, because I don't want to lose this job. It's bad enough that I have no chance of a real relationship with the first guy I've liked in a decade.

Tonight I'm hurrying to get dinner ready so I can have it on the table before Andrew comes home. But as I'm carrying the glasses of water to the dining room, I run smack into Andrew. Literally. One of the glasses slips out of my hand and shatters on the floor.

"Damn it!" I cry.

I hazard a look at Andrew. He's wearing a dark blue suit

with a dark tie, and yet again, he looks devastatingly handsome. He's been at work all day and he has a five o'clock shadow on his chin that only makes him more sexy. Our eyes meet for a split second, and against my will, I feel a jolt of attraction. His eyes widen, and I'm sure he feels it, too.

"I'll help you get this cleaned up," he says.

"You don't have to do that."

But he insists. I sweep up the large pieces of glass, and he holds the dustpan and disposes of them in the kitchen. Nina would never help me, but Andrew isn't like her. As he takes the broom from me, my fingers brush against his. Our eyes meet again, and this time we can't ignore the fireworks. It's physically painful that I can't be with this man.

"Millie," he says in a husky whisper.

My throat feels really dry. He's only a foot away from me. If I leaned forward, he would kiss me. I know he would.

"Oh no! What happened?"

At the sound of Nina's voice, Andrew and I jump away from each other like we were lit on fire. I grip the broom so tightly my fingers turn white. "I dropped a glass," I say. "Just, you know... getting it cleaned up."

Nina's eyes drop down to the floor, where little tiny shards of glass are glistening under the overhead lights. "Oh Millie," she says. "Please be more careful next time."

I have worked here for months and I have never once dropped or broken anything. Well, except for that night she caught me and Andrew watching *Family Feud* late at night. But she doesn't know about that. "Yes, I'm sorry. I'm just going to grab the vacuum."

Andrew's eyes follow me as I return to the utility closet (which is slightly larger than my bedroom upstairs), stuff the broom back inside, and grab the vacuum. He has a pained expression on his face. Whatever he wanted to say to me a minute ago, he still wants to say it. But he can't—not with Nina in the room.

Or maybe he can.

"We should talk later," he murmurs in my ear, just as he follows Nina into the living room to wait for me to clean up. "Okay?"

I nod. I don't know what he wants to talk to me about, but I take this as a good sign. We already agreed never to speak of what happened that night at The Plaza. So if he wants to revisit that...

I shouldn't get my hopes up though.

About ten minutes later, I've got everything cleaned up and I call Andrew and Nina back in from the living room. They're both sitting on the couch, but at opposite ends. They're looking at their phones, not even attempting to talk to each other. I've noticed they've started to do the same at dinner time.

They follow me back into the dining room and Nina takes her seat across from Andrew. She looks down at the plate of pork chop with applesauce and broccolini. She smiles at me, and that's when I notice her bright red lipstick looks a little bit off. It's smeared over the right side of her lips, which gives her almost a demonic clown appearance. "This looks delicious, Millie."

"Thank you."

"Doesn't it smell wonderful, Andy?" she says.

"Mmm." He picks up his fork. "Very nice."

"I'm sure," Nina continues, "you never got food like this in prison, did you, Millie?"

Mic drop.

Nina is smiling up at me pleasantly with those demonic lips. Andrew, sitting across from her, is gawking at me. Obviously, this is new information to him.

"Um," I say.

"What sort of food did they serve you there?" she presses

me. "I've always been curious about that. What's prison food like?"

I don't know what to say. I can't deny it. She knows my past. "It's okay."

"Well, I hope you don't get inspired by any meals you had there," she laughs. "Stick with what you've been doing. You're doing a good job."

"Thank you," I mutter.

Andrew's face is ashen. Of course, he had no idea I was ever in prison. I never even considered telling him. Somehow, when I'm with him, that time in my life seems like something from the distant past—another lifetime. But most people don't see it that way. To most people, I am only one thing. A convict.

And Nina wants to make sure I know my place.

Right now, I'm desperate to escape Andrew's shocked expression. I turn around to head back up to my room. I'm nearly at the stairwell when Nina calls out to me, "Millie?"

I stop, my back going rigid. It takes all my self-restraint to keep from snapping at her when I turn around. I slowly walk back to the dining room with an artificial smile on my face. "Yes, Nina?"

She frowns. "You forgot to put out the salt and pepper shaker. And unfortunately, this pork chop does need a bit of salt. I wish you would be more generous with the seasoning."

"Right. Sorry."

I walk into the kitchen and grab the salt and pepper shakers from the counter. They were roughly six feet away from where Nina was sitting in the other room. I bring them out to the dining room, and despite my efforts not to, I slam the shakers down on the table. When I look at Nina, the corners of her lips are twitching.

"Thank you *so* much, Millie," she says. "Please don't forget it again."

I hope she steps on a shard of broken glass.

I can't even look at Andrew. God knows what he must be thinking about me. I can't believe I was contemplating some sort of future with him. I wasn't really, but for a split second... Well, stranger things have happened. But that's out the window now. He looked horrified when she mentioned I had been in prison. If only I could explain...

I manage to make it to the stairs this time without Nina calling me over to tell me that, I don't know, I need to pass the butter from the other side of the table or something like that. I trudge up the steps to the second floor, then up the darker, narrow set of steps to my bedroom. I slam the door behind me, wishing not for the first time that I could lock it.

I plop down on my bed, trying to keep the tears from welling up. I wonder how long Nina has known about my past. Did she only recently discover it, or did she do a background check when she hired me after all? Maybe she liked the idea of hiring a convict. Someone she could boss around. Anyone else would have quit months ago.

While I am sitting on the bed, feeling sorry for myself, something on my nightstand catches my eye.

It's a copy of the playbill from *Showdown*.

I pick it up, confused. Why is the playbill on my nightstand? I put it in my purse after the show, and I've been keeping it in there as a reminder of that magical night. My purse is on the floor, leaning against the dresser. So how did the playbill get on the nightstand? I definitely didn't take it out. I'm sure of it.

Someone else must've put it there. I locked the door to the room, but I'm not the only one here who has the key.

I get a sinking feeling in my stomach. I finally understand why Nina blurted out that I had been in prison. She knows that I saw the show with Andrew. She knows we were in Manhattan together, all alone. I'm not sure if she knows we spent the night at The Plaza, but she knows we weren't home at eleven o'clock at night. And I'm sure if she's smart enough, she could find out whether or not we checked into the hotel.

Nina knows everything.

I have just made a dangerous enemy.

THIRTY-ONE

As part of my new daily regimen of torture, Nina has made it her goal to make shopping as challenging for me as she possibly can.

She has written out a list of items we need from the grocery store. But they are all very specific. She doesn't want *milk.* She wants organic milk from Queensland Farm. And if they don't have the exact item she wants, I have to text her to let her know and send her pictures of other possible replacements. And she takes her sweet time texting me back, but I have to stand there in the goddamn milk aisle waiting.

Right now, I'm in the bread aisle. I send Nina a text:

They are out of Nantucket sourdough bread. Here are some possible replacements.

I send her photographs of every single kind of sourdough bread they have in stock. And now I have to wait while she looks at them. After several minutes, I receive a text back from her:

Do they have any brioche?

Now I have to send her pictures of every brioche bread they have. I swear, I'm going to blow my brains out before I finish this shopping trip. She's deliberately tormenting me. But to be fair, I did sleep with her husband.

As I'm snapping photographs of the bread, I notice a heavyset man with gray hair watching me from the other end of the aisle. He's not even being subtle about it. I shoot him a look, and he backs off, thank God. I can't deal with a stalker on top of everything else.

As I wait for Nina to contemplate the bread a little further, I let my mind wander. As usual, it wanders to Andrew Winchester. After Nina's revelation that I had been in prison, Andrew never found me to "talk," like he said he would. He has been effectively scared off. I can't blame him.

I like Andrew. No, I don't just like him. I'm in love with him. I think about him all the time, and it's painful to share a home with him and not be able to act on my feelings for him. Moreover, he deserves better than Nina. I could make him happy. I could even give him a baby like he wants. And let's face it, anything is better than *her*.

But even though he knows we have a connection, nothing will ever happen. He knows I went to prison. He doesn't want an ex-convict. And he's going to keep on being miserable with that witch, probably for the rest of his life.

My phone buzzes again.

Any French bread?

It takes another ten minutes, but I manage to find a loaf of bread that meets Nina's expectations. As I roll my shopping cart to the checkout, I notice that heavyset guy again. He definitely is staring at me. And more unsettlingly, he doesn't have a shopping cart. So what exactly is he doing?

I check out as quickly as I possibly can. I load the paper bags filled with groceries back into my shopping cart, so I can push it out into the parking lot to my Nissan. It's only as I'm getting close to the exit that a hand closes around my shoulder. I lift my head and that heavyset man is standing over me.

"Excuse me!" I try to jerk away, but he holds tight to my arm. My right hand balls into a fist. At least a bunch of people are watching us, so I have witnesses. "What do you think you're doing?"

He points to a small ID badge hanging from the collar of his blue dress shirt, which I hadn't noticed before. "I'm supermarket security. Can you come with me, Miss?"

I'm going to be sick. It's bad enough I spent almost ninety minutes in this place, shopping for a handful of items, but now I'm being arrested? For *what*?

"What's wrong?" I gulp.

We have attracted a crowd. I notice a couple of women from the school pick-up, who I'm sure will gleefully report back to Nina that they saw her housekeeper being apprehended by supermarket security.

"Please come with me," the guy says again.

I push my cart with us because I'm scared to leave it behind. There are over two hundred dollars' worth of groceries in there, and I'm sure Nina would make me pay for all of them if they were lost or stolen. I follow the man into a small office with a scratched-up wooden desk and two plastic chairs set up in front of it. The man gestures for me to sit down, so I settle down in one of the chairs, which creaks threateningly under my weight.

"This has got to be a mistake..." I look at the man's ID badge. His name is Paul Dorsey. "What's this about, Mr. Dorsey?"

He frowns at me as his jowls hang down. "A customer alerted me that you were stealing items from the supermarket."

I let out a gasp. "I would never do that!"

"Maybe not." He sticks his thumb into the loop of his belt. "But I have to investigate. Can I see your receipt, please, Miss…?"

"Calloway." I dig around in my purse until I come up with the crumpled strip of paper. "Here."

"Just a warning," he says. "We prosecute all shoplifters."

I sit in a plastic chair, my cheeks burning, while the security guard painstakingly looks through all my purchases and matches them up with what's in the cart. My stomach churns as I consider the horrible possibility that maybe the clerk didn't ring something up properly, and he'll think I stole it. And then what? They prosecute all shoplifters. That means that they'll call the police. And that would be a violation of my parole for sure.

It hits me that this would work out pretty well for Nina. She would get rid of me without having to be the mean person who fired me. She would also get some pretty sweet revenge on me for having slept with her husband. Of course, it's a little harsh to be sent to jail for adultery, but I get the feeling Nina may look at it differently.

But that can't happen. I didn't steal anything from the grocery store. He's not going to find anything in that cart that isn't on my receipt.

Is he?

I watch him scrutinizing the strip of paper as the tub of pistachio ice cream in my cart likely turns to liquid. My heart is pounding in my chest and I can hardly breathe. I don't want to go back to jail. I don't. I *can't*. I'd rather kill myself.

"Well," he finally says, "everything seems to match up."

I almost burst into tears. "Right. Of course."

He grunts. "I'm sorry to bother you like that, Miss

Calloway. But we have a lot of problems with shoplifters, so I had to take it seriously. And I got a phone call alerting me that a customer matching your description might be planning to take something."

A phone call? Who would call the grocery store and describe what I look like, and tell the security guard I was planning to steal something? Who would do such a thing?

I can only think of one person who would do something like that.

"Anyway," he says, "thanks for your patience. You can go now."

Those are the four most beautiful words in the English language. *You can go now.* I get to leave this grocery store with my hands free, pushing my shopping cart. I get to go home.

This time.

But I have a terrible feeling this isn't the end of it. Nina has more in store for me.

THIRTY-TWO

I can't sleep.

It's been three days since I was nearly apprehended at the grocery store. I don't know what to do next. Nina has been pleasant enough, so maybe she feels like I've learned my lesson about who is boss in this house. Maybe she isn't trying to send me to jail.

But that's not the reason I'm tossing and turning.

The truth is, I can't stop thinking about Andrew. That night we spent together. The way I feel when I'm with him. I've never felt this way before. And until Nina dropped the bombshell about my past, he felt the same way. I could tell.

But not anymore. Now he thinks I'm nothing but a common criminal.

I kick the blankets off my legs. It's stiflingly hot in my room, even at night. If only I could open that stupid window. But I doubt Nina is going to do anything to make me feel more comfortable here.

I finally wander downstairs to the kitchen. I have that minifridge in my room, but I don't have much food in it. It's too small to fit much. Those three mini water bottles Nina left me are nearly all that's in there, still untouched.

As I'm walking to the kitchen, I notice the light is on for the back porch. I frown and approach the back door. That's when I realize there's a reason the light is on. Somebody is out there.

It's Andrew.

Sitting all alone in one of the chairs out there, drinking from a bottle of beer.

I quietly slide open the back door. Andrew blinks up at me in surprise, but he doesn't say anything. He just takes another swig from his bottle of beer.

"Hey," I say.

"Hey," he says.

I squeeze my hands together. "Can I sit here?"

"Sure. Knock yourself out."

I step out onto the cold wooden planks on the porch and lower myself into the seat next to his, wishing I had a beer as well. He doesn't even look at me. He just keeps drinking from his beer bottle, staring out into the huge backyard.

"I want to explain." I clear my throat. "I mean, why I didn't tell you about..."

"You don't have to explain." He glances in my direction then back down at his beer. "It's pretty obvious why you didn't tell me."

"I wanted to." That's not true. I didn't want to tell him. I didn't want him to ever know, even though that was entirely unrealistic. "Anyway, I'm sorry."

He swishes the beer around in his bottle. "So what were you in prison for?"

I really, really wish I had a beer. I open my mouth, but before I can figure out what to tell him, he says, "Forget it. I don't want to know. It's none of my business."

I chew on my lip. "Look, I'm sorry I didn't tell you. I wanted to try to put the past behind me. I didn't mean any harm."

"Yeah..."

"And..." I stare down at my hands in my lap. "I was embarrassed. I didn't want you to think less of me. Your opinion means a lot to me."

He rolls his head to look at me, his eyes soft under the dim porch light. "Millie..."

"I also want you to know..." I take a deep breath. "I had a really great time the other night. It was one of the best nights I've ever had. Because of you. So whatever else happens, thank you for that. I... I just had to tell you that."

There's a crease between his eyebrows. "I had a great time, too. I haven't felt that happy in..." He pinches the bridge of his nose. "A while. I hadn't even realized it."

We stare at each other for a moment. There's still electricity between us. I can see in his eyes that he feels it, too. He glances at the back door, and before I know what's happening, his lips are on mine.

He kisses me for what feels like an eternity, but it's probably more like sixty seconds. When he pulls away, there's regret in his eyes. "I can't..."

"I know..."

It's not meant to be between us. For so many reasons. But if he wanted to go for it, I would do it. Even if it meant making an enemy out of Nina. I would risk it. For him.

But instead, I get up and leave him behind on the porch with his beer.

The wood of the stairs is cold against my bare feet as I walk back up to the second floor. My head is still spinning from that kiss and my lips are tingling. That can't be the last time. It *can't*. I saw the way he was looking at me. He has real feelings for me. Even though he knows my past, he still likes me. The only problem is—

Wait. What's that?

I freeze at the top of the stairs. There is a shadow in the hallway. I squint at it, trying to make out the image in the darkness.

And then it moves.

I let out a screech and nearly go toppling down the stairs. I grab onto the banister and save myself at the last second. The shadow shifts closer to me, and now I can see what it is.

It's Nina.

"Nina," I gasp.

Why is she standing there in the hallway? Was she downstairs? Did she see me and Andrew kissing?

"Hello, Millie." It's dark in the hallway, but the whites of her eyes almost seem to be glowing.

"What… what are you doing here?"

She scowls at me, the light from the moon creating disturbing shadows on her face. "It's *my* home. I don't have to account for my whereabouts."

Of course, it's not really her home. Andrew owns the house. And if they weren't married, she couldn't live here. If he decided to choose me over her, this would be *my* house.

These thoughts are insane. Obviously, that isn't going to happen.

"I'm sorry."

She folds her arms across her chest. "What are *you* doing here?"

"I… I came down to get a glass of water."

"Don't you have water in your room?"

"I drank it all," I lie. And I'm sure she knows it's a lie, considering she snoops in my room.

She's silent for a moment. "Andy wasn't in bed. Did you see him downstairs anywhere?"

"I, uh… I think he was out on the back porch."

"I see."

"But I'm not sure. I didn't talk to him or anything."

Nina gives me a look like she doesn't believe one word I'm

saying. Which is fair enough, since it's all lies. "I'll go check on him."

"And I'll head up to my room."

She nods and pushes past me, jostling my shoulder. My heart is pounding. I can't push away the feeling that I've made a terrible mistake crossing Nina Winchester. Yet I can't seem to stop myself.

THIRTY-THREE

I have Sunday off, so I spend the day out of the house. It's a beautiful summer day—not too hot and not too cool—so I drive over to the local park and sit on a bench and read my book. When you're in prison, you forget those simple pleasures. Just going outside and reading at the park. Sometimes you want it so bad, it's physically painful.

I'm never going back there. Never.

I grab a bite to eat at a fast-food drive-through, then I drive back to the house. The Winchester estate is really beautiful. Even though I'm starting to despise Nina, I can't hate that house. It's a beautiful house.

I park on the street like always and walk up to the front door of the house. The sky has been darkening during my entire drive home, and just as I get to the door, the clouds break open and droplets of rain cascade out of the sky. I wrench the door open and slip inside before I get drenched.

When I get into the living room, Nina is sitting on the sofa in semi-darkness. She's not doing anything there. She's not reading, she's not watching TV. She's just sitting there. And when I open the door, her eyes snap to attention.

"Nina?" I say. "Everything okay?"

"Not really." She glances over at the other end of the sofa, and now I notice she's got a stack of clothing next to her. It's the same clothing that she insisted I take from her when I first started working here. "What is *my* clothing doing in your room?"

I stare at her as a flash of lightning brightens the room. "What? What are you talking about? You gave me those clothes."

"I gave them to you!" She lets out a barking laugh that echoes through the room, only partially drowned out by the crack of thunder. "Why would I give my *maid* clothing worth thousands of dollars?"

"You"—my legs tremble beneath me—"you said they were too small on you. You insisted that I take them."

"How could you lie like that?" She takes a step toward me, her blue eyes like ice. "You stole my clothing! You're a thief!"

"No..." I reach out for something before my legs give out under me. But I grasp only air. "I would never do that."

"Ha!" She snorts. "That's what I get for trusting a convict to work in my home!"

She's loud enough that Andrew hears the commotion. He dashes out of his office and I see his handsome face at the top of the stairs, lit by another bolt of lightning. Oh God, what is he going to think of me? It's bad enough that he knows about my prison record. I don't want him to think I stole from his own house.

"Nina?" He takes the stairs down two at a time. "What's going on here?"

"I'll tell you what's going on!" she announces triumphantly. "Millie here has been stealing from my closet. She stole all this clothing from me. I found it in her closet."

Andrew's eyes slowly grow wide. "She..."

"I didn't steal anything!" Tears prick at my eyes. "I swear to you. Nina gave me those clothes. She said they didn't fit her."

"As if we would believe your lies." She sneers at me. "I should call the police on you. Do you know what this clothing is worth?"

"No, please don't..."

"Oh, right." Nina laughs at the expression on my face. "You're on parole, aren't you? Something like this would send you right back to prison."

Andrew is looking down at the clothing on the couch, a deep crease between his eyebrows. "Nina..."

"I'm going to call them." Nina whips her phone out of her purse. "God knows what else she stole from us, right, Andy?"

"Nina." He lifts his eyes from the stack of clothing. "Millie didn't steal this clothing. I remember you emptying your closet. You put it all in trash bags and said you were donating it." He picks up a tiny white dress. "You haven't been able to fit into this in *years*."

It's gratifying the way Nina's cheeks turn pink. "What are you saying? That I'm too *fat*?"

He ignores her remark. "I'm saying there's no way she stole this from you. Why are you doing this to her?"

Her mouth falls open. "Andy..."

Andrew looks over at me, hovering by the sofa. "Millie." His voice is gentle when he says my name. "Would you go upstairs and give us some privacy? I need to talk to Nina."

"Yes, of course," I agree. Gladly.

The two of them stand there in silence while I mount the flight of stairs to the second floor. When I reach the top, I go over to the doorway to the attic and I open the door. For a moment, I stand there, contemplating my next move. Then I close the door without going through.

Much quieter this time, I creep over to the head of the stairs.

I stand at the edge of the hallway, just before the stairwell. I can't see Nina and Andrew, but I can hear their voices. It's wrong to eavesdrop, but I can't help myself. After all, this conversation will almost certainly involve Nina's accusations about me.

I hope Andrew continues to defend me, even when I'm out of the room. Will she convince him that I stole her clothes? I am, after all, a convict. You make one mistake in life, and nobody ever trusts you again.

"... didn't take these dresses," Andrew is saying. "I know she didn't."

"How could you take her side over mine?" Nina shoots back. "The girl was in prison. You can't trust somebody like that. She's a liar and a thief, and she probably deserves to be back in prison."

"How could you say something like that? Millie has been wonderful."

"Yes, I'm sure *you* think so."

"When did you become so cruel, Nina?" His voice trembles. "You've changed. You're a different person now."

"Everyone changes," she spits at him.

"No." His voice lowers so that I have to strain to hear it over the sound of raindrops falling outside and hitting the pavement. "Not like you. I don't even recognize you anymore. You're not the same person I fell in love with."

There's a long silence, broken by a bolt of thunder that cracks loud enough to shake the foundations of the house. Once it's faded, I hear Nina's next words loud and clear.

"What are you saying, Andy?"

"I'm saying... I don't think I'm in love with you anymore, Nina. I think we should separate."

"You're not in love with me anymore?" she bursts out. "How can you say that?"

"I'm sorry. I was just going along with things, living our lives, and I didn't even realize how unhappy I was."

Nina is quiet for a long time as she absorbs his words. "Does this have to do with Millie?"

I hold my breath waiting to hear his answer. There was something between us that night in New York, but I'm not going to kid myself that he's leaving Nina because of me.

"This isn't about Millie," he finally says.

"Really? So are you going to lie to my face and pretend nothing ever happened between you and her?"

Damn. She knows. Or at least, she thinks she knows.

"I have feelings for Millie," he says in a voice so quiet, I'm sure I must've imagined it. How could this rich, handsome, *married* man have feelings for *me*? "But that's not what this is about. This is about you and me. I don't love you anymore."

"This is bullshit!" The pitch of Nina's voice is going up to the point where soon only dogs will be able to hear her. "You're leaving me for our *maid*! This is the most ridiculous thing I've ever heard. This is an *embarrassment* to you. You're better than this, Andrew."

"Nina." His tone is firm. "It's over. I'm sorry."

"*Sorry?*" Another crack of thunder shakes the floorboards. "Oh, you don't know what sorry is..."

There's a pause. "*Excuse* me?"

"If you try to go through with this," she growls at him, "I will destroy you in court. I will make sure you are left penniless and homeless."

"Homeless? This is *my* home, Nina. I bought it before we even knew each other. I *allow* you to stay here. We have a prenup, as you recall, and after our marriage ends, it will be mine again." He pauses again. "And now I'd like you to leave."

I hazard a look around the stairwell. If I crouch, I can make out Nina standing in the center of the living room, her face pale.

Her mouth opens and closes like a fish. "You can't be serious about this, Andy," she sputters.

"I am very serious."

"But..." She clutches her chest. "What about Cece?"

"Cece is *your* daughter. You never wanted me to adopt her."

It sounds like she's speaking through gritted teeth. "Oh, I see what this is about. It's because I can't have another baby. You want somebody younger, who can give you a child. I'm not good enough anymore."

"That's not what this is about," he says. Although on some level, maybe it is. Andrew does want another child. And he can't have that with Nina.

Her voice trembles. "Andy, please don't do this to me... Don't humiliate me this way. *Please*."

"I'd like you to leave, Nina. Right now."

"But it's raining!"

Andrew's voice doesn't waver. "Pack a bag and get out."

I can almost hear her weighing her options. Whatever else I can say about Nina Winchester, she's not stupid. Finally, her shoulders sag. "Fine. I'll leave."

Nina's footsteps thud in the direction of the stairs. It occurs to me a second too late that I need to move out of sight. Nina lifts her eyes and sees me standing at the top of the stairs. Her eyes burn with anger like nothing I've ever seen. I should run back to my room, but my legs feel frozen as her heels bite into the steps one by one.

The lightning flashes one last time when she reaches the top of the stairs, and the glow on her face makes her look like she's standing at the gates of hell.

"Do..." My lips feel numb, it's almost hard to form the words. "Do you need help packing?"

There's such venom in her eyes, I'm afraid she's going to reach into my chest and yank my heart out with her bare hands. "Do I need help *packing*? No, I believe I can manage."

Nina goes into her bedroom, slamming the door behind her. I am not sure what to do. I could go up to the attic, but then I look downstairs where Andrew is still in the living room. He's looking up at me, so I descend the stairs to talk to him.

"I'm so sorry!" My words come out in a rush. "I didn't mean to..."

"Don't you dare blame yourself," he says. "This was a long time coming."

I glance at the window, which is drenched with rain. "Do you want me to... go?"

"No," he says. "I want you to stay."

He touches my arm and a tingle goes through me. All I can think is that I want him to kiss me, but he can't do it right now. Not with Nina right upstairs.

But soon she'll be gone.

About ten minutes later, Nina comes down the stairs, struggling with a bag on each shoulder. Yesterday, she would have made me carry those and laughed at how weak I was. Now she has to do it herself. When I look up at her, her eyes are puffy and her hair is disheveled. She looks terrible. I don't think I realized exactly how old she was until this moment.

"Please don't do this, Andy," she begs him. "*Please*."

A muscle twitches in his jaw. The thunder cracks again, but it's softer than it was before. The storm is moving away. "I'll help you put your bags in the car."

She chokes back a sob. "Don't bother."

She trudges over to the door to the garage that's just off the side of the living room, struggling with her heavy bags. Andrew tries to reach out to help her, but she shrugs him away. She fumbles to get the door open to the garage. Instead of putting her bags down, she's trying to juggle them both and get the door open. It takes her several minutes, and I finally can't stand it anymore. I sprint over to the door, and before she can stop me, I turn the knob and throw it open for her.

"Gee," she says. "Thanks *so* much."

I don't know how to respond. I just stand there as she pushes past me with her bags. Just before she goes through the door, she leans in close to me—so close that I can feel her hot breath on my neck.

"I will *never* forget this, Millie," she hisses in my ear.

My heart flutters in my chest. Her words echo in my ears as she tosses her bags into the back of her white Lexus, and then zooms out of the garage.

She left the garage door open. I can see the rain pouring down onto the driveway as a gust of wind whips me in the face. I stand there for a moment, watching Nina's car disappear into the distance. I nearly jump when an arm encircles my shoulders.

Of course, it's just Andrew.

"Are you okay?" he asks me.

He's so wonderful. After that miserable scene, he's considerate enough to ask me how I'm doing. "I'm okay. How about you?"

He sighs. "That could've gone better. But it had to be like that. I couldn't keep living that way. I didn't love her anymore."

I look back out at the garage. "Is she going to be okay? Where is she going to stay?"

He waves a hand. "She's got a credit card. She'll just get a hotel room. Don't worry about Nina."

Except I *am* worried about Nina. I'm very worried about Nina. But not in the way he thinks.

He lets go of my shoulders to hit the button to close the garage door. He grabs my hand to pull me away, but I keep watching the garage door until it closes completely, certain Nina's car will reappear at the last moment.

"Come on, Millie." There's a glint in Andrew's eyes. "I've been waiting to get you alone."

Despite everything, I smile. "You have?"

"You have no idea..."

He pulls me in for a kiss, and as I melt against him, the thunder cracks once again. I imagine I can still hear Nina's car engine in the distance. But that's impossible. She's gone.

For good.

THIRTY-FOUR

I wake up the next morning in the guest bedroom, with Andrew asleep beside me.

After Nina left last night, this is where we ended up. I didn't want to sleep in his bed, where Nina had been sleeping just the night before. And my cot upstairs was not very comfortable for two bodies. So this was the compromise.

I suppose if we continue like this—if things become more serious between us—I'll eventually have to sleep in the master bedroom. But not yet. It still smells like Nina in there. Her stench clings to everything.

Andrew's eyes crack open and a smile spreads across his face when he sees me lying there beside him. "Well, hello," he says.

"Hello yourself."

He runs a finger down my neck and over my shoulder, and my whole body tingles. "I love waking up next to you. Instead of *her*."

I feel the same way. I hope I get to wake up next to him tomorrow. And the morning after. Nina didn't appreciate this man, but I do. She took her life for granted.

It's crazy to think that now it will be mine.

He leans in and kisses me on the nose. "I better get up. I have to get to a meeting."

I struggle to sit up in bed. "I'll make you breakfast."

"Don't even think about it." He climbs out of bed, the blankets falling from his perfect body. He's in really good shape—he must work out. "You have been getting up and making breakfast for us every single day since you've been here. Today, you sleep in. And do whatever you want."

"I usually do the laundry on Mondays. I don't mind running a load and—"

"No." He gives me a look. "Look, I don't know exactly how to work this all out, but... I really like you. I want to give you and me a real try. And if we're going to do that, you can't be my maid. I'll find somebody else to clean and you can hang out here until you figure out what you want to do next."

My cheeks flush. "It's not that easy for me. You know I have a record. People don't want to hire someone who—"

"That's why you can stay here as long as you want." He holds up a hand to cut off my protests. "I mean it. I love having you here. And who knows—maybe it'll end up being, you know, a permanent thing."

He gives me this sweet, charming smile, and I just melt. Nina had to be insane to let this guy get away.

I'm still scared she's going to want him back.

I watch Andrew thread his muscular legs through his boxer shorts, although I pretend not to be watching. He winks at me one last time, then he leaves the room to take a shower. And I'm all alone.

I let out a yawn, stretching out in this luxurious double bed. I was thrilled when I got the cot upstairs, but this is on another level. I didn't even realize I had been walking around with a crick in my back, but after one night on this mattress, it feels better. A girl could get used to this.

I had abandoned my phone on the nightstand next to the bed, but now it starts buzzing with a phone call. I reach for it, and frown at the message on the screen:

Blocked Number.

My stomach fills with butterflies. Who is calling me at this hour of the morning? I stare at the screen until the phone goes silent again.

Well, that was one way to deal with it.

I drop my phone back down on the nightstand and snuggle up back in the bed. It's not just the mattress that's comfortable. The sheets feel like I'm sleeping on a bed of silk. And the blanket is warm yet somehow light. So much better than the itchy woolen thing I've been sleeping under upstairs. And that awful scrawny blanket I had at the prison. Nice, expensive blankets feel good—who knew?

My eyes start to drift shut again. But just before I fall asleep, my phone starts ringing yet again.

I groan and reach out for my phone. Once again, it has the same message:

Blocked Number.

Who could be calling me? I don't have any friends. Cecelia's school has my number, but school is out for the summer. The only person who ever calls me is...

Nina.

Well, if it's her, she's the last person I want to talk to right now. I press the red button to reject the call. But there's no way I'm falling asleep again, so I get out of bed and go upstairs to take a shower.

. . .

When I get downstairs, Andrew is already wearing his suit and sipping on a mug of coffee. I run my fingers self-consciously over my jeans, feeling incredibly underdressed compared with him. He's standing by the window, looking out at the front yard, his lips turned down.

"Everything okay?" I ask.

He jolts, surprised by my presence. He smiles. "Yeah, fine. It's just... That goddamn landscaper is out there again. What the hell is he doing all the time out there?"

I join him at the window. Enzo is bent over a flower bed, a spade in his hand. "Gardening?"

He looks down at his watch. "It's eight in the morning. He's *always* here. There are a dozen other families he works for—why is he always *here*?"

I shrug, but truthfully, he has a point. It does seem like Enzo is in our yard a lot. A disproportionate amount of time, even considering how much larger our yard is than many of the others.

Andrew seems to make his mind up about something and he puts his coffee cup down on the windowsill. I reach for it, knowing Nina will have an absolute fit if she sees a ring of coffee on the windowsill, but then I stop myself. Nina isn't going to give me a hard time anymore. I don't ever have to see her again. I can leave coffee cups wherever I want from now on.

Andrew strides into the front lawn, a determined expression on his face, and I follow him out of curiosity. Obviously, he's planning to say something to Enzo.

He clears his throat two times, but it's not enough to get Enzo's attention. Finally, he snaps, "Enzo!"

Enzo very slowly lifts his head and turns around. "Yes?"

"I want to talk to you."

Enzo lets out a long sigh and gets back on his feet. He ambles over to us, going as slow as humanly possible. "Eh? What you want?"

"Listen." Andrew is tall, but Enzo is taller, and he has to lift his head to look at him. "Thank you for all your help here, but we don't need you anymore. So please just get your things and go to your next job."

"*Che cosa*?" Enzo says.

Andrew's lips set into a straight line. "I said, we don't need you. Done. Finished. You can leave."

Enzo's head tilts to the side. "Fired?"

Andrew sucks in a breath. "Yes. Fired."

Enzo contemplates this for a moment. I take a step back, aware that as strong and muscular as Andrew is, Enzo has him beat by a mile. If the two of them were in a fight, I don't even think it would be a close call. But then he just shrugs.

"Okay," Enzo says. "I go."

He seems to care so little about the whole thing that I wonder if Andrew feels silly for having made a big deal out of him working here so often. But Andrew nods, relieved, "*Grazie.* I appreciate your help the last few years."

Enzo just stares at him blankly.

Andrew mutters something under his breath and turns around to go back into the house. I start to follow him, but just as Andrew disappears through the front door, something restrains me. It takes me a second to realize that Enzo has grabbed my arm.

I turn around to look at him. His expression has completely changed since Andrew went back into the house. His dark eyes are wide as they stare into mine. "Millie," he breathes, "you must get out of here. You are in terrible danger."

My mouth falls open. Not only because of what he said, but how he said it. Since I've been working here, he hasn't managed to string together more than a couple of English words. And now he said two entire sentences. And not just that, but the Italian accent that is usually so thick that I can barely understand him, is far more subtle. It's the accent of a man who is *very* comfortable with the English language.

"I'm okay," I say. "Nina is gone."

"No." He shakes his head firmly, his fingers still wrapped around my arm. "You are wrong. She is not—"

Before he can get any other words out, the front door to the house swings open again. Enzo quickly releases my arm and backs away.

"Millie?" Andrew pokes his head out the front door. "Everything okay?"

"Fine," I manage.

"You coming back inside?"

I want to stay out here and ask Enzo what exactly he meant by his ominous warning and what he was trying to tell me, but I have to go back inside the house. I don't have a choice.

As I follow Andrew through the front door, I look back at Enzo, who has made himself busy gathering his equipment. He doesn't even look up at me. It's almost like I imagined the entire thing. Except when I look down at my arm, I can see the angry red marks his fingers left behind.

THIRTY-FIVE

Andrew told me that I shouldn't be doing any work for the house, but Monday I usually go grocery shopping, and we're low on a lot of supplies. And after I flip through a few books I pulled out of the bookcase and watch a little TV, I'm itching for something else to do with myself. Unlike Nina, I like keeping busy.

I have been meticulously avoiding the grocery store where that security guard tried to apprehend me. Instead, I go to a different grocery store in another part of town. They're all the same anyway.

The best part is pushing my cart around the store and not having to follow Nina's stupid pretentious grocery list. I can buy whatever I want. If I want to get brioche bread, I'll get brioche. And if I want to get sourdough, I'll get that. I don't have to send her a hundred pictures of every kind of bread. It's so liberating.

While I am looking through the dairy aisle, my phone rings inside my purse. Again, I get that unsettled feeling. Who could be calling me?

Maybe it's Andrew.

I reach into my purse and pull out the phone. Again, there's that blocked number. Whoever called me this morning is trying to call me again.

"Millie, is it?"

I nearly jump out of my skin. I look up and it's one of those women Nina had over for her PTA meeting—I can't remember her name. She's pushing her own shopping cart, and she's got a phony smile on her plump, painted lips.

"Yes?" I say.

"I'm Patrice," she says. "You're Nina's girl, right?"

I bristle at the label she gave me. *Nina's girl*. Wow. Wait till she finds out that Andrew dumped Nina and she's going to be screwed over in the divorce thanks to the prenup. Wait till she finds out that I am Andrew Winchester's new girlfriend. Soon maybe *I'll* be the one she has to suck up to.

"I work for the Winchesters," I say stiffly. But not for long.

"Oh, good." Her smile broadens. "I've been trying to get in touch with Nina all morning. She and I were supposed to get together for brunch—we always have brunch Monday and Thursday at Kristen's Diner—but she never showed up. Is everything okay?"

"Yes," I lie. "Everything is fine."

Patrice purses her lips. "I guess she must've just forgotten then. You know Nina can be a bit flaky, I'm sure."

Oh, she's a lot more than that. But I keep my mouth shut.

Her eyes fall on the phone in my hand. "Is that the phone Nina gave you to use?"

"Uh, yeah. It is."

She throws her head back and laughs. "I have to say, it's nice of you to let her keep track of where you are at all times. I don't know if I would be okay with that if I were you."

I shrug. "She mostly just texts me. It's not that bad."

"That's not what I mean." She nods at the phone. "I'm

talking about the tracking app she installed. Doesn't it drive you crazy that she wants to know where you are all the time?"

I feel like I got sucker-punched in the stomach. *Nina tracks me on my phone*? What the hell?

I'm so stupid. Of *course* she would do something like that. It makes perfect sense. And now I realize that she didn't have to go through my purse to find that playbill or call the house the night of the show. She knew exactly where I was.

"Oh!" Patrice clasps a hand over her mouth. "I'm so sorry. Did you not realize…?"

I want to slap her across her Botoxed face. I'm not sure whether she knew that I knew about it or not, but she looks like she's taking great pleasure in being the one to tell me. A cold sweat breaks out in the back of my neck. "Excuse me," I say to Patrice.

I push past her, leaving my grocery cart behind. I race out into the parking lot and I can only breathe again when I'm out of the store. I put my hands on my knees and lean forward until my breathing returns to normal.

When I straighten up again, a car is making a quick exit from the parking lot. I recognize the white Lexus.

It looks like Nina's car.

And then my phone starts to ring again.

I rip it out of my purse. Again, it says blocked number. Fine, if she wants to talk to me, she can go ahead and say what she wants to say. If she wants to threaten me and call me a homewrecker, let her do it.

I jab at the green button. "Hello? Nina?"

"Hello!" a cheerful voice says. "It's come to our attention that your vehicle warranty may have recently expired!"

I pull the phone away from my ear and stare at it in disbelief. It wasn't Nina after all. It was a stupid spam caller. I just completely overreacted to the entire thing.

But I still can't push away the feeling that I'm in danger.

THIRTY-SIX

Andrew is stuck at work tonight.

He sent me a regretful text at a quarter to seven:

Problem at work. I'm stuck here at least another hour. Eat without me.

I texted back:

No problem. Drive safely.

But inside, I was reeling with disappointment. I had so much fun having dinner in Manhattan with Andrew, and I had been attempting to re-create one of the meals we had at that French restaurant. Steak au poivre. I used black peppercorns that I picked up at the supermarket (after I worked up the nerve to go back in), minced shallot, cognac, red wine, beef broth, and heavy whipping cream. The smell was incredible, but it wasn't going to keep for another hour or two—steak just isn't the same reheated. I had no choice but to eat my magnificent dinner all alone. And now it's sitting in my stomach like a rock while I flick through stations of the television.

I don't like being in this house alone. When Andrew is here, it feels like *his* house, which it is. But when he's not here, the whole place reeks of Nina. Her perfume emanates from every crack and crevice—she's marked her territory with her scent, like an animal.

Even though Andrew told me not to, I did a deep clean of the house after my shopping trip, trying to get rid of her perfume. But I can still smell it.

As obnoxious as Patrice was in the supermarket, she did me one big favor. Nina *was* tracking me. I found the tracking app hidden in a random folder, somewhere I never would've seen it. I deleted it immediately.

But I still can't shake the feeling that she's watching me.

I close my eyes and I think of the warning Enzo gave me this morning. *You must get out of here. You are in terrible danger*. He was afraid of Nina. I could see it in his eyes when he and I were talking and she passed within earshot.

You are in terrible danger.

I push away a wave of nausea. She's gone now.

But maybe she could still hurt me.

The sun has gone down and when I look out the window, all I can see is my reflection. I stand up from the sofa and walk over to the window, my heart pounding. I press my forehead against the cool glass, peering into the dark outside.

Is that a car parked outside the gates?

I squint into the darkness, trying to figure out if I'm just imagining things. I suppose I could go outside and get a closer look. But that would involve unlocking the doors to the house.

Of course, what's the difference if the door is unlocked when Nina has a key?

My thoughts are interrupted by the sound of my phone ringing on the coffee table. I hurry over to grab it before I miss the call and frown when I find another blocked number on the screen. I shake my head. Another spam call. Just what I need.

I press the green button to accept the call, expecting to hear that obnoxious recorded voice. But instead, I hear a distorted, mechanical voice:

"*Stay away from Andrew Winchester!*"

I suck in a breath. "Nina?"

I couldn't tell if it was a man or a woman, much less whether it was Nina. Then there's a click on the other line. It's gone dead.

I swallow. I've had enough of Nina's games. Starting tomorrow, I'm taking back this house. I'm calling a locksmith to change the locks on the doors. And tonight, I'm spending the night in the master bedroom. Enough of this guest bedroom bullshit. I'm not a guest here anymore.

Andrew said he wanted this to become permanent. So now, this is my home too.

I head for the stairs, taking them two at a time. I keep going until I get up to the stuffy room in the attic—my bedroom. Except it won't be my bedroom after tonight. I'm packing everything up and moving downstairs. This will be my last time in this claustrophobic little room with the weird lock on the outside of the door.

I grab one of my pieces of luggage out of the closet. I start throwing clothing inside, not bothering to be too careful, given that I'm just carrying it down one flight of stairs. Of course, I'll have to ask Andrew's permission before I clean out a drawer downstairs. But he can't expect me to live up here anymore. It's inhuman. This room is like some sort of torture chamber.

"Millie? What are you doing?"

The voice from behind me nearly gives me a heart attack. I clutch my chest and turn around. "Andrew. I didn't hear you come in."

His gaze darts over my luggage. "What are you doing?"

I shove the handful of bras I was holding into the luggage. "Well, I thought I might move downstairs."

"Oh."

"Is… is that okay?" I feel suddenly awkward. I had assumed Andrew would be fine with it, but maybe I shouldn't have made that assumption.

He takes a step toward me. I bite down on my lip until it hurts. "Of course it's okay. I was going to suggest it myself. But I wasn't sure if you would want to."

My shoulders sag. "I definitely want to. I… I had kind of a rough day."

"What have you been up to? I saw some of my books on the coffee table. Have you been reading?"

I wish that's all I had been doing today. "Honestly, I don't want to talk about it."

He takes another step closer and reaches out to trace my jaw with the tip of his finger. "Maybe I could make you forget about it…"

I shiver at his touch. "I bet you could…"

And he does.

THIRTY-SEVEN

Despite how incredibly uncomfortable my cot is compared with the incredible mattress in the guestroom, I pass out soon after Andrew and I make love up there, wrapped tightly in his arms. I never thought I would be having sex in this room. Especially since Nina was so strict about letting me have any guests over.

That rule certainly didn't work out too well for her.

I wake up again at around three in the morning. The first sensation I become aware of is my bladder—full and slightly uncomfortable. I've got to hit the bathroom. Usually, I go right before bed, but Andrew wore me out and I fell asleep before I could muster up the energy.

And that's the other sensation I become aware of. A sense of emptiness. Andrew isn't in the cot anymore.

I suspect after I fell asleep, he decided to relocate to his own bed. I can't blame him. This cot is hardly comfortable for one person, much less two, and the room is so claustrophobic. Maybe he tried to tough it out, but after tossing and turning, he migrated downstairs. Andrew is more than ten years older than me, and my back can barely make it through the night with this mattress, so I can hardly blame him.

I'm so glad this is the last night I'll be sleeping here. Maybe after I use the bathroom, I'll go join Andrew downstairs.

I rise to my feet, the floorboards groaning under my weight. I make my way to the door and turn the doorknob. As usual, it sticks. So I turn it more firmly.

It still doesn't turn.

Panic mounts in my chest. I press myself against the door, the scratch marks in the wood splintering into my shoulder, and place my right hand squarely on the knob. I try once again to turn it clockwise. But it doesn't budge. Not even a millimeter. And that's when I realize what's going on.

The door isn't stuck.

It's locked.

PART II

THIRTY-EIGHT

NINA

If a few months ago, someone had told me I would be spending tonight in a hotel room while Andy was at *my* house with another woman—the maid!—I wouldn't have believed it.

But here I am. Dressed in a terry cloth bathrobe I found in the closet, stretched out in the queen-size hotel bed. The television is on, but I'm barely aware of it. I've got my phone out and I click on the app I have been using for the last several months. *Find my friends.* I wait for it to tell me the location of Wilhelmina "Millie" Calloway.

But under her name, it says: location not found. The same as it has since the afternoon.

She must've figured out I was tracking her and disabled the app. Smart girl.

But not smart enough.

I pick up my purse from where I put it down on the nightstand. I dig around inside until I find the one paper photograph I have of Andy. It's a few years old—a copy of the photographs he had professionally taken for the company website, and he gave me one of them. I stare into his deep brown eyes on the shiny piece of paper, his perfect mahogany hair, the hint of a cleft in his strong chin. Andy is the most handsome man I've ever known in real life. I fell half in love with him the first moment I saw him.

And then I find one other object inside my purse and drop it into the pocket of my robe.

I get up off the queen-size bed, my feet sinking into the plush carpet of the hotel room. This room is costing Andy's credit card a fortune, but that's okay. I won't be here long.

I go into the bathroom and I hold up the photograph of Andy's smiling face. Then I pull out the contents of my pocket.

It's a lighter.

I flick the starter until a yellow flame shoots out of it. I hold the flickering light to the edge of the photograph until it catches. I watch my husband's handsome face turn brown and disintegrate, until the sink is full of ashes.

And I smile. My first real smile in almost eight years.

I can't believe I finally got rid of that asshole.

* * *

How to Get Rid of Your Sadistic, Evil Husband—A Guide by Nina Winchester

Step One: Get Knocked Up by a Drunken One-Night Stand, Drop Out of School, and Take a Crappy Job to Pay the Bills

My boss, Andrew Winchester, is ever so dreamy.

He's not actually my boss. He's more like, my boss's boss's boss. There may be a few other layers in there of people in the chain between him—the CEO of this company since his father's retirement—and me—a receptionist.

So when I'm sitting at my desk, outside my actual boss's

office, and I admire him from afar, it's not like I'm crushing on an *actual* man. It's more like admiring a famous actor at a movie premiere or possibly even a painting at the fine arts museum. Especially since I have zero room in my life for a date, much less a boyfriend.

He is just *so* good-looking though. All that money and also so handsome. It would say something about life just being unfair, if the guy wasn't so *nice*.

Like for example, when he went in to talk to my own boss, a guy at least twenty years his senior named Stewart Lynch, who clearly resents being bossed around by a guy who he calls "the kid," Andrew Winchester stopped at my desk and smiled at me and called me by name. He said, "Hello, Nina. How are you today?"

Obviously, he doesn't know who I am. He just read my name off my desk. But still. It was nice that he made the effort. I liked hearing my ordinary four-letter name on his tongue.

Andrew and Stewart have been in his office talking for about half an hour. Stewart instructed me not to leave while Mr. Winchester was in there, because he might need me to fetch some data from the computer. I can't quite figure out what Stewart does, because I do all his work. But that's fine. I don't mind, as long as I get my paychecks and my health insurance. Cecelia and I need a place to live, and the pediatrician says there's a set of shots she requires next month (for diseases she doesn't even have!).

But what I mind a little more is that Stewart didn't warn me he was going to ask me to wait around. I'm supposed to be pumping now. My breasts are full and aching with milk, straining at the clips of my flimsy nursing bra. I'm trying my best not to think about Cece, because if I do, the milk will almost certainly burst through my nipples. And that's just not the kind of thing you want to happen when you're sitting at your desk.

Cece is with my neighbor Elena right now. Elena is also a single mother, so we trade babysitting duties. My hours are more regular, and she works evening shifts at a bar. So I take Teddy for her, and she takes Cece for me. We are making it work. Barely.

I miss Cece when I'm at work. I think about her all the time. I had always fantasized that when I had a baby, I would be able to stay home for at least the first six months. Instead, I just took my two weeks of vacation and went right back to work, even though it still sort of hurt to walk. They would have allowed me twelve weeks off, but the other ten would have been unpaid. Who could afford ten weeks unpaid? Certainly not me.

Sometimes Elena resents her son for what she gave up for him. I was in graduate school when I got that positive pregnancy test, leisurely working on a Ph.D. in English as I lived in semi-poverty. It hit me when I saw those two blue lines that my eternal graduate school lifestyle would never provide for me and my unborn child. The next day, I quit. And I started pounding the pavement, looking for something to pay the bills.

This isn't my dream job. Far from it. But the salary is decent, the benefits are great, and the hours are steady and not too long. And I was told there's room for advancement. Eventually.

But right now, I just have to get through the next twenty minutes without my breasts leaking.

I'm *this* close to running off to the bathroom with my little pumping backpack and my tiny little milk bottles when Stewart's voice crackles out of the intercom.

"Nina?" he barks at me. "Could you bring in the Grady data?"

"Yes, sir, right away!"

I get on my computer and load up the files he wants, then I hit print. It's about fifty pages' worth of data, and I sit there, tapping my toes against the ground, watching the printer spit out each page. When the final page finishes printing, I yank out the sheets of paper and hurry over to his office.

I crack open the door. "Mr. Lynch, sir?"

"Come in, Nina."

I let the door swing the rest of the way open. Right away, I notice both men are staring at me. And not in that appreciative way I used to get at bars before I got knocked up and my whole life changed. They're looking at me like I've got a giant spider hanging off my hair and I don't even know it. I'm about to ask them what the hell both of them are staring at when I look down and figure it out.

I leaked.

And I didn't just leak—I squirted milk out like the office cow. There are two huge circles around each of my nipples, and a few droplets of milk are trickling down my blouse. I want to crawl under a desk and die.

"Nina!" Stewart cries. "Get yourself cleaned up!"

"Right," I say quickly. "I… I'm so sorry. I…"

I drop the papers on Stewart's desk and hurry out of the office as fast as I can. I grab my coat to hide my blouse, all the while blinking back tears. I'm not even sure what I'm more upset about. The fact that my boss's boss's boss saw me lactating or all the milk I just wasted.

I take my pump to the bathroom, plug it in, and relieve the pressure in my breasts. Despite my embarrassment, it feels *so* good to empty all that milk. Maybe better than sex. Not that I remember what sex feels like—the last time was that stupid, stupid one-night stand that got me into this situation to begin with. I fill two entire five-ounce bottles and stick them in my bag with an ice pack. I'll put it in the refrigerator until it's time to go home. Right now, I've got to get back to my desk. And leave my coat on for the rest of the afternoon, because I have recently discovered that even if it dries, milk leaves a stain.

When I crack open the door to the bathroom, I'm shocked

to see someone standing there. And not just anyone. It's Andrew Winchester. My boss's boss's boss. His fist is raised in the air, poised to knock on the door. His eyes widen when he sees me.

"Uh, hi?" I say. "The men's room is, um, over there."

I feel stupid saying that. I mean, this is *his* company. Also, there's a stencil of a woman with a dress on the door to the bathroom. He should realize this is the women's room.

"Actually," he says, "I was looking for you."

"For me?"

He nods. "I wanted to see if you were okay."

"I'm fine." I try to smile, hiding my humiliation from earlier. "It's just milk."

"I know, but..." He frowns. "Stewart was a jerk to you. That was unacceptable."

"Yeah, well..." I'm tempted to tell him of a hundred other instances when Stewart was a jerk to me. But it's a bad idea to talk shit about my boss. "It's fine. Anyway, I was just about to grab some lunch, so..."

"Me too." He arches an eyebrow. "Care to join me?"

Of course I say yes. Even if he wasn't my boss's boss's boss, I would've said yes. He's gorgeous, for starters. I love his smile—the crinkling around his eyes and the hint of a cleft in his chin. But it's not like he's asking me out on a date. He just feels bad because of what happened before in Stewart's office. Probably someone from HR told him to do it to smooth things over.

I follow Andrew Winchester downstairs to the lobby of the building that he owns. I assume he's going to take me to one of the many fancy restaurants in the neighborhood, so I'm shocked when he leads me over to the hotdog cart right outside the building and joins the line.

"Best hotdogs in the city." He winks at me. "What do you like on yours?"

"Um... mustard, I guess?"

When we get to the front of the line, he orders two hotdogs, both with mustard, and two bottles of water. He hands me a hotdog and a bottle of water, and he leads me to a brownstone down the block. He sits on the steps and I join him. It's almost comical—this handsome man sitting on the steps of the brownstone in his expensive suit, holding a hotdog covered in mustard.

"Thank you for the hotdog, Mr. Winchester," I say.

"Andy," he corrects me.

"Andy," I repeat. I take a bite of my hotdog. It's pretty good. Best in the city? I'm not so sure about that. I mean, it's bread and mystery meat.

"How old is your baby?" he asks.

My face flushes with pleasure the way it always does when somebody asks me about my daughter. "Five months."

"What's her name?"

"Cecelia."

"That's nice." He grins. "Like the song."

Now he has scored big points because the Simon and Garfunkel song is why I named her that, although the spelling is different. It was my parents' favorite song. It was *their* song before that plane crash took them from me. And it made me feel close to them again to honor them that way.

We sit there for the next twenty minutes, eating our hotdogs and talking. It surprises me how down-to-earth Andy Winchester is. I love the way he smiles at me. I love the way he asks me questions about myself, like he's really interested. I'm not surprised he's done so well with the company—he's good with people. Whatever HR told him to do with me, he's done a good job. I'm definitely not upset anymore about the incident in Stewart's office.

"I better get back," I tell him, when my watch reads half past one. "Stewart will kill me if I get back late from lunch."

I don't point out the fact that Stewart works for *him*.

He stands up and brushes crumbs off his hands. "I have a

feeling hotdogs were not the lunch you were expecting from me."

"It's fine." And it is. I had a great time eating hotdogs with Andy.

"Let me make it up to you." He looks me in the eyes. "Let me take you to dinner tonight."

My jaw drops. Andrew Winchester could have any woman he wants. *Anyone.* Why would he want to take *me* out to dinner? But he asked.

And I want to go so badly, which makes it almost painful to have to turn him down. "I can't. I don't have anyone to babysit."

"My mother is going to be in the city tomorrow afternoon anyway," he says. "She loves babies. She'd be thrilled to watch Cecelia for you."

Now my mouth is hanging open. Not only did he invite me to dinner, but when I presented him with a barrier, he came up with a solution. Involving his *mother*. He really does want to go to dinner with me.

How could I say no?

THIRTY-NINE

Step Two: Naively Marry Sadistic, Evil Man

Andy and I have been married for three months, and sometimes I have to pinch myself.

Our courtship was quick. Before I met Andy, all the men I dated just wanted to play games. But Andy wasn't about games. From the night of our magical first date, he made his intentions clear to me. He was looking for a serious relationship. He had been engaged before, a year earlier, to a woman named Kathleen, but it hadn't worked out. He was ready to get married. He was willing to take on both me and Cecelia.

And from my perspective, he was everything I was looking for. I wanted a secure home for me and my daughter. I wanted a man with a steady job, who would be a father figure for my little girl. I wanted a man who was kind and responsible and... well, yes, attractive. Andy checked off every single box.

In the days leading up to our wedding, I kept looking for flaws. Nobody could possibly be as perfect as Andy Winchester. He had to have a secret gambling problem or maybe a whole other family stashed away in Utah. I even contemplated calling Kathleen, the former fiancée. He'd shown me photographs of her—she had blond hair like me and a sweet face—but I didn't know her last name and I couldn't locate her on social media. But at least she wasn't talking trash about him all over the internet. I took that as a good sign.

The only thing about Andy that isn't ideal is... well, his mother. Evelyn Winchester is around a little bit more than I would like. And I wouldn't call her the warmest person in the world. Despite Andy's assurance that she "loves babies" and is "thrilled" to watch Cece, she always seems a bit put out when we ask her to babysit. And the evening invariably concludes with a set of criticisms of my parenting, thinly veiled as "suggestions."

But I am marrying Andy, not his mother. No one likes their mother-in-law, right? I can deal with Evelyn, especially since she doesn't have that much interest in me in general outside my apparent lack of parenting skills. If that's the only thing wrong with Andy, I'm in good shape.

So I married him.

And even three months later, I haven't quite come down from my cloud yet. I can't believe that I have the financial stability to stay home with my little girl. I do want to go back to graduate school eventually, but right now I want to soak up every minute of my family. Cece and Andy. How could one woman get so lucky?

And in return, I try to be a perfect wife. In my little free time, I work out at the gym to make sure I'm in perfect shape. I bought a wardrobe of absolutely impractical white clothing because he adores me in white. I've studied recipes online and I'm trying to cook for him as much as I can. I want to be worthy of this incredible life he's given me.

Tonight I kiss Cecelia on her baby-smooth cheek, taking a few extra seconds to stare down at her and take in the sound of her deep breathing and the scent of baby powder. I tuck a strand of her soft blond hair between one of her nearly translucent ears. She is so beautiful. I love her so much, sometimes I feel like I could just eat her up.

When I come out of her bedroom, Andy is waiting for me outside. He is smiling at me, his dark hair without even a strand out of place, every bit as gorgeous as that first day I met him. I still don't understand why he picked me. He could have had any woman in the world. Why me?

But maybe I shouldn't question it. I should just be happy.

"Hey," he says. He tucks a strand of my own blond hair behind my ear. "I can see your roots starting to show a bit."

"Oh." I touch my hairline self-consciously. Andy loves blond hair, so I started going to the salon after we got engaged to lighten my hair to more of a golden shade. "Gosh, I guess I've been so busy with Cece, it just slipped my mind."

I can't quite read the expression on his face. He's still smiling, but there's something off about it. It doesn't bother him that much that I missed a hair appointment, does it?

"Listen," he says. "I need your help with something first."

I lift an eyebrow, glad he doesn't seem too upset about my hair. "Sure. What is it?"

He raises his eyes in the direction of the ceiling. "There are some papers from work that I stashed in the upstairs storage area. I was wondering if you could help me try to find them. I've got to get this contract done tonight. And then after, we can..." He grins at me. "You know."

He doesn't have to tell me twice.

I've been living in this house for about four months now, and I've never been up to the storage area in the attic. I climbed the stairs up there once, while Cece was taking a nap, but the door was locked, so I turned back. Andy says it's just a bunch of papers. Nothing too exciting.

And the truth is, I don't love going up there. I don't have any crazy phobias about attics, but the staircase leading up there is kind of creepy. It's dark, and the stairs creak with every step. As I follow Andy up the staircase, I stay close to him.

When we get to the top of the stairs, Andy leads me down the small hallway to the locked door at the end. He gets out his set of keys and fits one of the small ones into the lock. Then he throws the door open and tugs on a cord to turn on the light.

I blink as my eyes adjust to the light and I take in my surroundings. This is not a storage closet like I thought it would be. It's more like a tiny room, with a cot pushed up into one corner. There's even a little dresser and a mini-fridge. There's a single tiny window at the far end of the room.

"Oh." I scratch my chin. "This is a *room*. I thought it would just be junk and storage stuff."

"Well, I store everything in the closet over there," he explains, pointing to the closet near the bed.

I walk over to the closet and peer inside. There's nothing inside except a blue bucket. There are no papers at all, much less enough for searching through them to be a two-person job. I don't quite understand what he would like me to do.

Then I hear a door slam shut.

I lift my head and turn around. Suddenly, I'm all alone in this tiny room. Andy has left the room and shut the door behind him.

"Andy?" I call out.

I cross the room in two strides and reach for the doorknob. But it doesn't turn. I try harder, throwing my weight into it, but still no luck. The doorknob doesn't budge even an inch.

It's locked.

"Andy?" I call out again. No answer. "Andy!"

What the hell is going on here?

Maybe he went downstairs to get something and the door blew shut. But that doesn't explain why there aren't any papers in this room when he said that's what we were coming up here to get.

I pound on the door with my fist. "Andy!"

Still no answer.

I press my ear against the door. I hear footsteps, but they're not coming closer. They're getting further away, disappearing down the stairwell.

He must not hear me. That's the only explanation. I pat my pockets, but my phone is in the bedroom. There's no way to call him.

Damn it.

My eyes fall on the window. There's one tiny little window in the corner of the room. I walk over and look outside, realizing that the window looks out on to the backyard. So there's no way to get anybody's attention outside. I'm stuck here until Andy returns.

I'm not exactly claustrophobic, but this room is very small with a low ceiling that slants over the bed. And the idea that I'm locked in here is starting to freak me out. Yes, Andy will come back shortly, but I don't like this enclosed space. My breathing quickens and my fingertips start to tingle.

I've got to get that window open.

I push against the bottom of the window, but the window doesn't budge. Not even a millimeter. For a moment, I think maybe it swings out, but it doesn't. What the hell is wrong with the stupid window? I take a deep breath, trying to calm myself down. I look closer at the window and...

It's painted shut.

When Andy comes back up here, I am going to give it to him. I consider myself pretty even-tempered, but I do *not* like being locked in this room. We've got to do something about this lock on the door, to make sure it doesn't lock automatically again. I mean, what if both of us had been in here? We would've really been stuck.

I go back to pounding on the door. "Andy!" I scream at the top of my lungs. "Andy!"

After fifteen minutes, my voice is hoarse from screaming. Why hasn't he come back? Even if he can't hear me, he must've realized I'm still in the attic. What could I possibly be doing up here by myself? I don't even know what papers he wants.

I mean, was he walking down the stairs, tripped, then fell the rest of the way down the stairs, and is now lying unconscious in a pool of blood at the bottom? Because that's the only thing that makes sense to me.

Thirty minutes later, I'm about to go out of my mind. My throat aches and my fists are red from pounding on the door. I want to burst into tears. Where is Andy? What is going on here?

Just when I feel like I'm about to lose my mind, I hear a voice from the other side of the door. "Nina?"

"Andy!" I cry. "Thank God! I got locked in here! Didn't you hear me screaming?"

There's a long silence on the other side of the door. "Yes. I did."

I don't even know what to say to that. If he heard me, why didn't he let me out? But I can't deal with that right now. I just want to get out of this room. "Can you please open the door?"

Another long silence. "No. Not yet."

What?

"I don't understand," I sputter. "Why can't you let me out? Did you lose the key?"

"No."

"So let me out!"

"I said *not yet*."

I flinch at the sharpness of the last two words. I don't understand. What's going on here? Why won't he let me out of the attic?

I stare at the door between us. I try the doorknob one more time, hoping maybe it's some kind of joke. It's still locked. "Andy, you need to let me out of here."

"Don't tell me what to do in my own house." His voice has an odd intonation that I barely recognize as him. "You have to learn your lesson before you can be let out."

A cold, sick feeling runs down my spine. While Andy and I were engaged, he seemed so perfect. He was sweet, romantic, handsome, wealthy, and good to Cecelia. I had been searching for his one fatal flaw.

I have found it.

"Andy," I say. "Please let me out of here. I don't know what you're upset about, but we can work it out. Just unlock the door and we'll talk."

"I don't think so." His voice is calm and even—the exact opposite of how I'm feeling right now. "The only way to learn is to see the consequences of your actions."

I suck in a breath. "Andy, you let me out of this fucking room *right now*."

I kick the door hard, although my bare feet don't make too much of an impact. Mostly, it just hurts my toes. I wait to hear the door unlocking, but there's nothing.

"I swear to God, Andy," I growl. "Let me out of this room. Let. Me. Out."

"You're upset," he acknowledges. "I'll come back when you've calmed down."

And then his footsteps grow more distant—he's walking away.

"Andy!" I scream. "Don't you dare walk away! Come back! Come back and let me the fuck out of here! Andy, if you don't let me out of here, I'm leaving you! Let me out!" I pound with both fists. "I'm calm! Let me out!"

But the footsteps grow fainter until they finally disappear.

FORTY

Step Three: Discover Your Husband is Pure Evil

It's midnight. Three hours later.

I pounded at the door and scraped at the wood until I had splinters under my fingernails. I screamed until I lost my voice. I figured even if he wasn't going to let me out, maybe the neighbors would hear. But after an hour, I gave up hope of that.

Now I'm sitting on the cot in the corner of the room. Springs poke into my butt cheeks as I finally let the tears roll down my cheeks. I don't know what he plans to do to me, but all I can think about is Cecelia, asleep in her crib. Alone with that psychopath. What will he do to me? What will he do to *her*?

If I ever get out of here, I'm going to grab Cece and run as far as I can away from this man. I don't care how much money he has. I don't care if we're legally married. I want *out*.

"Nina?"

Andy's voice. I jump off the bed and sprint over to the door. "Andy," I choke out with what's left of my voice.

"You lost your voice," he acknowledges.

I don't know what to say to that.

"You shouldn't bother screaming," he tells me. "Everything is soundproofed below the attic. So nobody will hear you. I could be having a dinner party downstairs and they would never hear you screaming."

"Please let me out," I whimper.

I'm willing to do whatever it takes. I'll agree to whatever he wants if he'll let me out of here. Of course, once the door's open, I'm leaving him. I don't care if the prenup says I'll get nothing for ending the marriage within the first year. Anything to get the hell out of here.

"Don't worry, Nina," he says. "I'm going to let you out. I promise."

I let out a breath.

"Just not *yet*," he adds. "You have to learn the consequences of what you've done."

"What are you talking about? Consequences of *what*?"

"Your hair." His voice is filled with disgust. "I can't have my wife walking around like a slob with dark roots showing."

My roots. I can't believe he was that upset over it. I mean, it's just a few millimeters of hair. "I'm so sorry. I promise, I'll make an appointment with the hairdresser right away."

"That's not enough."

I press my forehead against the door. "I'll go first thing tomorrow morning. I swear."

He yawns on the other side of the door. "I'm going to sleep now. You just hang tight and we'll talk more in the morning about your punishment."

His footsteps fade as he walks away. Even though my hands are aching from banging on the doors, I do it again. I slam my fist against the door so hard, I can't believe I don't break every bone in my hand. "Andy, don't you dare leave me here overnight! Come back here! Come back!"

But he ignores me like he did before.

• • •

I sleep in that room. Of course I do. What choice do I have?

I didn't think I would end up drifting off, but somehow I did. Between all the screaming and pounding on the door, the adrenaline gave way to exhaustion and I passed out on that uncomfortable old cot. The cot isn't that much worse than the bed I used to sleep in back in the tiny apartment I had when it was just me and Cecelia, but I've gotten used to Andy's memory foam mattress.

I think back to when it was just me and Cece. I was always overwhelmed, always on the brink of tears. I had no idea how good I had it before I was married to a psychopath who would lock me in a room overnight just because I missed a hairdresser appointment.

Cece. I hope she's okay. If that asshole touches even one hair on her head, I swear I will kill him. I don't care if I go to jail for the rest of my life.

My back is aching when I wake up in the morning. And my head is pounding. But worst of all, my bladder is full. Painfully full. This is the most pressing need of all.

Except what can I do? The bathroom is outside this room.

Then again, if I wait much longer, I'm going to pee in my pants.

I get up and pace the room. I try the doorknob one more time, hoping maybe I just imagined everything that happened last night and it will open magically. No such luck. It's still locked.

I remember when I looked in the closet, there was only one item in there. A bucket.

Andy set this whole thing up. He tricked me into coming up here. He installed a lock on the outside of the door. And he also put that bucket there for a reason.

I'm really going to have to do this.

I suppose there are worse things than peeing in a bucket. I

drag it out of the closet and I do what I have to do. Then I stick it back in there. Hopefully, I won't have to use it again.

My mouth feels parched and my stomach is growling, even though eating would make me sick. Considering how he set up the bucket, I wonder if he put that same consideration into other parts of the room. I throw open the mini-fridge, hoping for some sort of bounty of food in there.

Instead, there are three mini water bottles.

Three beautiful water bottles.

I almost faint from relief. I grab one of the bottles, crack it open, and guzzle it practically in one gulp. My throat still feels dry and raw, but slightly better.

I eye the other two bottles. I would love to have another one, but I'm scared. How long will Andy leave me here? I have no idea. I should conserve my resources.

"Nina? Are you awake?"

Andy's voice at the door. I stumble over to it, my head pounding with each step. "Andy..."

"Good morning, Nina."

I shut my eyes against a wave of dizziness. "Is Cecelia okay?"

"She's fine. I told my mother you went to visit some family and she's watching Cecelia until you get back."

I let out a breath. At least my daughter is safe. Evelyn Winchester isn't my favorite person in the world, but she is a vigilant babysitter. "Andy, please let me out."

He ignores my request—it doesn't even surprise me at this point. "Did you find the water in the fridge?"

"Yes." And even though it kills me, I add, "Thank you."

"You're going to have to make it last. I can't give you any more."

"Then let me out," I croak.

"I will," he says. "But you have to do something for me first."

"What? Anything."

He pauses. "You need to understand that hair is a privilege."

"Okay, I understand that."

"Do you, Nina? Because I feel like if you did understand it, you wouldn't walk around like a slob, with your dark roots showing."

"I... I'm sorry for that."

"Because you couldn't take care of your hair, now you will give it to me."

I have a horrible, sick feeling in the pit of my stomach. "What?"

"Not all of it." He chuckles, because of course *that* would be ridiculous. "I want a hundred strands."

"You... you want a hundred strands of my hair?"

"That's right." He taps on the door. "Give me one hundred strands of your hair, and I'll let you out of the room."

This is the strangest request I've ever heard. He wants to punish me for my dark roots by giving him a hundred strands of my hair? There's that much nestled in my hairbrush. Does he have some sort of hair fetish? Is that what this is about? "If you look in my brush—"

"No," he interrupts me. "I want it from your scalp. I want to see the root."

I stand there, stunned. "Are you serious?"

"Does it sound like I'm joking?" he snaps. His voice then softens. "There are a few envelopes in the dresser drawer. You put the hairs in there and slide them under the door. If you do that, you'll have learned your lesson and I'll let you out."

"Okay," I agree. I run a hand through my blond hair and two strands come loose in my fingers. "I'll have it for you in five minutes."

"I have to go to work now, Nina," he says irritably. "But when I get home, you should have the strands ready for me."

"But I can do it fast!" I tug at my hair again and another strand comes free.

"I'll be home by seven," he says. "And remember, I want fully intact hair. I have to see the root or it doesn't count!"

"No! Please!" I grasp at my hair more violently this time—my eyes water but only a few more strands rip loose. "I'll do it now! Just wait!"

But he's not going to wait. He's leaving. His footsteps disappear the way they did earlier.

I've learned no amount of screaming or pounding on the door is going to get him to come back. There's no point in wasting my energy and aggravating my already agonizing headache. I have to focus on getting him what he wants. Then I can get back to my daughter. And I can escape this house forever.

FORTY-ONE

By seven o'clock, I have accomplished the task.

I obtained about twenty strands by running my fingers repeatedly through my hair. After that, I knew I was going to have to pluck the rest out by the root. About eighty times, I grabbed a strand of my hair, braced myself, and pulled. I tried doing a few strands at once, but that was agonizing. Thankfully, my hair is healthy, so most of the strands yanked free with the hair follicle intact. After I had Cecelia, I would have had to pluck myself bald before I got enough usable hair.

So when seven o'clock hits, I am sitting on the cot, clutching an envelope containing a hundred strands of my hair. I can't wait to hand it over to him and get out of here. And serve him with divorce papers. That sick bastard.

"Nina?"

I look down at my watch. Seven o'clock on the dot. He's prompt—I'll give him that.

I jump off the bed and press my head against the door. "I have it," I say.

"Slide it under."

I slide the envelope under the gap below the door. I imagine him on the other side. Ripping the envelope open, examining my hair follicles. I don't care what he does at this point, as long as he lets me out. I've done what he wanted me to do.

"Okay?" I say. My throat feels painfully parched. I finished the other two water bottles over the course of the day, saving the last one for the final hour. When I get out of here, I'm going to drink five glasses of water all in a row. And pee in an actual toilet.

"Give me a minute," he says. "I'm checking."

I grit my teeth, ignoring the angry growl in my stomach. I haven't eaten in twenty-four hours now and I'm dizzy with hunger. It got to the point where the hair was starting to look tasty.

"Where is Cece?" I choke out.

"She's in her playpen downstairs," he says. We created a gated, safe area in the living room where she could play without worrying about her hurting herself. It was Andy's idea. He's so thoughtful.

No, he's not thoughtful. That was all an illusion. An act.

He's a monster.

"Hmm," Andy says.

"What?" I croak. "What is it?"

"See," he says, "*almost* all of the strands are fine, but one of them doesn't have a hair follicle on it."

Bastard. "Fine. I'll give you a new one."

"I'm afraid not," he sighs. "You'll have to start all over again. I'll check in on you tomorrow morning. Hopefully by then, you'll have one hundred intact hairs for me. Otherwise, we'll have to just keep trying."

"No..." His footsteps disappear down the hall, and it hits me he's really leaving me. With no food and no water. "Andy!" My voice is hoarse and not much better than a whisper. "Don't do this! Please! Please don't do this!"

But he's gone.

. . .

I have the extra hundred strands ready by bedtime, on the off chance he returns, but he doesn't. I even put in an extra ten strands. Somehow, they're coming out easier now. I barely feel it anymore as the hair separates from my scalp.

All I can think about is water. Food and water, but mostly water. And of course, my Cecelia. I'm not sure I'll ever see her again. I don't know how long a person can go without water, but it can't be very long. Andy swore he was going to let me out of here, but what if he was lying? What if he's going to let me die here?

All because I missed a hairdresser appointment.

When I drift off at night, I dream of a pool of water. I lower my head to the pool and the water moves away from me. Each time I try to drink, the water escapes me. It's like one of the tortures of hell.

"Nina?"

Andy's voice wakes me. I'm not sure if I fell asleep or passed out. But I've been waiting for him all night long, so I need to get up and give him what he wants. It's the only way I'll ever get out of here.

Get up, Nina!

As soon as I sit up in bed, my head spins violently. Everything goes black for a second. I clutch the edge of the thin mattress, waiting for my vision to clear. It takes a good minute.

"I'm afraid I can't let you out unless I get those hairs," Andy says from the other side of the door.

The sound of his horrible voice sparks a wave of adrenaline that boosts me to my feet. My fingers are trembling as I grab the envelope and stumble over to the door. I slide the envelope under the door, then collapse against the wall, sliding to the floor.

I wait while he counts. It seems to take an eternity. If he

says I haven't done it, I don't know what I'll do. I can't last another twelve hours here. That will be the end. I'll die in this room.

No, I have to keep going no matter what. For Cece. I can't leave her to this monster.

"Okay," he finally says. "Good job."

And then the lock turns. And the door swings open.

Andy is dressed in his suit, already ready for work. I had imagined the moment I saw this man after being stuck in this room for two nights, I would jump up and scratch his eyes out. But instead, I remain on the floor, too weak to move. Andy crouches beside me, and that's when I notice he's holding a large glass of water and a bagel.

"Here," he says. "I brought you this."

I should throw the water in his face. I want to. But I don't think I can get out of this room if I don't eat and drink something. So I accept his gift, gulping down the cup of water and stuffing chunks of the bagel down my throat until it's all gone.

"I'm sorry I had to do that," he says, "but it's the only way you'll learn."

"Go to hell," I hiss at him.

I try to get to my feet, but I stumble again. Even after drinking that water, my head is still spinning. I can't walk in a straight line. I doubt I can get down the stairs to the second floor.

So even though I hate myself for it, I let Andy help me. I let him lead me downstairs, and I have to lean on him heavily the whole way. When I get to the second floor, I can hear Cecelia singing downstairs. She's okay. He didn't hurt her. Thank God.

I'm not going to let him have another chance.

"You need to lie down," Andy says sternly. "You're not well."

"No," I croak. I want to be with Cecelia. My arms ache for her.

"You're too sick right now," he says. Like I'm getting over the flu rather than him trapping me in a room for two days. He's talking to me like *I'm* the crazy one. "Come on."

But whatever else, he's right that I need to lie down. My legs are trembling with every step and my head won't stop spinning. So I let him lead me to our king-size bed and he tucks me in under the covers. If there was any chance I might make it out of here, that chance is gone once I get in the bed. It feels like sleeping on a cloud after passing out on that cot for the last two nights.

My eyelids feel like lead—I can't fight the urge to fall asleep. Andy sits beside me, at the edge of the bed, running his fingers through my hair. "You just haven't been feeling well," he says. "You need a day of sleep. Don't worry about Cecelia. I'll make sure she's taken care of."

His voice is so kind and gentle, I start to wonder if maybe I imagined the whole thing. After all, he's been such a good husband. Would he really lock me up in a room and make me pull out my hair? That doesn't sound like something he would do. Maybe I just have a fever and this is all a horrible hallucination?

No. It wasn't a hallucination. It was real. I know it was.

"I hate you," I whisper.

Andy ignores my statement as he continues to stroke my hair until my eyes drift shut. "Just get some sleep," he says gently. "That's all you need."

FORTY-TWO

Step Four: Make the World Believe You're Crazy

I wake up to the distant sound of water running.

I still feel groggy and out of it. How long does it take the body to recover from being deprived of food and water for two days? I look at my watch—it's the afternoon.

I rub my eyes, trying to identify the location of the running water. It seems to be coming from the master bathroom, which is closed. Is Andy in there showering? If he is, I don't have much time to get the hell out of here.

My phone is sitting on the nightstand by the bed. I snatch it up, tempted to call the police about what Andy did to me. But no, I'm going to wait. Until I'm far away from him.

Except the phone is filled with text messages from Andy. The sound of his messages must've been what woke me up. I scroll through them, frowning at the screen.

Are you OK?

You seemed to be acting really strangely this morning. Please give me a call and let me know you're all right.

Nina, is everything OK? About to go into a meeting, but let me know you're OK.

How are you and Cece doing? Please call or text me.

The last text is what gets my attention. Cecelia. I haven't seen her in two days. Before that, I had never gone one day without her. I wouldn't even leave her to go on a honeymoon. Where is she right now?

After all, Andy wouldn't have left me alone with her if I was asleep, would he?

I look up at the closed bathroom door. Who is inside the master bathroom? I had assumed it was Andy, but it couldn't be. He's been texting me from work. Did I leave the water running by accident somehow? Maybe I got up and used the bathroom and forgot to turn the sink off. It seems possible, considering how out of it I am.

I throw the covers off my legs. My hands look pale and shaky. I try to get up, but it's hard. Even though I've had water and rest, I still feel awful. I have to hold onto the bed to walk. I'm not sure if I can make it from the bed to the master bathroom.

I take a deep breath, swallow my dizziness, and walk as slowly as I can. I get about two-thirds of the way there before I collapse to my knees. God, what is wrong with me?

But I need to know what that sound is. Why is there water running in the bathroom? And now that I'm closer, I can see that the light is on inside the closed door. Who is in there? *Who is in my bathroom?*

I crawl the rest of the way there. When I finally make it to the bathroom door, I reach for the handle and push the door open. And what I see when I get inside is something I'll never forget for the rest of my life.

It's Cece. She's inside the bathtub. Her eyes are closed and she's propped up in the tub. The water is rapidly filling the tub, rising above the level of her shoulders. In another minute or two, it will be over her head.

"Cecelia," I gasp.

She doesn't say a word. She doesn't cry or call for me. But her eyelids flutter slightly.

I've got to save her. I've got to shut off the water and drag her from the tub. But I can't get my feet to work, and every movement is like going through molasses. I'm going to save her though. I'll save my daughter if it takes every ounce of my strength. If it kills me.

I crawl across the bathroom floor. My head is spinning so badly, I'm not sure if I can hold onto consciousness. But I can't pass out. My baby needs me.

I'm coming, Cece. Please hold on. Please.

When my fingers graze the porcelain of the tub, I almost cry with relief. The water is almost up to her chin now. I start to reach for the faucet, but a harsh voice makes my fingers freeze.

"Mrs. Winchester. Don't move."

I reach for the faucet anyway. Nobody is going to stop me from saving my baby. I manage to get the water off, but before I can do anything else, strong hands grasp my arms, yanking me to my feet. In a haze, I see a man in uniform pulling Cecelia out of the tub.

"What are you doing?" I try to ask, but my speech is slurred.

The man who rescued Cecelia ignores my question. Another voice says, "She's alive, but it looks like she's been drugged."

"Yes," I manage. "Drugged."

They know. They know what Andy has been doing to us. And now he's drugged both of us. Thank God the police came.

And now a paramedic has Cecelia on a stretcher, and they're lifting me onto one as well. We're going to be okay. They've come to save us.

A man in a police uniform shines a light in my eyes. I look away, wincing at the unbearable brightness. "Mrs. Winchester," he says sharply. "Why were you trying to drown your daughter?"

I open my mouth but no sound comes out. *Drown my daughter?* What is he talking about? I was trying to *save* her. Can't they see that?

But the policeman just shakes his head. He turns to one of his colleagues. "She's too out of it. Looks like she took a bunch of the drugs herself. Get her to the hospital. I'll call the husband and let him know we got here in time."

Got here in time? What's he talking about? I've just been sleeping all day. For God's sake, *what do they think I've done*?

FORTY-THREE

The next eight months of my life are spent in Clearview Psychiatric Hospital.

The story, which has been repeated to me countless times, is that I took a bunch of sedatives that my physician prescribed to me and also gave my daughter some in her bottle. Then I placed her in the bathtub and turned on the water. My intention, apparently, was to kill both of us. Thank God my wonderful husband Andy suspected something was wrong and the police arrived in time to save us.

I have no memory of any of this. I have no memory of taking pills. I have no memory of putting Cecelia in the bathtub. I don't even have a memory of my physician prescribing that medication for me, but the family doctor Andy and I go to assured us he did.

According to the therapist I see at Clearview, I suffer from major depression and delusions. The delusions are what led me to believe my husband was keeping me captive in a room for two days. The depression was what caused me to make the murder-suicide attempt.

At first, I didn't believe it. My memories of being up in the attic are so vivid, I could almost feel the sting on my scalp from the hairs I pulled out. But Dr. Barringer keeps explaining to me that when you're having delusions, it can feel very real even when it's not.

So now I'm on two medications to keep this from happening ever again. An anti-psychotic and an anti-depressant. When I have my sessions with Dr. Barringer, I own up to my part in what I did. Even though I still don't remember it at all. I only remember waking up and finding Cecelia in the bathtub.

But I must've done it. There was no one else there.

The part that finally convinced me I'd done it myself is that Andy could never have done something like that to me. Since the day I met him, he has been nothing but wonderful. And through my entire stay at Clearview, he has visited me every chance he could get. The staff love him. He brings muffins and cookies for the nurses. And he always saves one for me.

Today he brought me a blueberry muffin. He knocks on the door of the private room at Clearview, an expensive facility for people with psychiatric issues who also have money. He's come straight from work, and he's wearing a suit and tie, and he looks achingly handsome.

When I first came here, I was locked in the room. But I've done so much better with the medication that they've given me the privilege of an unlocked room. Andy perches at the other end of my bed while I stuff the muffin into my mouth. The anti-psychotic has ramped up my appetite, and I've put on twenty pounds since I've been here.

"Are you ready to come home next week?" he asks.

I nod, wiping blueberry crumbs from my lips. "I... I think so."

He reaches for my hand, and I flinch but manage not to pull away. When I first came here, I couldn't bear for him to touch me. But I've managed to push my feelings of revulsion aside.

Andy didn't do anything to me. It was my screwed-up brain that imagined it all.

But it felt so real.

"How is Cecelia doing?" I ask.

"She's doing great." He squeezes my hand. "She's so excited you're coming home."

I would have thought she might forget me while I was in here, but she never forgets. I wasn't allowed to see her for the first several months I was here, but when Andy finally brought her to me, the two of us clung to each other, and when visiting hours ended, she wailed her head off until my heart broke in two.

I've got to get home. I've got to get back to my life the way it was. Andy has been so great about everything. He took on more than he bargained for with me.

"So I'm going to pick you up at noon on Sunday," he says. "And then I'll drive you home. My mother will stay with Cece."

"Great," I say.

As much as I'm excited about coming home and seeing my daughter, the thought of returning to that house gives me a sick feeling in the pit of my stomach. I'm not looking forward to setting foot back there. Especially in the attic.

I'm never going up there again.

FORTY-FOUR

"What are you afraid of, Nina?"

I look up at Dr. Hewitt's question. I've been going to these sessions for the last four months, two times a week, ever since my discharge from Clearview. Dr. Hewitt would not have been my first choice. For starters, I probably would have picked a female therapist and someone younger—like without a full head of gray hair. But Andy's mother highly recommended Dr. John Hewitt, and I didn't feel comfortable saying no, considering Andy has paid through the teeth for all my psychiatric care.

Anyway, Dr. Hewitt has turned out to be very good. He does press me with some hard questions. Like right now we are addressing the fact that I have not gone near the attic of our house since I've been home.

I shift on his leather sofa. The expensive furnishing in this office is a testament to my therapist's great success. "I don't know what I'm afraid of. That's the problem."

"Do you really think there's a dungeon up in the attic?"

"Not a dungeon, but..."

After all my claims about what had been done to me in our house, a police officer was sent to check out the attic. He found the room up there and verified it was nothing more than a storage closet. Filled with boxes and papers.

It was a delusion. Something went wrong with the chemicals in my brain and I imagined Andy was holding me hostage. I mean, making me pluck out my hair and put them in an envelope just because I missed a hairdresser appointment? That's completely insane, in retrospect.

But it felt so real at the time. And I have been diligent about coloring my hair ever since I got home. Just in case.

Andy has been keeping the door to the stairwell up to the attic closed. As far as I know, he hasn't opened it since I came home.

"I think it would be therapeutic for you to go up there," Dr. Hewitt tells me, his thick white eyebrows knitted together. "That way the place won't hold any power over you anymore. You'll see for yourself that it's just a storage closet."

"Maybe..."

Andy has been encouraging me to go up there as well. *Just see for yourself. There's nothing to be scared of.*

"Promise me you'll try, Nina," he says.

"I'll try."

Maybe. We'll see.

Dr. Hewitt escorts me into the waiting area, where Andy is sitting on one of the wooden chairs, reading something on his phone. When he sees me, his face breaks into a smile. He has rearranged his schedule to take me to every single one of these appointments. I don't know how he could still love me so much after the terrible things I accused him of. But we are working together to heal.

And he waits until we're in his BMW to ask about the session. "So how did it go?"

"He thinks I should go visit the attic room."

"And?"

I swallow as I watch through the window as the scenery flies by. "I'm considering it."

Andy bobs his head. "I think it's a good idea. Once you get up there, you'll realize the whole thing was all just a delusion. It will be like a revelation, you know?"

Or I could have another complete breakdown and try to kill Cecelia again. Of course, that would be difficult since I'm not currently allowed to be alone with her. Either Andy or his mother are around at all times. That was one of the conditions of my coming home. I don't know how long I'm going to need to be babysat when I'm with my own daughter, but right now it's clear that nobody trusts me.

Cece is on the floor, playing with one of the educational games Evelyn bought her. When my daughter sees us come in, she abandons her game and hurls herself at me until her little body makes contact with my left leg. It almost knocks me off my feet. Despite the fact that I'm not allowed to be alone with her, Cece has been achingly clingy with me since I've been home.

"Mama, up!" She raises her arms to me until I gather her up. She's wearing a frilly white dress that is a bit preposterous for such a little girl playing in the living room—Evelyn must have dressed her in it. "Mama home."

Evelyn is not as quick as Cece to rise to her feet. She slowly stands up from the couch, brushing off her pristine white slacks. I never noticed before how frequently Evelyn dresses in white, which has always been Andy's favorite color on me. It suits her though. Her hair looks like it might have once been blond, but now she's just at that precipice between blond and white, her hair surprisingly thick and healthy for a woman her age. Evelyn is, in general, incredibly well preserved and flawless. I have never seen her with so much as a loose thread on her sweater.

"Thanks for watching Cece, Mother," Andy says.

"Of course," Evelyn says. "She was well behaved today. But..." Her eyes drift up toward the ceiling. "I noticed you left the lights on in the bedroom upstairs. Such a terrible waste of electricity."

She gives him a disapproving look and Andy's entire face turns bright red. I've noticed how desperate he is for her approval.

"It was my fault," I speak up. I'm not sure it was, but what the hell—I might as well take the blame since Evelyn already dislikes me. "I left the light on."

Evelyn tuts at me. "Nina, producing electricity takes a lot of our planet's resources. You should remember to shut off the lights when you leave any room."

"I absolutely will," I promise.

Evelyn gives me a look like she's not quite sure I mean it, but what is she going to do? She's already failed to stop her son from marrying me. Of course, maybe she was right about me after the terrible thing I did.

"We stopped off to get food, Mother," Andy says. "We got extra. Do you want to join us?"

I'm relieved when Evelyn shakes her head. She's not a pleasant dinner guest. Having her stay for the meal guarantees a string of criticisms about our dining area, the cleanliness of our dishes and utensils, and the food itself.

"No, I should be heading out," she says. "Your father is expecting me."

She hesitates in front of Andy. For a moment, I almost think she's going to kiss him on the cheek, which is something I've never seen her do before. But instead, she reaches out and adjusts his collar, smoothing out his shirt. She cocks her head, examining him, then nods an approval. "All right, I'm off."

After Evelyn is gone, we enjoy a nice dinner together, just the three of us. Cecelia sits in her highchair and eats noodles with her fingers. Halfway through the meal, one of the noodles somehow makes it onto her forehead and adheres there for the rest of the dinner. But even as I try to enjoy the meal, something isn't sitting right in the pit of my stomach. I keep thinking about what Dr. Hewitt said. He thinks I should go up to the attic. So does Andy.

Maybe they're both right.

So after I put Cecelia down for the night, when Andy brings it up, I say yes.

FORTY-FIVE

Step Five: Find Out You're Not Crazy After All

"We'll take it slow," Andy promises me as we stand together at the door to the attic staircase. "But this will be good for you. To see yourself that there's nothing there to be scared of. That this was all completely in your head."

"Right," I manage. I know he's right. But it felt *so* real.

Andy takes my hand in his. I don't cringe anymore when he touches me. We started making love again. I trust him again. This will be the final step to getting back to where we were before I did this terrible thing. Before my brain broke.

"Ready?" he says.

I nod.

We hold hands as we ascend the creaky staircase together. We need to put in a lightbulb here somewhere. The rest of the house is so nice—maybe if this entire area were less frightening, I would feel better. Not that it's any excuse for what I did.

Far too soon, we reach the room in the attic. The storage closet that I somehow turned into a dungeon in my head. Andy raises his eyebrows at me. "Are you okay?"

"I… I think so."

He turns the doorknob and nudges the door open. The light is out, and the room is pitch black. Which is strange, because there's a window and I know there's a full moon tonight—I had admired it from the bedroom window. I step inside, squinting into the shadows of the room.

"Andy." I swallow a lump in my throat. "Can you turn the light on?"

"Of course, sweetheart."

He pulls on the cord for the lights, and the room lights up. But it's not normal light. The light coming from overhead is almost blinding. It's super bright, like nothing I've ever experienced before. I let go of Andy's hand and clasp my own hands over my eyes to block it out.

And then I hear the sound of the door slamming shut.

"Andy!" I call out. "Andy!"

My eyes have adjusted to the super bright light just barely enough to be able to make out the contents of the room if I squint. And… it's just as I remember it. The dingy cot in the corner of the room. The closet with the bucket. The mini fridge that had contained three tiny bottles of water.

"Andy?" I croak.

"I'm out here, Nina." His voice is muffled.

"Where?" I grasp around blindly, still squinting. "Where did you go?"

My fingers make contact with the cold metal of the doorknob. I twist it to the right and…

No. *No*. It can't be.

Am I having another breakdown? Is this all in my head? It can't be. It feels so real.

"Nina." Andy's voice again. "Can you hear me?"

I shield my eyes with my hand. "It's so bright in here. Why is it so bright?"

"Turn out the light."

I grasp around until I find the cord for the lights, then I give it a good tug. I feel a surge of relief as I'm plunged back into blackness. It lasts for about two seconds, until I realize I'm completely blind in here.

"Your eyes will adjust a bit," he says. "But it won't help much. I boarded up the window last week and put in new lights. If you turn off the light, the world will be pitch black. Turn it on and... well, those ultra-bright lightbulbs are pretty intense, huh?"

I close my eyes and see nothing but blackness. I open them, and it's exactly the same. No difference. My breathing quickens.

"Light is a privilege, Nina," he says. "My mother has noticed before that you failed to turn off the lights. Did you know in other countries, there are people who don't even have electricity? And what do you do? You waste it."

I press my palm against the door. "This is really happening, isn't it?"

"What do you think?"

"I think you're a crazy, sick asshole."

Andy laughs on the other side of the door. "Maybe. But *you* were the one who was in a loony bin for trying to kill yourself and your daughter. The police saw you doing it. You *admitted* to having done it. And by the time they came here to check things out, this room looked exactly like a storage closet."

"It was real," I gasp. "It was real the whole time. You..."

"I wanted you to know what you're dealing with." His tone is amused. He finds this *entertaining*. "I wanted you to know what would happen if you tried to get away."

"I understand." I clear my throat. "I swear to you, I won't leave. Just let me out of here."

"Not yet. First you have to be disciplined for wasting electricity."

The sound of those words brings back an overwhelming

feeling of déjà vu. I feel like I'm going to throw up. I sink to my knees.

"So here's how it's going to work, Nina," he says. "Because I am *such* a nice guy, I'm giving you two choices. You can have the lightbulb or you can have blackness. It's entirely up to you."

"Andy, please..."

"Good night, Nina. We'll talk more tomorrow."

"Please! Andy, don't do this!"

Tears spring to my eyes as his footsteps fade away. Shouting won't make a difference. I know it because this exact same thing happened to me one year ago. He locked me in here the same way he has today.

And somehow I've let him do it again.

I imagine things unfolding the same way as last time. Emerging from this room, weak and groggy. Him making it seem like I was trying to hurt myself, or worse, hurt Cecelia. Everyone will be so quick to believe his story after the last time. I imagine being wrenched away from my daughter again. I just got her back. I can't let that happen. I *can't*.

I'll do anything.

Once again, Andy has left three water bottles for me in the refrigerator. I decide to save them for the next day, because it's all I'll get and I have no idea how long I'll be in here. I'm going to save them for when I can't stand it another minute. When my tongue starts to feel like it's made of sandpaper.

The light situation is driving me completely crazy. There are two naked bulbs on the ceiling, and both of them are these ultra-bright lights. If I turn on the light, it is agonizingly bright in here. But with them off, it's pitch black. I get the idea to push the dresser over below the lightbulbs, and I climb up there and manage to unscrew one of them. It's a little better with just the single lightbulb, but still bright enough that I have to squint.

Andy doesn't come back in the morning either. I sit in that room the entire day, worrying about Cecelia, wondering what the hell I'm going to do when and if I get out of here. But this isn't a delusion. This isn't a hallucination. This is really happening to me.

I have to remember that.

It's bedtime when I finally hear footsteps outside the room. I've been lying in the bed, choosing the darkness option. When it was daylight, a few tiny cracks of sunlight had gotten through, and I could almost make out the shadow of objects in the room. But now that the sun has gone down, it's pitch black again.

"Nina?"

I open my mouth but my throat is too dry to say anything. I have to clear my throat. "I'm here."

"I'm going to let you out."

I wait for him to add "but not yet," but he doesn't.

"But first," he says, "there are going to be some ground rules."

"Anything you say." *Just please let me out of here.*

"For starters, you don't tell anyone what went on in this room." His voice is firm. "You don't tell your friends, you don't tell your doctor, you don't tell *anyone*. Because nobody will believe you, and if you talk about it, it's just going to be a sign that you're having delusions again and poor Cecelia could be in danger."

I stare into the blackness. Even though I knew what he was going to say, hearing it fills me with fury. How can he expect me not to talk about what he just did to me?

"*Do you understand, Nina*?"

"Yes," I manage.

"Good." I can almost imagine his satisfied smirk. "Second, from time to time, if you need to be disciplined, that will take place in this room."

Is he kidding me? "No way. Forget it."

"I don't think you're in a position to negotiate, Nina." He snorts. "I'm just telling you how it's going to be. You are my wife now, and I have very specific expectations. Really, it's for your own good. I taught you a valuable lesson about wasting electricity, didn't I?"

I gasp for air in the blackness. I feel like I'm choking.

"This is *for* you, Nina," he says. "Look at the horrible choices you made in your life before I came along. You had a dead-end minimum-wage job. You got knocked up by some loser who didn't stick around. I'm just trying to teach you how to be a better person."

"I wish I had never met you," I spit out.

"That's not a very nice thing to say." He laughs. "I guess I can't blame you. I'm impressed that you managed to unscrew one of those lightbulbs though. I didn't even think of that."

"You... How did you...?"

"I'm watching you, Nina. I'm always watching." I can hear him breathing behind the door. "This is going to be our lives from now on. We will be a happily married couple like everyone else. And you will be the best wife in the entire neighborhood. I'll make sure of that."

I press my fingers into my eyeballs, trying to extinguish the headache that's blooming in my temples.

"Do you understand, Nina?"

Tears prick at my eyes, but I can't cry. I'm too dehydrated; nothing comes out.

"*Do you understand, Nina?*"

FORTY-SIX

Step Six: Try to Live With It

I crack the window open in Suzanne's Audi so that the wind tousles my light hair as she drives me home from our lunch date. We were supposed to be discussing PTA issues, but we got distracted and started gossiping. It's hard not to gossip. There are so many bored housewives in this town.

People think I'm one of them.

Andy and I have been married for seven years now. And he has kept every one of his promises. He has, in many ways, been a wonderful husband. He has supported me financially, he has been a father figure to Cecelia, he's even-tempered and agreeable. He doesn't drink heavily or mess around behind my back like so many other men in this town. He's almost perfect.

And I hate his guts.

I have done everything I possibly can to get out of this marriage. I bargained with him. I told him I would leave with just Cecelia and the clothing on my back, but he just laughed. With my history of mental health problems, it would be easy for him to tell the police I'd kidnapped Cece and was going to hurt her again. I tried playing the part of the perfect wife, hoping not to give him an excuse to take me up to the attic. I cooked delicious homemade dinners, kept the house spotless, and even pretended not to be repulsed when we had sex. But he always found something. Something I never would have even imagined I did wrong.

Eventually, I gave up. I wasn't going to try to be nice if it didn't even affect how often he took me up there. My new strategy became to repel him. I started behaving like a shrew, snapping at him for every little thing that annoyed me. He didn't care—he almost seemed to enjoy the abuse. I stopped going to the gym and started eating whatever the hell I wanted, hoping if I couldn't turn him off with my behavior, I could turn him off with my appearance. On one occasion, he caught me indulging in a chocolate cake and he dragged me up to the attic and starved me for two days as a punishment. But after that, he didn't seem to care anymore.

I tried finding Kathleen, his former fiancé, hoping she might back up my story so that I could finally go to the police without sounding like a crazy person. I had an idea of what she looked like and her approximate age—I thought I could find her. But do you know how many people roughly aged thirty to thirty-five have the name Kathleen? Quite a lot. I couldn't find her. I finally gave up trying.

On average, he makes me go up to the attic once every other month. Sometimes it's more frequent, sometimes less. Once six months went by without a trip up there. I don't know if it's better or worse that I don't know when it's coming. It would be awful if I knew the exact day and had to dread it, but it's also awful to never know if I'll be spending that night in my own bed or in that uncomfortable cot. And of course, I never know what sort of torture he's got waiting for me in the room because I never know what transgression I have committed.

And it's not just me. If Cecelia does something unacceptable, I'm the one who gets punished. He has purchased a wardrobe of itchy, frilly dresses that she hates, that the other children make fun of her for wearing, but she knows if she doesn't wear them or gets them dirty, her mother will disappear for days (likely naked, to teach me clothing is a privilege). So she obeys.

I'm scared that someday he will start punishing her instead, but in the meantime, I'm happy to accept my fate if he spares my daughter.

And he's very clear that if I try to get away from him, Cecelia will pay the price. He already almost drowned her. His other favorite way to taunt me is keeping a jar of peanut butter in our pantry, even though he knows that she's allergic. I have thrown it away dozens of times, and it always reappears–and sometimes I get punished for the transgression. Thankfully, it's not a life-threatening allergy–she just breaks out in welts all over her body. Every once in a while, he slips a little bit into her dinner, just to prove a point when the itchy, uncomfortable rash sprouts after our meal has ended.

If I knew I wouldn't go to jail for it, I would pick up a steak knife and drive it through his neck.

Andy has prepared for that contingency though. Of course, he knows that my temptation to arrange for his death or outright kill him myself might become overwhelming. He has informed me that in the event of his death from any cause, a letter will be sent from his attorney to the police department, informing them of my unstable behavior and homicidal threats against him. Not that he needs to do it, with my psychiatric history.

So I stay with him. And I don't murder him in his sleep. Or hire a hitman. But I do fantasize. When Cecelia is older, when she doesn't need me, maybe I could get away. Then he won't have a threat against me anymore. Once she is safe, I don't care what happens to me.

"Here we are!" Suzanne announces cheerfully as we pull

up in front of the gate to our home. Funny how the first time I saw those gates, I thought how charming it was to have a home with a gate surrounding it. Now it seems like exactly what it is: a prison.

"Thanks for the ride," I say. Even though she didn't thank me for paying for lunch.

"You're welcome," she chirps. "Hopefully, Andrew will be home soon."

I grimace at the tinge of worry in her voice. A few years ago, when I was getting very close with Suzanne, we had a few too many drinks at her house and I confessed everything. *Everything*. I begged her to help me. I told her I wanted to go to the police, but I couldn't. Not without anyone supporting me.

We talked for hours. Suzanne had held my hand and sworn to me it was going to be okay. She told me to go home and we would figure this out together. I cried with relief, believing my nightmare was finally over.

But when I got home, Andy was waiting for me.

Apparently, every time I made a new friend, Andy sought out that friend. He sat down with them and clued them in to my history of mental health problems. He told them what I had tried to do years earlier. And he told them if they had any reason for concern to call him immediately. Because I might be having another episode.

Unbeknownst to me, Suzanne had slipped away briefly during our conversation, under the guise of needing the bathroom, and she called Andy. She warned him that I was having delusions again. So when I came home, he was ready for me. It was another two-month stay at Clearview, where I discovered at least one of the directors was a golfing buddy of his father.

When I got out, Suzanne apologized profusely. *I was just worried about you, Nina. I'm so glad you got help.* I forgave her, of course. She was tricked the same way I was. But it was never the same between us again after that. And I was never able to trust anyone ever again.

"So I'll see you Friday, right?" Suzanne says. "At the school play."

"Sure," I say. "What time does it start again?"

Suzanne doesn't answer me, suddenly distracted by something.

"Does it start at seven?" I press her.

"Mm-hmm," she says.

I glance over her shoulder to see what has grabbed her attention. I roll my eyes when I figure it out. It's Enzo, the local landscaper who we hired to work on our yard a couple of months ago. He does a good job—always works hard and never makes excuses—and he's admittedly pretty easy on the eyes. But it's crazy the way everyone who comes to our house when he's working slobbers over him and then suddenly remembers they have some yard work they need done.

"Wow," Suzanne breathes. "I heard your yard guy was hot, but *damn*."

I roll my eyes. "He just works on our lawn—that's it. He doesn't even speak English."

"I'm okay with that," Suzanne says. "Hell, that might be a plus."

She won't let up until I hand over Enzo's phone number. Not that I mind. He seems like a nice enough guy, and I'm glad he's getting some extra business. Even if it's only because he's hot, and not because of what he does.

When I get out of the car and pass through the gates, Enzo looks up from his hedge clippers and waves his hand in greeting. "*Ciao, Signora.*"

I return his smile. "*Ciao*, Enzo."

I like Enzo. Even though he doesn't speak any English, he seems like a kind person—you can just tell. He plants all these beautiful flowers in our yard. Cece sometimes watches him, and when she asks him about the flowers, he patiently points to them and says their names. She repeats the names, and he nods and smiles. A few times she asked if she could help him, and he looked at me and asked, "Is okay?" When I agreed, he gave her a job to do in the flower bed, even though it probably slowed him down.

He has tattoos all over his upper arms, mostly concealed by his shirt. One time when I was watching him work, I saw the name Antonia etched in a heart on his biceps. It made me wonder who Antonia was. I'm pretty sure Enzo isn't married.

There's something about him. If only he spoke English, I feel like I could confide in him. That he might be the one person who would believe me. Who might actually help me.

I stand there, watching him clip our hedges. I haven't worked since the day I moved in here—Andy won't let me. I miss it. Enzo would understand. I know he would. Too bad he doesn't speak any English. But in a way, that makes it easier to confide in him. Sometimes I feel like if I don't say the words out loud, I'm going to lose my mind for real.

"My husband is a monster," I say aloud. "He tortures me. He holds me hostage in the attic."

Enzo's shoulders stiffen. He lowers his clippers, his brow furrowed. "*Signora*... Nina..."

My stomach turns to ice. Why did I say that? I should never have said those words. It's just that I knew he wouldn't understand me, and I felt like I needed to tell *somebody* who wouldn't rat me out to Andy. I thought it would be safe to tell Enzo. After all, he doesn't even know English. But when I look into his dark eyes, there's understanding there.

"Never mind," I say quickly.

He takes a step toward me, and I shake my head, backing away. I made a huge mistake. Now I'm probably going to have to fire Enzo.

But then he seems to get it. He picks up his clippers again and goes back to work.

I hurry into the house as fast as I can and slam the door behind me. Right by the window, there's a spectacular arrangement of flowers. I would say every color of the rainbow represented. Andy brought it home last night from work to surprise me, to show me what a spectacular husband he is when I am "well behaved."

I peer beyond the flowers out the window into the front yard. Enzo is still working out there, the sharp clippers in his gloved hands. But he pauses for a moment and looks up at the window. Our eyes meet for a split second.

And then I look away.

FORTY-SEVEN

I have been in the attic for about twenty hours.

Andy marched me up here right after Cecelia went to bed last night. I've learned not to argue. If I do, it's another stay at Clearview. Or maybe when I try to pick Cece up at the school the next day, she won't be there and I won't see her for a whole week, while she's "out of town." He doesn't want to hurt Cecelia, but he absolutely will. After all, if the police didn't arrive exactly when they did, she could've drowned in that bathtub all those years ago. I brought it up with him once, and he just smiled at me. *That would've taught you a lesson, wouldn't it?*

Andy wants another child. Another little person who I will love and want to protect, who he will use to control me for years to come. I can't let that happen. So I drove to a clinic in the city, gave a fake name, and paid in cash for them to insert an IUD. I've practiced my perplexed expression when the pregnancy tests come back negative.

This time my transgression was spraying too much air freshener in our bedroom. It was exactly the same amount I always spray, and if I hadn't used it at all, he would have locked me in there with something malodorous, like a rotting fish. I know how his mind works now.

Anyway, somehow last night the air freshener was too much and it irritated his eyes. My punishment? I had to pepper-spray myself.

Oh yes.

He left the bottle of pepper spray in the dresser drawer. *Point it at your eyes and pull the trigger.*

Also, keep your eyes open. Or it won't count.

So I've done it. I sprayed myself with pepper spray just to get out of this goddamn room. Have you ever been pepper-sprayed? I don't recommend it. It stings terribly, and right away, my eyes started to tear up like crazy. My face felt like it was burning. And then my nose started to run. A minute later, I felt it dripping into my mouth where it stung and tasted terrible. For several minutes, I sat on the bed, just struggling to breathe. I could barely open my eyes for nearly an hour.

It was definitely worse than a little air freshener.

But now it's several hours later. I can open my eyes again. I still feel like I have a sunburn on my face and my eyes feel puffy, but I don't feel like I'm going to die anymore. I'm sure Andy will want to wait until I look more like my usual self before he lets me out of here.

Which means it could be one more night. But hopefully not.

The window isn't boarded up, like he keeps it sometimes, so at least I have some natural light in the room. It's the only thing keeping me from going completely crazy. I walk over to the window and peer out into the backyard, wishing I were out there instead of in here.

That's when I realize the backyard isn't empty.

Enzo is working out there. I start to back away, but he happens to look up at the window at the exact moment I'm standing there. He stares at me, and even from the third floor of the house, I can make out the darkening look on his face. He yanks off his gardening gloves and stalks out of the yard.

Oh no. This isn't good.

I don't know what Enzo is going to do. Will he call the police? I'm not sure if that would be a good thing or not. Andy has always managed to flip these things around on me. He's always one step ahead. About a year ago, I started stashing some money in one of my boots in my closet, saving up in hopes of escaping him. Then one day, all the money disappeared, and the day after, he forced me up to the attic.

About a minute later, a fist pounds on the attic door. I step back, cowering against the wall. "Nina!" It's Enzo's voice. "Nina! I know you are in there!"

I clear my throat. "I'm fine!"

The doorknob jiggles. "If you are fine, open the door and show me you are fine."

It hits me at that moment that Enzo is speaking pretty good English. I had been under the impression that he understood some English and spoke far less, but his English seems excellent right now. His Italian accent isn't even that thick.

"I... I'm busy," I say in an abnormally high voice. "But I'm fine! Just getting some work done."

"You told me your husband tortures you and locks you in the attic."

I suck in a breath. I only said that to him because I thought he didn't understand. But now it's clear he understood everything I said. I have to do damage control. I can't do anything to anger Andy. "How did you get into the house anyway?"

Enzo lets out an exasperated sound. "You leave a key under the potted plant by the front door. Now, where is the key to this room? Tell me."

"Enzo..."

"*Tell me.*"

I do know where the key to the attic door is. It doesn't do me a lot of good when I'm in here, but I could direct him to it. If I wanted to. "I know you're trying to help, but this isn't helping. Please—just stay out of it. He'll let me out later today."

There's a long silence on the other side of the door. I hope he's thinking about whether it's worth it to get involved in a client's personal life. And I don't know what his immigration status is, but I know he wasn't born here. I'm sure Andy and his family have enough money and power to get him deported if they want.

"Step back," Enzo finally says. "I will break down the door."

"No, you can't!" Tears jump to my eyes. "Look, you don't understand. If I don't do what he says, he'll hurt Cecelia. And he'll have me locked up—he's done it before."

"No. This is just excuses."

"No, they're not!" A single tear rolls down my cheek. "You don't understand the kind of money he has. You don't understand what he could do to you. Do you want to get deported?"

Enzo is quiet again. "This is wrong. He is hurting you."

"I'm fine. I swear to you."

It's mostly true. My face still feels like it's burning, and my eyes still sting, but Enzo doesn't need to know that. In another day, I'll be completely fine. Like it never happened. And then I can go back to my normal, miserable life.

"You want me to leave," he acknowledges.

I don't want him to leave. I want nothing more for him to break the door down, but I know how Andy will twist it around. God knows what he'll accuse the two of us of doing. I never thought he could get me locked up in a mental institution multiple times just for trying to tell the truth. I don't want that to become Enzo's life too. Except Andy had reason to want me to get out—he would have no problem with locking Enzo up indefinitely.

"Yes," I say. "Please go."

He lets out a long sigh. "I will go. But if I do not see you tomorrow morning, I will come up here and break the door down. And I will call the police."

"That's fair." I'm down to my last tiny bottle of water, so if Andy hasn't let me out by the morning, I'll be in bad shape.

I wait to hear his footsteps walking away. But I don't hear them. He is still standing on the other side of the door. "You do not deserve to be treated this way," he finally says.

Then his footsteps disappear down the hallway as the tears run down my cheeks.

Andy lets me out of the room that night. When I finally get to a mirror, I'm shocked at how swollen my eyes look from the pepper spray, and my face is bright red like I was scalded. But by the next morning, I look almost back to normal. My cheeks are pink, like I got a little too much sun the day before.

Enzo is working in the front yard when Andy pulls out of the garage, with Cece strapped into the backseat. He's dropping her off at school while I rest today. He's usually very nice to me for several days after he lets me out of the attic. I'm sure tonight he'll come home with flowers and maybe some jewelry for me. As if that could make up for any of it.

I watch from the window as Andy drives through the gate, pulling out onto the road. After the car disappears, I notice Enzo staring at me. He isn't usually in our yard two days in a row. He's here for a reason that has nothing to do with the state of our flower beds.

I come out through the front door to where Enzo is standing with his clippers. It occurs to me how sharp the clippers are. If he drove them through Andy's chest, that would be the end. Of course, he wouldn't need to do that. He could probably kill Andy with his bare hands.

"See?" I offer a forced smile. "I told you I'm fine."

He doesn't return my smile.

"Really," I say.

His eyes are so dark, it's impossible to make out his pupils. "Tell me the truth."

"You don't want to hear the truth."

"Tell me."

In the last five years, every single person I have told about the things Andy has done to me—the police, the doctors, my best friend—has called me crazy. *Delusional*. I have been locked up for talking about what he has done to me. But here is a man who wants to hear the truth. He will believe me.

So as we stand on my front lawn on this beautiful sunny day, I tell Enzo everything. I tell him about the room in the attic. I tell him some of the ways Andy has tormented me. I tell him about finding Cecelia unconscious in the bathtub. It was years ago but I remember her face under the water like it was yesterday. I tell him everything as his face grows darker and darker.

Before I even finish, Enzo lets loose with a string of Italian. I don't know the language, but I know curse words when I hear them. His fingers squeeze on the clippers until they turn white. "I kill him," he hisses. "Tonight, I will kill him."

All the blood drains out of my face. It felt so good to tell him everything that happened to me, but it was a mistake. He is beyond furious. "Enzo…"

"He is a monster!" he bursts out. "You do not *want* me to kill him?"

Yes, I want Andy dead. But I don't want to deal with any of the consequences. Especially the letter that will go to the police in the event of his death. I want him dead, but not enough to spend my life in prison.

"You can't do it." I shake my head firmly. "You'll go to jail. We'll both go to jail. Is that what you want?"

Enzo mumbles more Italian under his breath. "Fine. Then you leave him."

"I can't."

"You *can*. I will help you."

"What can you do?" It's not entirely a rhetorical question. Maybe Enzo is secretly rich. Maybe he's got some mob connections I don't know about. "Can you get me a plane ticket? A new passport? A new identity?"

"No, but..." He rubs his chin. "I will find a way. I know some people. I will help."

I want so badly to believe him.

FORTY-EIGHT

Step Seven: Try to Escape

A week later, I meet up with Enzo to make plans.

We are careful about it. In fact, when I have friends over from the PTA, I make a show of snapping at him that he's ruining my geraniums, just to ward off any potential gossip. I'm almost certain Andy put a tracking device somewhere in my car, so I can't drive to his house. Instead, I drive to a fast-food restaurant, park in the lot, and hop into his vehicle before anyone can see. I leave my phone behind.

I'm not taking any chances.

Enzo has a small basement apartment that he rents, but it has a private entrance. He leads me to his tiny kitchenette with a round circular table and rickety chairs, and the chair groans threateningly as I sit down. I feel self-conscious about how much nicer our house is than his living quarters, but then again, I don't think he's the kind of person who would care about stuff like that.

Enzo goes over to his fridge. He pulls out a beer and holds it up. "You want?"

I start to say no, but I change my mind. "Yes, please."

He returns to the table with two beer bottles. He uses a bottle opener on his keychain to pop them both open and then he slides one of them across the table to me. I rest my fingers on the bottle, feeling the cold condensation under my hand.

"Thank you," I say.

He shrugs. "Is not great beer."

"I don't mean for the beer."

He cracks his knuckles. As the muscles in his arms flex, it's hard not to be aware of how incredibly sexy this man is. If the women in my neighborhood knew I was in his apartment, they would all be incredibly jealous. They would assume he was ripping my clothes off as we speak and getting ready to ravish me—they would probably be angry that he picked me out of all the other women on the block who are more attractive than I am. *Enzo could do so much better.* They have no clue. It's so far off from the truth, it's almost funny. But not really.

"I had a feeling," he says. "Your husband—I could tell he is bad guy."

I take a long swig from the beer bottle. "I didn't even know you spoke English."

Enzo laughs. He's been working in my yard for two years now, and this is the first time I've heard him laugh. "It is easier to pretend I don't understand. Otherwise, the housewives do not ever leave me alone. You get me?"

Despite everything, I laugh too. He's right about that. "You're from Italy originally?"

"Sicily."

"So..." I swish my beer around in the bottle. "What brought you here?"

His shoulders sag. "It is not a good story."

"And mine is?"

He looks down at his own beer bottle. "My sister Antonia's husband—he was like yours. A bad guy. A rich, powerful bad guy, who made himself feel better by slapping her around. I tell her, leave... but she would not. Then one day, he pushed her down the stairs and she never woke up at the hospital." He grabs the sleeve of his T-shirt and pulls it up to reveal the tattoo I have seen of the heart with the name Antonia inscribed in it. "Now this is how I remember her."

"Oh." I clasp a hand over my mouth. "I'm so sorry."

His Adam's apple bobs. "There is no justice for men like him. No jail. No punishment for murdering my sister. So I decided to punish him. Myself."

I remember the dark look in his eyes when I told him what Andy did to me. *I will kill him.* "Did you...?"

"No." He cracks his knuckles again—the sound echoes through the tiny apartment. "I did not go that far. And I regret this. Because after that, my life was worth nothing. *Niente.* I had to take everything I had and use it to get out." He takes a drink from his beer bottle. "If I ever go back, I will be killed before I leave the airport."

I don't know what to say. "Was it hard for you to leave?"

"Will it be hard for you to leave here?"

I think about it for a moment and shake my head. I want to leave. I want to put as many miles as I can between me and Andrew Winchester. If that means going to Siberia, I'll do it.

"You will need passports for you and Cecelia." He ticks it off on his fingers. "A driver's license. Birth certificates. Enough cash to keep you going until you can find work. And two plane tickets."

My heart speeds up. "So I need money..."

"I have some saved up I can give you," he says.

"Enzo, I couldn't possibly—"

He waves off my protest. "It is not enough though. You will need more. Can you get it?"

I'll have to find a way.

* * *

A few days later, I drive Cecelia to school like I do almost every day. She's got her yellow hair in flawless twin braids behind her head and she's wearing one of her pale frilly dresses that make her stand out among her classmates. I'm scared other kids make fun of her because of those dresses, and she can't play in them like she wants to. But if she doesn't wear them, Andy punishes me for it.

Cece taps her fingers on the glass pane of the back window absently as I turn onto the street for the Windsor Academy. She never gives me a hard time about going to school, but I don't think she enjoys it. I wish she had more friends. I put her in so many activities to distract her and help her meet people, but it doesn't help.

But it doesn't matter anymore. Soon everything will change.

Very soon.

When I get to the school drop-off area, Cece lingers in the back of the car, her blond eyebrows knitted together. "You're picking me up, right? Not Dad?"

Andy is the only father she's ever known. And she doesn't know what he does to me, but she knows that sometimes when she does something he doesn't like, I disappear for days at a time. And when I do, he's the one who picks her up. It scares her. She won't say the words out loud, but she hates him.

"I'll pick you up," I say.

Her small face relaxes. I want to blurt out the words out loud: *Don't worry, honey. We will be out of here soon. And he won't be able to hurt us ever again.* But I can't yet. I can't take that chance. Not until the day I pick her up and we go straight to the airport.

After Cecelia gets out of the car, I turn around and drive home. I have one week left here. One week before I pack a bag, then make the ninety-minute drive to where my safe-deposit box is waiting with my new passport, my new driver's license, and a big wad of cash. I'll purchase the tickets at the airport using cash, because the last time I bought a ticket in advance, Andy was waiting for me at the gate. Enzo has helped me plan this in a way to minimize the chances of Andy figuring out what I'm doing. So far, he's still in the dark.

Or so I believe until I walk into my living room. To find Andy sitting at the dining table. Waiting for me.

"Andy," I gasp. "Um, hi."

"Hello, Nina."

That's when I see the three piles laid out in front of him. The passport, the driver's license, and the stack of cash.

Oh no.

"So what were you planning to do with this..." He looks down and reads off the name on the driver's license. "Tracy Eaton."

I feel like I'm choking. My legs tremble beneath me and I have to hold onto the wall to keep from collapsing. "How did you get that?"

Andy rises from his seat. "Haven't you figured out yet that you can't keep any secrets from me?"

I take a step back. "Andy..."

"Nina," he says. "It's time to go upstairs."

No. I'm not going. I'm not breaking my promise to my daughter that I would pick her up today. I'm not allowing myself to be locked up there for days when I thought I would be on my way to freedom soon. I won't. I can't do this anymore.

Before Andy can come any closer, I dash out the front door and back into my car. I speed out of the driveway so fast I nearly bash into the gate on the way out.

I have no idea where I'm going. Part of me wants to go straight to Cecelia's school and grab her. Then just start driving until I hit the Canadian border. But it's going to be hard to evade him without that passport or driver's license. I'm sure he's calling the police right now and feeding them a story about how his crazy wife is having a relapse.

There's only one positive in this situation. He only found one of the two safety deposit boxes. The two separate boxes were Enzo's idea. He found the one with the passport and the driver's license. But there's still a second stack of cash he doesn't know about.

I keep driving until I get to Enzo's neighborhood. I park two blocks away from his apartment and then I walk the rest of the way. He's just climbing into his truck when I sprint over to him. "Enzo!"

He jerks his head up at the sound of my voice. His face drops when he sees the look on mine. "What happened?"

"He found one of the safe deposit boxes." I pause to catch my breath. "It... it's over. I can't leave."

My face crumbles. Before I started talking to Enzo, I had accepted that this would be my life. At least until Cecelia turned eighteen. But now I don't think I can do it. I can't live like this. I *can't*.

"Nina..."

"What am I going to do?" I whimper.

He holds out his arms and I fall into them. We should be more careful. Somebody could see us. What if Andy thought I was having an affair with Enzo?

We are not having an affair, by the way. Not even a little bit. He thinks of me like Antonia—his sister he couldn't save. He hasn't touched me in a way that is anything other than brotherly. It's the absolute last thing either of us is thinking about. Right now, all I can think of is the future I thought I might have had being flushed down the toilet. Another decade living with that monster.

"What am I going to do?" I say again.

"Is simple," he says. "We go to plan B."

I lift my tear-streaked face. "What's plan B?"

"I kill the bastard."

I shiver because I can see in his dark eyes that he means it. "Enzo..."

"I will do it." He pulls away from me and his jaw is rigid. "He deserves to die. This is not right. I'll do for you what I should have done for Antonia."

"And we both go to jail?"

"You won't go to jail."

I smack him in the arm. "I'm not okay with you going to jail either."

"So then what do you suggest?"

And then the idea hits me. It's so beautifully simple. And even though I hate Andy, I know him very well. This will work.

FORTY-NINE

Step Eight: Find a Replacement

I can't pick just anyone.

First of all, she has to be beautiful. More beautiful than I am, which shouldn't be hard since I've deliberately let myself go the last few years. She has to be younger than me—young enough to give Andy the children he so badly wants. She has to look good in white. He loves that color.

And most of all, she has to be desperate.

Then I meet Wilhelmina Calloway. She's everything I wanted. The dowdy clothing she wears to her interview can't conceal how young and pretty she is. She's desperate to please me. And then when the simple background check I run reveals a criminal record, I know I've hit paydirt. This is a girl who will be desperate for a decent, high-paying job.

"I am not on board with this," Enzo tells me when I come out to my backyard to ask for the name of the private detective he knows. "This is not right."

When I told him my plan a few weeks ago, he was not

happy. *You would sacrifice somebody else?* But he didn't understand.

"Andy controls me because of Cece," I say. "This girl has no children. No attachments. Nothing he can hold over her. She can leave."

"You know it doesn't work that way," he grumbles.

"Will you help me or not?"

His shoulders sag. "Yes. You know I will help."

So I hire the private investigator Enzo recommended to me using some of the remaining money I had squirreled away. And the detective tells me everything I need to know about Wilhelmina Calloway. He tells me that she got fired from her last job—and they were close to calling the police on her. He tells me she's living in her car. And he tells me one other tidbit that changes everything. Right after I hang up with the detective, I call Millie and offer her the job.

The only problem is Andy.

He won't want a stranger living in our house. He has reluctantly allowed people to come in for a few hours to clean, but that's it. He never even allows anyone to babysit for Cecelia except for his mother. But the timing works out very well. Andy's father recently retired and after taking a bad fall on a patch of ice, they decided to move down to Florida. I could tell Evelyn was not enthusiastic about the idea and they decided to retain their old house for the summer, but most of their friends had relocated to southern Florida by now. And Andy's father was looking forward to spending his retirement playing golf every day with his buddies.

What it comes down to is that we need help.

The trickiest part is that Millie's new bedroom will be in the attic. He won't like that at all. But it has to be that way. He has to see her up there if I want him to think of her as my replacement. I have to entice him.

I set the stage before I spring her on him. I wake up every

morning complaining of migraines that make it impossible for me to cook or clean. I work hard to leave the house a complete mess. Another few days and our house would be ready to be condemned. We need help. Desperately.

Still, right after Andy discovers I've hired Millie, he corners me outside my car. His fingers bite into my biceps as he gives me a good hard yank. "What the hell do you think you're doing, Nina?"

"We need help." I lift my chin defiantly. "Your mother isn't around. We need someone to watch Cece and to help clean."

"You put her in the attic," he growls. "That's *your* room. You should put her in the guest room."

"And where will your parents stay when they come to visit us? The attic? The living room sofa?"

I see his jaw working as he considers this. Evelyn Winchester would *never* sleep on the living room sofa.

"Just let her stay for two months," I say. "Until the school year is over and I have more free time to clean, and your mother will come back up from Florida."

"Forget it."

"So fire her if you want." I blink at him. "I can't stop you."

"Believe me, I will."

Except he doesn't fire her. Because when he comes home that night, for the first time, the house is clean. And she serves him a dinner that isn't burned. And she is young and beautiful.

So Millie stays in the attic.

This will only work if three things happen:

1. Millie and Andy have a mutual attraction.
2. Millie hates me enough to sleep with my husband.
3. They have the opportunity.

The attraction part is easy. Millie is gorgeous—even more attractive than I was when I was younger—and although Andy is getting on in years compared with her, he is still devastatingly handsome. Sometimes Millie looks at me like she can't quite figure out what he sees in me. I do my best to pack on the pounds. Since Andy doesn't have the option of locking me in the attic, I dare to skip my hair appointment and let the darker roots start to show.

And most of all, I treat Millie like crap.

It doesn't come easily to me to treat her that way. Deep down, I'm a nice person. Or at least, I used to be before Andy wrecked me. Now everything is a means to an end. Millie might not deserve it, but I can't do this anymore. I have to get out.

She starts hating me on her first morning at our house. I've got a PTA meeting in the evening, and I march into the kitchen first thing in the morning. I have left a mess over the last couple of weeks, and Millie did an amazing job cleaning up. She worked really hard. Every surface is shining.

I feel terrible about this. I really do.

I rip the kitchen apart. I pull out every dish and every cup I can find. I throw pots and pans on the floor. Just as Millie arrives, I'm getting to the refrigerator. Growing up, I was responsible for my fair share of chores, and it's physically painful for me to take a milk carton and throw it on the ground, letting the milk spill out everywhere. But I force myself. Means to an end.

When Millie enters the kitchen, I turn around and look at her accusingly. "Where is it?"

"Where... where is *what*?"

"My notes!" I bring my hand to my forehead like the horror of it all might make me faint. "I left all my notes for the PTA meeting tonight on the kitchen counter! And now they're gone!" And then accusingly: "What did you do with them?"

I do have notes for the meeting. But they are safely tucked

away on my computer. Why would my only copies be here in a pile on the kitchen counter? It makes no sense, but I keep insisting it's true. She knows I didn't leave the notes there, but she doesn't know that I know that.

I yell loud enough to get Andy's attention. He feels sorry for her. His heart goes out to her because I'm accusing her of something he knows she didn't do. He's attracted to her because I'm turning her into the victim.

The same way I was the victim when I got yelled at for my breasts leaking milk all those years ago.

"I'm so sorry, Nina," Millie stammers. "If there's anything I can do..."

My eyes sweep down to the disaster I created on the kitchen floor. "You can clean up this disgusting mess you left in my kitchen while I fix this problem."

And at that moment, I have accomplished all three of my goals. First, the mutual attraction: her in skinny jeans and effortlessly beautiful. Second, Millie hates me. Third, when I storm out of the room, they have an opportunity to be alone together.

But it's not quite enough. I have one other ace up my sleeve.

Andy wants a baby.

It won't happen with me. Not with the IUD sitting snugly in my uterus. And Andy is going to discover I'm barren, because the private investigator Enzo found for me managed to get a few great photographs of the fertility specialist with a woman who isn't his wife of twenty-five years. All the good doctor has to do is tell Andy there's no chance I'll ever get pregnant, and those photographs go in the garbage.

The day before our appointment with Dr. Gelman, I give Evelyn a call down in Florida. As always, she seems less than thrilled to hear from me.

"Hello, Nina," she says drily. *What do you want from me?* is implied.

"I just want you to be the first to know," I say, "that my period is late. I think I'm pregnant!"

"Oh..." She pauses, torn between wanting to be excited for her first biological grandchild and hating the idea that I would be the mother of that grandchild. "How lovely."

Lovely. It's probably the opposite of what she's thinking.

"Hopefully you're taking prenatal multivitamins," she says. "And you need to follow a strict diet when you're pregnant. It's not good for the baby if you have lots of calorie-laden treats, like you usually do. Andy is lax about letting you get away with it, but for the good of the baby, you should try to control yourself."

"Yes, of course." I smile thinly, delighted that Evelyn will never be the grandmother of my child. "Also, I was wondering... It would be *so* great if you could send us some of Andy's old baby stuff. He was talking the other day about wanting to pass on his old baby blankets and stuff like that to the new baby. Do you think you could send it?"

"Yes, I'll call Roberto and ask him to send over the box."

"*Lovely*."

Andy is shaken by the revelation from Dr. Gelman. I watch his face in the doctor's office as the bombshell drops. *I'm afraid Nina will never be able to carry a pregnancy to term.* His eyes fill with tears. If he were anyone else, I might feel sorry for him.

Then that night, I pick a fight with him. And not just any fight. I remind him of the very reason why he will never father a child with me.

"It's all my fault!" I summon tears to my eyes by remembering the time when he locked me in the attic and turned the furnace up full blast, until I was clawing at my skin. "If you were with a younger woman, you could have a child. I'm the one who's the problem!"

A younger woman like Millie. I don't say it, but he must be thinking it. I see the way he looks at her.

"Nina." He reaches out to touch me, and there's still love in his eyes. *Still*. I hate him so much for loving me. Why couldn't he have chosen someone else? "Don't say that. It's not your fault."

"Yes, it is!" The rage builds up inside me like a volcano, and before I know what I'm doing, I've smashed my fist into the vanity mirror. The crash echoes through the room. It's only a second later that my hands sting with pain, and I notice the blood dripping from my knuckles.

"Oh Jesus." Andy's face turns pale. "Let me get you some tissues."

He grabs some tissues from the bathroom, but I resist him, and by the time he gets my hand wrapped, there's blood all over his hands as well. When he goes into the bathroom to wash it off, I hear the sound outside the door. Did Cecelia hear our fight? I hate the idea that my temper tantrum might've scared her.

I pull the door open, but it isn't my daughter standing there. It's Millie. And I can see all over her face that she heard every word of our argument. She notices the blood on my hands and her eyes become saucers.

She thinks I'm insane. It's become a familiar feeling.

Millie thinks I'm crazy. Andy thinks I'm too old. After that, it's just a matter of opportunity. Andy will want to get me tickets to *Showdown* after how much I've talked about it—he loves to do things to please me, alternating with the horrors he subjects me to. But it will be Millie who will see the show—not me. The show and then the hotel room overnight. It's almost too perfect. And it gives me a chance to get Cecelia out of the way to camp, so Andy can't use her against me.

When the GPS tracker on Millie's phone registers that she's

in Manhattan that night, I know I've won. I see the way they look at each other after that. It's over. He's in love with her now. He's her problem.

I'm free.

FIFTY

It will never happen again. He will never lead me up to the attic again. He will never warn everybody in the neighborhood that I'm crazy and they need to watch my behavior. He'll never have me locked up again.

Of course, even though he kicked me out, I won't feel entirely confident until we're divorced. I have to be careful about that one. He needs to file first. If he gets even a hint that this is my idea, it's all over.

I lie in the queen-size bed in my hotel room, planning my next move. I'm going to drive up to the camp to pick up Cecelia tomorrow. And then we'll go... somewhere. I don't know where, but I need a fresh start. Thank God, Andy never adopted her. He has no claim to her. I can take her wherever I want. I don't even need to worry about fake identities, but I'll definitely revert to my maiden name. I don't want any memories of that man.

There's a knock at the door to the hotel room. For one horrible moment, I think it must be Andy. I imagine him standing at the door to the hotel room. *Did you really think it would be that easy, Nina? Come on.*

Up you go to the attic.

"Who is it?" I ask warily.

"It is Enzo."

I feel a rush of relief. I crack open the door, and he's standing there in a T-shirt and soil-dusted jeans, his brow scrunched together. "Well?" he says.

"It's done. He threw me out."

His eyes light up. "Yes? Really?"

I swipe at my moist eyes with the back of my hand. "Really."

"That is... incredible..."

I take a breath. "I have to thank you. Without you, there's no way I could have..."

He nods slowly. "It was my pleasure to help you, Nina. My duty. I..."

We stand there for a moment, staring at each other. Then he leans forward, and a second later, he's kissing me.

I didn't expect this. I mean, yes, I thought Enzo was hot. I have *eyes*. But we were always so absorbed by the common purpose of getting me away from Andy. And the truth is, after so many years of being married to that monster, I thought I was dead inside. Andy and I still had sex, because it was required of me, but it was always very mechanical—I might as well have been washing the dishes or doing the laundry. I felt nothing. I didn't think it was possible to have those kinds of feelings for anyone anymore. I was entirely in survival mode.

But now—now that I've survived—it turns out I'm not dead inside after all. Far from it.

I'm the one who tugs Enzo by his T-shirt into the queen-size bed. But he's the one who unbuttons my blouse—except for the one button he rips clear off. And pretty much everything that happens after is a joint effort.

It's so nice. Better than nice. *Amazing*. Amazing to be with a man who I don't despise with every fiber of my being. A man who is good and kind. A man who helped save my life. Even if it's just for one night.

And God, he's a good kisser.

When it's over, both of us are sweaty and hot and happy. Enzo puts his arm around me and I cuddle up beside him. "Is good?" he says.

"*Really* good." I bury my cheek in his bare chest. "I didn't think you felt that way about me."

"I always did," he says. "From when I first saw you. But I try to be, you know, *good guy*."

"I figured you thought of me like a sister."

"Sister!" He looks aghast. "No. Not sister. Definitely not sister."

I have to laugh at the expression on his face. But just as fast, my laughter dies. "I'm leaving town tomorrow. You know that, right?"

He's quiet for a long moment. Is he thinking about asking me to stay? I care about him a lot, but I can't stay for him. I can't stay here for anybody. He should know that better than anyone.

Maybe he's going to offer to go with me. I'm not sure how I would feel about that if he offered. I like him a lot. But I need to be alone for a while after this. It's going to be a long time before I can really trust a man ever again, although I suspect if there's anyone I can trust, it's Enzo. He has proven himself to me.

But he doesn't ask me to stay. He doesn't offer to come with me. He says something entirely different:

"We can't leave her, Nina."

"Excuse me?" I say.

"Millie." He looks down at me with his dark eyes. "We can't leave her with him. It is not right. I won't allow it."

"You won't *allow* it?" I repeat incredulously as I pull away from him. My post-sex euphoria has evaporated. "What is that supposed to mean?"

"I mean..." His jaw tightens. "Millie does not deserve him any more than you did."

"She's a criminal!"

"Listen to yourself. She's a human being."

I sit up in bed, clutching the blankets to my bare chest. Enzo is breathing hard and a vein is standing out in his neck, and I suppose I don't blame him for being upset. But he doesn't know anything.

"We have to tell her," he insists.

"No, we don't."

"I will tell her." A muscle twitches in his jaw. "If you don't do it, I will tell her. I will warn her."

My eyes fill with tears. "You wouldn't dare..."

"Nina." He shakes his head. "I'm sorry. I... I do not want to hurt you, but this is not right. We can't do this to her."

"You don't understand," I say.

"I understand."

"No," I say, "you don't."

PART III

FIFTY-ONE

MILLIE

"Andrew?" I call out. "Andrew!"

Silence.

I grasp the cold metal of the doorknob once again and twist it with all my strength, hoping it was just a case of the metal sticking. No luck. The door is locked. But how?

The only thing I can think of is that maybe when Andrew left the room to sleep in his own bed (I can't entirely blame him, given how uncomfortable the cot is for one person, much less two), he locked the door automatically, thinking it was still a closet. If he was half asleep, it's a reasonable mistake to make, I suppose.

That means I'll have to call him and wake him up to let me out of the room. I'm not excited to wake him up, but it's his damn fault I'm locked in here. I'm not staying trapped in here all night, especially since I have to pee.

I flick on the light, and that's when I see three textbooks that are in the middle of my room, right on the floor. It's the strangest thing. I bend down beside them, reading off the hardcover titles. *A Guide to U.S. Prisons. The History of Torture.* And a copy of the phone book.

These books weren't here when I went to bed last night. Did Andrew bring them up here and stuff them in the room, thinking I would be moving out of here by the morning and he could convert this room back into a closet again? That's the only thing that makes sense.

I kick the heavy books out of the way and search the top of the dresser where I plugged in my phone to charge last night. Or at least, I thought I had. It's not there anymore.

What the hell?

I grab the blue jeans that I abandoned on the floor and start searching through the pockets. No trace of my phone. Where did it go? I rip apart my dresser drawers, looking for that little rectangle that has become my lifeline. I even strip the sheets and blankets off the bed, wondering if it got lost during our recreational activities last night. Then I get down on my hands and knees and look *under* the bed.

Nothing.

I must've left it downstairs, although I feel like I have a memory of using it up here last night. I guess not. What terrible timing to forget my phone downstairs—when I'm locked up here in this stupid attic and I've got to use the bathroom.

I settle back into the bed, trying not to think about my full bladder. I don't know how I'm ever going to fall asleep though. When Andrew comes to find me here in the morning, I'm going to give him hell for accidentally locking me in here.

"Millie? Are you awake?"

My eyes fly open. I don't know how I managed to fall asleep, but somehow I did. But it's still early in the morning. The tiny room is dim, with only a few streaks of sunlight peeking in through my small window.

"Andrew." I sit up in bed, the tug in my bladder now more

than urgent. I scurry off the bed and stumble closer to the door. "You locked me in here last night!"

There's a long silence on the other side of the door. I expect an apology, a jingle of keys while he tries to locate the one that will let me out. But I don't hear any of that. He's completely silent.

"Andrew," I say. "You have the key, right?"

"Oh, I have the key," he confirms.

And that's when I get a sick feeling. Last night, I kept telling myself this was an accident. It had to be an accident. But suddenly, I'm not so sure. After all, how do you accidentally lock your girlfriend in a room and not even realize it until hours later? "Andrew, can you please open the door?"

"Millie." His voice sounds strange. Unfamiliar. "Do you remember yesterday you were reading some of my books from the bookcase?"

"Yes..."

"Well, you took out a few books, and then you just left them on the coffee table. Those were my books, and you didn't treat them very well, did you?"

I don't know what he's talking about. Yes, I did take a few books out of the bookcase. Three, at the most. And maybe I got distracted and never put them back. But is it really that big a deal? Why does he sound so upset?

"I... I'm sorry," I say.

"Hmm." His voice still sounds strange. "You say you're sorry, but this is my house. You can't just do anything you want without any consequences. I thought you would know better, since you're a *maid* and all."

I flinch at the disparaging way he says my job description, but I'll say anything to get him to calm down. "I'm sorry. I didn't mean to make a mess. I'll go clean it up."

"I already cleaned it up. You're too late."

"Listen, can you open the door so we can talk about this?"

"I'll open the door," he says. "But you need to do something for me first."

"What?"

"Do you see the three books I left you on the floor of the room?"

The textbooks he left in the middle of my room, the ones I almost tripped over last night, are still right where he left them. "Yes..."

"I want you to lie on the floor of your room and balance them on your stomach."

"*Excuse* me?"

"You heard me," he says. "I want you to balance those books on your stomach. For three straight hours."

I stare at the door, imagining the twisted expression on Andrew's face. "You're joking, right?"

"Not even a tiny bit."

I have no idea why he's doing this. This isn't the Andrew I fell in love with. It's like he's playing some sort of bizarre game with me. I don't know if he realizes quite how much he's upsetting me. "Listen, Andrew, whatever you want to do, whatever game you want to play, just let me out of this room and let me go to the bathroom at least."

"Can I make this any clearer?" He clucks his tongue. "You carelessly left my books in the living room, and I had to put them back for you. So now I want you to take these books and bear their weight."

"I'm not going to do that."

"Well, that's unfortunate. Because you're not getting out of this room until you do what I tell you to do."

"Fine. I'm probably going to pee my pants then."

"There's a bucket in the closet if you need to relieve yourself."

When I first moved in here, I noticed that blue bucket in the corner of the closet. I just left it there, never giving it a second thought. I look over at the closet and it's still sitting there. My bladder spasms and I cross my legs.

"Andrew, I mean it. I really have to go to the bathroom."

"I just told you what you can do."

He isn't giving in. I don't understand what's going on here. *Nina* was always the crazy one. Andrew was the one who was *reasonable*, who saved me when Nina was accusing me of stealing her clothes.

Are they both crazy? Are they both in on this?

"Fine." Let's just get this over with. I sit down on the ground and pick up one of the books so he can hear it. "All right, I've got the books on top of me. Can you let me out now?"

"You don't have the books on top of you."

"Yes, I do. "

"Don't lie."

I let out a huff of exasperation. "How do you know whether I'm lying or not?"

"Because I can see you."

My spine turns to liquid. He can *see* me? My gaze darts from wall to wall, searching for a camera. How long has he been watching me? Has he been spying on me the entire time I've been here?

"You're not going to find it," he says. "It's well hidden. And don't worry, I haven't been watching you all along. Only since a few weeks ago."

I scramble to my feet. "What the hell is your problem? You need to let me out *right now*."

"Here's the thing," Andrew says calmly. "I don't think you're in any position to be making demands."

I lunge at the door. I pound my fists against the wood, hard enough to make my hands red and sore. "I swear to God, you better let me out of here! This isn't funny!"

"Hey. *Hey*." Andrew's calm voice interrupts my pounding. "Settle down. Look, I'm going to let you out. I promise."

I let my arms drop to my sides. My fists are throbbing. "*Thank* you."

"Just not *yet*."

Heat rises in my cheeks. "Andrew..."

"I told you what you need to do to get out," he says. "This is an extremely fair punishment for what you did."

I press my lips together, too angry to even respond.

"Why don't I give you a little while to think about it, Millie? I'll come back later."

I swear to God, I still believe he's got to be joking until his footsteps disappear down the hallway.

FIFTY-TWO

MILLIE

It's been an hour since Andrew was here.

I used the bucket. I don't want to talk about it. But it got to a point where if I didn't use the bucket, I was going to have pee running down my legs. It was an interesting experience, to say the least.

After I got that need taken care of, my stomach started rumbling. I checked the mini-fridge, where I usually keep a couple of snacks like yogurt. But somehow, it had been emptied in the last few days. The only thing left in there was three of those mini bottles of water. I chugged the contents of two of the bottles, although immediately after, I regretted it. What if he leaves me here for several more hours? Or *days*? I might need that water.

I throw on my jeans and a fresh T-shirt, then I examine the pile of books on the floor. Andrew said he wanted me to keep those books resting on my belly for three hours and then he would let me out of the room. I don't quite understand the purpose of this ridiculous game, but maybe I should just do it. Then he'll let me out and I can get the hell out of here forever.

I stretch out on the uncarpeted floor. It's the beginning of summer, which means the attic is unbearably stuffy, but the floor is still cool. I rest my head against the ground and pick up the book on prisons. It's a thick textbook that has got to weigh several pounds. I lower it onto my belly.

It's pressure, but not exactly uncomfortable. If I had done this before my trip to the bucket, I would probably have peed my pants by now. But this isn't so bad. Then I pick up the second book.

This is the one on torture. I suppose the title of this textbook isn't entirely a coincidence. Or maybe it is. Who knows?

I lower the second book onto my belly. This time the pressure becomes more uncomfortable. The books are heavy. And the protuberance of my scapula and my tailbone bite into the hard, uncarpeted floor. This isn't enjoyable, but it's tolerable.

But he wanted all three books.

I pick up the final book—the phonebook. This one is not only heavy, but bulky. It's hard to even lift it with two other books already on top of me. It takes a couple of tries, but I manage to get the phonebook balanced on my abdomen.

The weight of all three books almost takes my breath away. Two was doable, but three is awful. This is very, *very* uncomfortable. It's hard to take a deep breath. And the edge of the bottom book bites into my rib cage.

No, I can't do it. I *can't*.

I shove all three books off me. My shoulders heave as I suck in air. He can't expect me to keep all three books balanced on me for hours. Can he?

I get back on my feet and immediately start pacing the room. I don't know what game Andrew is playing here, but I'm not going to do this. He's going to let me out of here. Or else I'm going to find a way out myself. There must be a way out of this room. This isn't *prison*.

Maybe there's a way I can unscrew the door hinges. Or the screws on the doorknob. Andrew has a tool kit downstairs stashed in the garage, and I would give anything to get my hands on that right now. But I've got lots of stuff in my dresser drawers. Maybe there's something I can use as a makeshift screwdriver.

"Millie?"

It's Andrew's voice again. I abandon my search for tools and rush over to the door. "I put the books on top of me. Please let me out."

"I told you three hours. You only did it for about a minute."

I have had enough of this shit. "Let. Me. Out. Now."

"Or else what?" He laughs. "I told you what you need to do."

"I'm not doing it."

"Fine. Then you can stay locked in there."

I shake my head. "So you'll let me die in here?"

"You're not going to die. When the water runs out, you'll realize what you have to do."

This time I can barely hear his footsteps retreating over the sound of my own screams.

I have had the three books on my abdomen for two hours and fifty minutes.

Andrew was right. After the third water bottle had been drained, my desperation to leave the room heightened considerably. When fantasies of waterfalls started dancing before my eyes, I knew I had to complete the task he wanted. Of course, there's no guarantee he'll let me out if I do it, but I hope he will.

The books are really, really uncomfortable. I'm not going to lie. There are moments when I feel like I can't stand it another second, that the weight is going to literally crush my pelvis, but then I take a breath—best I can with these stupid books on top of me—and I hang in there. It's almost over.

And when I get out of here...

At the three-hour mark, I shove the books off of my belly. It's a massive relief, but when I try to sit up, my abdomen aches badly enough to bring tears to my eyes. There are going to be bruises left behind. Still, I push forward and pound on the door. "I did it!" I yell. "I'm done! Let me out of here!"

But of course, he doesn't come. He might be able to see me, but I have no idea where he is. Is he in the house? At work? He could be anywhere. He knows where I am, but I don't have the same privilege.

That bastard.

It's an hour later when I hear footsteps outside my door. I want to cry with relief. I've never been claustrophobic before, but this experience has changed me. I'm not sure if I'll be able to ride in elevators after this.

"Millie?"

"I did it, you asshole," I spit at the door. "Now let me out."

"Hmm." His lackadaisical tone makes me want to wrap my fingers around his neck and squeeze. "I'm afraid I can't do that."

"But you promised! You said if I kept the books on my belly for three hours, you would let me out."

"Right. But here's the thing. You pushed them off a minute too early. So I'm afraid you'll have to start over."

My eyes fly open. If there were a moment when I would morph into the Incredible Hulk and rip the door right off by the hinges, that would be this moment. "You've got to be kidding me."

"I'm so sorry. But these are the rules."

"But..." I sputter. "I don't have any water left."

"That's a shame," he sighs. "Next time, you'll have to learn to conserve your water."

"Next time?" I kick the door. "Are you out of your mind? There's not going to be a next time."

"Actually, I think there will be," he says thoughtfully. "You're on parole, right? If you were to take something from our house—and I'm sure Nina would back me up on that—where do you think you would end up? One offense and you're right back in jail! Whereas you only have to stay in this room for a day or two every once in a while if you misbehave. I think this is a much better deal, don't you?"

Okay, *this* would be the moment I would turn into the Incredible Hulk.

"So," he says, "I would get back to work. Because soon you're going to get pretty thirsty."

This time I wait three hours and ten minutes. Because I don't want there to be any chance that Andrew will claim that I need to do it a third time. That will kill me.

My belly feels like somebody has been punching me in the abdomen for the last several hours. It hurts so much, at first I can't even sit up. I have to roll onto my side and push myself into a sitting position using my arms. And my head aches from lack of water. I have to crawl over to the cot and pull myself onto it. I sit there and wait for Andrew to come.

It's another half an hour before his voice reappears behind the door. "Millie?"

"I did it," I say, although my own voice is barely a whisper. I can't even stand up.

"I saw you." There's a patronizing edge to his voice. "Excellent job."

And then I hear the most beautiful sound I've ever heard. It's the sound of the door unlocking. It's even better than when I got out of prison.

Andrew comes into the bedroom, clutching a glass of water. He hands it over to me, and for a moment, it hits me that he could've slipped some sort of drugs into the water, but I don't even care. I gulp it down. All of it.

He sits down beside me on the cot. He rests a hand on the small of my back and I cringe. "How are you doing?"

"My belly hurts."

He tilts his head. "I'm sorry."

"Are you?"

"You do have to be taught a lesson when you do something wrong—it's the only way you'll learn." His lips twitch. "If you had done it right the first time, I wouldn't have had to ask you to do it again."

I look up and study his handsome features. How could I have fallen in love with this man? He seemed nice and normal and wonderful. I hadn't even the slightest clue what a monster he is. His goal isn't to marry me—it's to make me his prisoner.

"How could you tell exactly how long I was doing it?" I say. "You can't possibly be able to see that well."

"On the contrary." He pulls his phone out of his pocket and brings up an app. A crisp color image of my room fills the screen. I can see the two of us sitting together on the bed in incredible resolution. The image of myself shows me looking pale and hunched over, with stringy hair. "Isn't that a great image? Like a movie."

That bastard. He watched me suffer in here for the entire day. And he has every intention of doing this to me again. Except next time it will be longer. And God knows what he'll make me do next time. I've already been a prisoner once—I won't let it happen again. No way.

So I reach into the pocket of my jeans.

And I pull out the bottle of pepper spray I found in the bucket.

FIFTY-THREE

NINA

When I hired that private investigator to dig into Wilhelmina Calloway's past, I found some very interesting information.

I had assumed Millie went to jail for some sort of drug crime or maybe theft. But no. Millie Calloway went to jail for something entirely different. She was in prison for murder.

She was only sixteen years old at the time of her arrest and was in prison by seventeen, so it took some effort for the detective to get all the information. Millie was in boarding school. No, not just a boarding school. A school specifically for teenagers with disciplinary problems.

One night, Millie and one of her girlfriends snuck out to a party at the boys' dormitory. Millie was passing by a bedroom and heard her friend screaming for help behind the door. She entered the dark room and found one of their classmates—a two-hundred-pound football player—forcing himself on her friend.

So Millie picked up a paperweight from on top of a desk and bashed the boy in the head with it. Multiple times. The boy was dead before he even got to the hospital.

The detective had photographs. Millie's attorney argued

that she had been trying to defend her friend, who was being assaulted. But if you look at those photographs, it would be hard to argue she hadn't meant to kill him. His skull was visibly crushed.

She eventually pleaded guilty to lesser manslaughter charges, given her age and the circumstances. The family of the boy was in agreement—they wanted vengeance for their son's death, but they also didn't want him branded a rapist all over the internet.

Millie took the deal because there were other incidents. Things that would have come to light if she had gone to trial.

In grade school, she was expelled when she got into a fight with a little boy in her class who was calling her names—she shoved him off the monkey bars and broke his arm.

In middle school, she slashed the tires of her math teacher's car when he gave her a failing grade. Soon after that, she was sent to boarding school.

And then even after her prison sentence, the incidents continued. Millie wasn't laid off from her waitressing job. She was fired after she smashed her fist into the nose of one of her coworkers.

Millie seems like a sweet girl. That's what Andrew sees when he looks at her. He won't dig into her past the way I did. He doesn't know what she's capable of.

And here's the truth:

I initially wanted to hire a maid in hopes that she would become my replacement—that if Andrew fell in love with another woman, he would finally let me go. But that's not why I hired Millie. That's not why I gave her a copy of the key to the room. And that's not why I left a bottle of pepper spray in the blue bucket in the closet.

I hired her to kill him.

She just doesn't know it.

FIFTY-FOUR

MILLIE

Andrew screams when the pepper spray gets him in the eyes.

The nozzle is about three inches away from his eyes, so he gets a good dose of it. And then I press it a second time for good measure. While I do it, I turn my own head away and close my eyes. The last thing I need is to get pepper spray in my eyes, although it's hard not to get a little bit of residue.

When I look up again, he's clawing at his face, which has turned bright red. His phone has fallen from his hands onto the floor, and I scoop it up, being very careful not to touch anything else. Everything has to go exactly right in the next twenty seconds. I have spent over six hours planning this while three books were resting on my belly.

My legs are wobbly when I stand up, but they work. Andrew is still writhing on the cot, and before he can get his sight back, I slip out of the room and close the door behind me. Then I take the key Nina gave me and fit it into the lock. I turn the key and pocket it. Then I take a step back.

"Millie!" Andrew screams on the other side of the door. "What the hell?"

I look down at the screen of his phone. My fingers are shaking, but I'm able to get into settings, and I shut off the Lock Screen setting before the phone locks automatically, so the phone won't require a password anymore.

"Millie!"

I take another step back, as if he could reach through the door and grab me. But he can't. I'm safe on the other side of the door.

"Millie." His voice is a low growl now. "Let me out of here *right now*."

My heart is beating fast in my chest. It's the same way I felt when I walked into that bedroom all those years ago and found Kelsey screaming at that asshole football player, *Get off of me!* And Duncan was laughing drunkenly. I stood there for a second, my body paralyzed as my chest filled with rage. He was so much bigger than either one of us—it wasn't like I could pull him off of her. The room was dark and I felt around on the desk until my hands made contact with a paperweight and...

I will never forget that day. How good it felt to smash the paperweight against that bastard's skull until he became still. It was almost worth all those years in prison. After all, who knows how many other girls I saved from him?

"I'll let you out," I say. "Just not *yet*."

"You've got to be kidding me." The outrage in his voice is palpable. "This is *my* house. You can't keep me hostage here. And you're a criminal. All I have to do is call the police and you're right back in jail."

"Right," I say. "But how can you call the police when I have your phone?"

I look down at the screen of his phone. I can see him standing there, in vivid color. I can even see how red his face is from the pepper spray and the tears on his cheeks. He checks his pockets, then scans the floor with his swollen eyes.

"Millie," he says in a slow, controlled voice. "I want my phone back."

I let out a hoarse laugh. "I'm sure you do."

"Millie, give me my phone back right now."

"Hmm. I don't think you're in any position to be making *demands*."

"*Millie*."

"Just a moment." I slip his phone into my pocket. "I'm going to grab a bite to eat. I'll be back *real* soon."

"Millie!"

He's still calling my name as I walk down the hall and go downstairs. I ignore him. There's nothing he can do when he's stuck in that room. And I have to figure out my next move.

The first thing I do is exactly what I said I was going to do—I go to the kitchen, where I drink two heaping glasses of water. Then I make myself a bologna sandwich. No, not *abalone*. Bologna. With lots of mayonnaise, and white bread. After I've got some food in my belly, I feel a lot better. I can finally think straight.

I pick up Andrew's phone. He is still in the attic room, pacing back and forth. Like a caged animal. If I were to let him out, I can't even imagine what he would do to me. The thought of it makes a cold sweat break out at the back of my neck. While I'm watching him, a text message pops up on his phone from "Mom."

Are you going to serve Nina with divorce papers?

I scroll through some of the previous messages. Andrew has told his mother all about his falling-out with Nina. I've got to answer her, because if he doesn't, she might come over here—and then I'm screwed. Nobody can suspect something has happened to Andrew.

Yes. Just speaking with my lawyer right now.

The reply from Andrew's mother comes back almost instantly:

Good. I never liked her. And I always did the best I could with Cecelia, but Nina was extremely lax on discipline and the little girl became quite a brat.

I get a jab of sympathy in my chest for Nina and Cecelia. It's bad enough that Andrew's mother never liked Nina. But to speak that way of her own grandchild? And I wonder what Andrew's mother had in mind for "discipline." If it's anything like Andy's idea of punishment, I'm glad Nina never went through with it.

My hands are trembling as I type my reply:

Looks like you were right about Nina.

Now I have to deal with that asshole.

I shove his phone back in my pocket, then I climb the stairs to the second floor, then all the way up to the attic. When I get to the top floor, the footsteps in the attic room go silent. He must've heard me.

"Millie," he says.

"I'm here," I say stiffly.

He clears his throat. "You made your point about the room. I'm sorry about what I did."

"Are you?"

"Yes. I realize now I was wrong."

"I see. So you're sorry?"

He clears his throat. "Yes."

"Say it."

He is silent for a bit. "Say what?"

"Say you're sorry that you did a terrible thing to me."

I watch his expression on the screen. He doesn't want to tell me he's sorry because he's not. All he's sorry for is that he gave me the chance to get the better of him.

"I'm so sorry," he finally says. "I was absolutely wrong. I did an awful thing to you, and I will never do it again." He pauses. "Will you let me out now?"

"Yes. I will."

"Thank you."

"Just not *yet*."

He inhales sharply. "Millie..."

"I'm going to let you out." My calm voice belies the pounding in my chest. "But before I do, you have to be punished for what you did to me."

"Don't play this game," he growls. "You don't have the stomach for it."

He wouldn't talk to me that way if he knew I beat a man to death with a paperweight. He has no idea. But I'm betting that Nina knows. "I want you to lie down on the floor and put those three books on top of you."

"Come on. This is ridiculous."

"I'm not letting you out of this room until you do it."

Andrew lifts his eyes to look into the camera. I always thought he had nice eyes, but there's venom in them as he stares at me. *Not at me,* I remind myself. He's looking at the camera. "Fine. I'll humor you."

He lies down on the floor. One by one, he picks up each book and stacks them on his abdomen, the same way I did only hours earlier. But he's bigger and stronger than I am, and he only looks mildly uncomfortable with those books on top of him, even when all three are stacked on him.

"Happy?" he calls out.

"Lower," I say.

"What?"

"*Move the books lower*."

"I don't know what you—"

I press my forehead against the door as I speak: "You know *exactly* what I mean."

Even through the door, I can hear the sharp inhale of his breath. "Millie, I can't—"

"If you want to get out of that room, you're going to do it."

I stare down at the screen of his phone, watching him. He pushes the books down his chest so they are squarely on top of his genitals. He didn't look very uncomfortable before, but that has changed now. His face is frozen in a grimace.

"Jesus Christ," he gasps.

"Good," I say. "Now stay that way for three hours."

FIFTY-FIVE

MILLIE

As I sit on the couch, watching television and waiting for the three hours to be up, I think about Nina.

All along, I believed she was the crazy one. Now I don't know what to think. She must have left me the pepper spray in that room. She suspected what he was going to do to me. Which makes me think he's done it to her. Maybe many times before.

Was Nina ever really jealous? Or was it all just an act? I'm still not entirely sure. Part of me wants to call her and find out, but I suspect that wouldn't be a good idea. After all, Kelsey never spoke to me again after I killed Duncan. I don't understand why, because I killed him *for her*. He was forcing himself on her. But the next time I saw my former best friend, she looked at me with disgust.

Nobody ever understood. After I got in trouble for slashing Mr. Cavanaugh's tires, I tried to explain to my mother how he had told me I was going to fail math class unless I let him feel me up. She didn't believe me. Nobody believed me. She shipped me off to boarding school because I kept getting in trouble. That didn't work out so well. After the incident at the boarding school, they wiped their hands of me for good.

And then when I finally got a decent job after getting out of prison, I had to deal with that bartender Kyle, who kept grabbing my ass every chance he got. So one day, I spun around and slammed my fist into his nose. He only didn't press charges because he was so embarrassed that he got beat up by a girl. But they told me not to come back. And soon after that, I was living in my car.

The only person I can trust is myself.

I yawn and shut off the television. It's been just over three hours and Andrew hasn't budged from the floor. He's followed all the rules, even though he must be in agony. I take my time walking up the steps to the top floor. Just as I get there, he shoves the books off his genitals. For a moment, he just lies there, doubled over.

"Andrew?" I say.

"*What?*"

"How are you feeling?"

"How do you *think* I'm feeling?" he hisses. "Let me out of here, you bitch."

He doesn't seem nearly as calm and smug as he was last time I was here. Good. I lean against the door, watching his face on my screen. "I really don't appreciate swearing. I would've thought since you're counting on me to help you, you could be a little nicer."

"Let. Me. Out." He sits up on the floor, cradling his head in his hands. "I swear to God, Millie. If you don't let me out right now, I'm going to kill you."

He says it so casually. *I'm going to kill you.* I stare at the screen of my phone, wondering how many other women have been in this room. I wonder if any of them have died in this room.

It seems entirely possible.

"Relax," I say. "I'm going to let you out."

"Good."

"Just not *yet*."

"Millie..." he growls. "I did exactly what you said. Three hours."

"Three hours?" I raise my eyebrows even though he can't see them. "I'm sorry if you heard three hours. I actually said *five* hours. So I'm afraid you're going to have to start over."

"Five..." I love that the full-color display allows me to see the way his face blanches. "I can't do that. I can't do five more hours. Come on. You've got to let me out of here. This game is over."

"This isn't a *negotiation*, Andrew," I say patiently. "If you want to get out of this room, you're going to keep those books on your junk for the next five hours. The choice is yours."

"Millie. *Millie*." His breathing is jagged. "Look, there is always room to negotiate. What do you want? I'll give you money. I'll give you a million dollars right now if you let me out of this room. How about that?"

"No."

"Two million."

It's easy for him to offer me money he has no intention of ever giving me. "I'm afraid not. I'm going to go to bed now, but maybe in the morning I'll see you again."

"Millie, be reasonable!" His voice breaks. "At least I left you with some water. Can't I have some water?"

"I'm afraid not," I say. "Maybe next time, you should leave the girl you lock in the room with more water, so some will be left for you."

With those words, I walk down the hallway as he screams my name. As soon as I get down to the bedroom, I google: *How long can a person live without water?*

FIFTY-SIX

NINA

When I greet Cecelia at her camp, it's the happiest I've seen her look in a while. She's with some new friends she's made, her round face shining. She's got a sunburn on her shoulders and cheeks, and there's a scrape on her elbow with a Band-Aid half hanging off. Instead of one of those horrible frilly dresses Andy always insists on, she's wearing a comfy pair of shorts and a T-shirt. I'll be happy if she never wears a dress again.

"Hi, Mom!" She bounces over to me, her ponytail swinging behind her. Suzanne said that when her youngest started calling her "Mom" instead of "Mommy," it was a dagger in her heart. But I was happy Cece was growing up, because it meant that soon she'd be old enough that *he* wouldn't have any power over her. Over *us*. "You're early!"

"Yes..."

The top of her head comes up to my shoulder now. Did she grow during the time she was here? She wraps her skinny arms around me, resting her head against my shoulder. "Where are we going now?"

I smile. When Cece was packing her things for camp, I told her to pack a bunch of extra clothes because I wasn't sure if we would be coming straight home. That maybe we would be going somewhere else after this. So I've still got some of her bags in the trunk of my car.

I wasn't sure if it would happen. I didn't know that it would all go according to plan. Every time I think about it, my eyes fill with tears. We're free.

"Where would you like to go?" I ask.

She tilts up her head. "Disneyland!"

We could go to California. I would love to put three thousand miles between me and Andrew Winchester. Just in case he somehow gets it in his head that we should be together again.

Just in case Millie doesn't do what I'm hoping she's going to do.

"Let's do it!" I say.

Cece's face lights up, and she starts jumping up and down. She still has that childlike happiness. The ability to live in the moment. He hasn't completely stolen it from her. Not yet, anyway.

Then she stops jumping as her face gets serious. "What about Dad?"

"He's not coming."

The relief on her face mirrors my own. He never laid a finger on her as far as I know, and I watched carefully. If I had seen even the tiniest suspicious bruise on my child, I would have told Enzo to go ahead and kill him. But I never saw anything. Still, she knew some of her own transgressions resulted in me being punished. She's a smart girl.

Of course, the fact that she always had to be so perfect around her father meant that she rebounded when he wasn't around. She doesn't really trust any adults except me, and she can sometimes be difficult. She's been called a brat before. But it's not her fault. My daughter has a good heart.

Cece runs into her cabin to grab her bags. I start to follow her, but then my phone buzzes in my purse. I rifle through the messy contents of my bag until I find my phone. It's Enzo.

I debate if I should answer. Enzo helped save my life, and I can't argue he didn't give me an unforgettable night. But I'm ready to leave that part of my life behind. I don't know what he's calling about, and I'm not sure I want to know.

Then again, I owe him at least to pick up the phone.

"Hello?" I lower my voice a few notches. "What's going on?"

Enzo's tone is low and serious. "We need to talk, Nina."

In my lifetime, those four words have never led to anything good.

"What is it?" I say.

"You need to come back here. You need to help Millie."

I snort. "Out of the question."

"Out of the question?" I've heard Enzo angry before, but never directed at me. This is a first. "Nina, she is in trouble. You put her in that situation."

"Right, because she slept with my husband. Am I supposed to feel *sorry* for her?"

"You pushed her into it!"

"She didn't have to take the bait. Nobody twisted her arm. Anyway, she'll be fine. Andy never did anything to me for months. Not until after we got married." I sniff. "I'll write her a letter after the divorce, okay? I'll warn her about him. Before she marries him."

He's quiet for a few beats on the other line. "Millie hasn't left the house in three days."

My eyes dart up to Cecelia's cabin. She's still inside packing and probably gabbing with her new friends. I look around at the other parents arriving for pick-up. I scurry off to the side, lowering my voice further. "What do you mean?"

"I was worried about her. So I put a red mark on the tire of her car. It's been three days and the mark is still in the exact same spot. She hasn't gone anywhere in three days."

I let out a huff. "Look, Enzo. That could mean anything. Maybe the two of them went on a trip together."

"No. I've seen his car move."

I roll my eyes. "So maybe they're carpooling. Maybe she just doesn't feel like driving anywhere."

"The light is on in the attic."

"The..." I clear my throat, taking another step away from the other parents. "How do you know that?"

"I went in the backyard."

"After Andy fired you?"

"I had to check, okay? There is somebody up there."

I squeeze the phone so tightly my fingers start to tingle. "So what? The attic was her bedroom. Is it really such a big deal that she's up there?"

"I don't know. You tell me."

A dizzy sensation comes over me. When I planned this whole thing out, back when I wanted Millie to be my replacement and then later when I wanted her to kill that bastard, I never really thought it out. I left her the pepper spray and I gave her the key to the room, and I thought she would be fine. But now I realize I may have made a huge mistake. I think of her trapped in the room in the attic, having to endure whatever torture Andy has come up with. The thought of it makes me sick.

"What about you?" I say. "Can't you go in and check on her?"

"I rang the bell. No answer."

"What about the key under the flowerpot?"

"It wasn't there."

"What about—"

"Nina," Enzo growls, "are you saying you want me to break into that house? Do you know what would happen to me if I got caught? *You* have a key. You have every right to go in there. I'll go with you, but I can't go alone."

"But—"

"This is all just excuses!" he bursts out. "I can't believe you would let her suffer the way you suffered."

I take one last look up at Cecelia's cabin. She's just coming out now, lugging her bags behind her.

"Fine," I say. "I'll come back. But only on one condition."

FIFTY-SEVEN

MILLIE

When I wake up in the guest bedroom the next morning, the first thing I do is reach for Andrew's phone.

I bring up the app for the camera in the attic. Right away, the room jumps into focus. I stare at the screen and my blood turns cold. The room is deathly still. Andrew isn't in there anymore.

He's gotten out of the room.

I clutch the blankets in my left hand. My eyes dart around the bedroom, searching for him, maybe lurking in the shadows. There's a sudden movement at the window, and I almost have a heart attack before I realize it's a bird.

Where is he? And how did he get out? Is there some sort of failsafe button that I didn't know about? A way for him to escape if he ever found himself in this situation? But it's hard to imagine. He kept those books on his groin for hours on end. Why would he have done that if he had been able to get out all along?

Either way, if he's gotten out of the room, he's got to be pissed.

I've got to get out of this house. *Now.*

My eyes drop down to the phone. And then something moves on the screen. I let out a slow breath. Andrew is in the room after all. He's under the covers on the cot. I just didn't see him because he was so still.

I use the function to rewind the video of the room. I watch Andrew lying on the floor of the room, grimacing at the weight on top of him. Five hours. He did it for five hours. So if I am to hold up my end of the bargain, I have to let him out now.

I take my time getting ready. I take a long, hot shower. The tension in my neck melts away as the warm water runs over my body. I know what I have to do next. And I'm ready.

I put on a comfortable T-shirt and a pair of jeans. I gather my dirty-blond hair back into a ponytail and slide Andrew's phone into my pocket. Then I pick up something that I grabbed from the garage yesterday and hide it in my other pocket.

I climb up the creaky steps to the attic. I've climbed up here enough times that I've noticed not every step creaks. Only certain ones. The second step is very loud, for example. And the top step.

When I get to the top, I rap on the door. I look down at his phone, at the color image of the room. He doesn't move from the bed.

Worry prickles the base of my neck. Andrew hasn't had anything to drink in about twelve hours. He must be feeling pretty weak by now. I remember how I was feeling yesterday when I was starved for water. What if he's unconscious? What then?

But then Andrew stirs on the mattress. I watch as he struggles into a sitting position and rubs his eyes with the balls of his hands.

"Andrew," I say. "I'm back."

He lifts his eyes and looks directly at the camera. I shiver, imagining exactly what he would do to me if I opened this door. If I opened the door, he would drag me in there by my ponytail.

He would make me do horrible things before he let me out. If he *ever* let me out.

He rises unsteadily to his feet. He walks over to the door and collapses against it. "I did it. Let me out."

Yeah. Right.

"So here's the thing," I say. "The video feed didn't come through from overnight. Frustrating, right? So I'm afraid you're going to have to—"

"*I'm not doing it again.*" His face is bright pink, and it isn't from the pepper spray. "You need to let me out *right now*, Millie. I'm not joking around."

"I'm going to let you out." I pause. "Just not *yet*."

Andrew takes a step back, staring at the door. Then he takes another step back. And another. And then he starts running.

He rams himself at the door so hard, it shakes on his hinges. But it doesn't budge.

Then he starts backing up again. Shit.

"Listen," I say. "I'm going to let you out. There's just one other thing you need to do."

"Fuck you. I don't believe you."

He rams himself at the door again. It shakes, but it doesn't splinter. The house is relatively new and well-made. I wonder if he is capable of knocking the door down. Maybe at his best, when he's well hydrated. But not now. And it would be hard to knock it down from the inside because that's where the hinges are.

He's breathing hard now. He leans against the door, trying to catch his breath. His face is even redder than it was before. I don't think he has it in him to break the door down. "What do you want me to do?" he manages.

I pull the object I grabbed from the garage out of my pocket. I found it in Andrew's tool kit. It's a pair of pliers. I slide it under the gap below the door.

On the other side of the door, he reaches down and picks up

the pliers. He turns them back and forth. He frowns. "I don't understand. What do you want me to do?"

"Well," I say, "it was just so hard to tell exactly how long you had those books on top of you. This will be easier. A one-time deal."

"I don't understand."

"It's simple. If you want to get out of the room, all you have to do is pull out one of your teeth."

I watch Andrew's face on the screen. His lips pull into a grimace and he throws the pliers on the floor. "You're joking. There's no way. I'm not doing that."

"I think," I say, "that another few hours without water and you might feel differently."

He takes another few steps back again. He's summoning all his strength. He runs at the door and rams against it as hard as he can. Once again, it shakes but doesn't budge. I watch as he draws back a fist and slams it against the wooden door.

Andrew howls with pain. Honestly, he would've been better off just pulling out a tooth. At the bar where I used to work, a guy got drunk and punched the wall, and he broke a bone in his hand. I wouldn't be surprised if Andrew has done the same.

"Let me out!" he screams at me. "Let me out of this fucking room *right now*."

"I'll let you out. You know what you have to do."

He's cradling his right hand with his left. He falls to his knees, almost doubled over. I watch on the phone screen as he picks up the pliers with his left hand. I hold my breath as he brings them to his mouth.

Is he going to do it? I can't stand this. I close my eyes, unable to watch.

He howls with agony. It's the same sound Duncan made when I brought that paperweight down on his skull. My eyes fly open and Andrew is still on the screen. He's still on his knees. I watch as he bows his head and bawls like a little baby.

He's close to breaking point. He can't stand it. He's willing to rip his own teeth out of his mouth just to get out of this room.

He has no idea this is just the beginning.

FIFTY-EIGHT

NINA

Something has gone wrong.

I feel it the second I pull up in front of Andrew's house. Something terrible has happened inside that house. I sense it with every fiber of my being.

I agreed to return here on one condition. Enzo was to stay with Cece and *protect her with his life*. There was nobody else in the world I would trust with my daughter. I know a lot of women in this town, and every single one of them was taken in by my husband's charm. I wouldn't trust any of them not to hand her over to him.

But that means I am here alone.

The last time I was here was a week ago, but it feels like an eternity. I park outside the gates, on the street behind Millie's car. I crouch down behind her vehicle and notice the red mark Enzo made on her tire. It's still there. Is it in the same place it was yesterday and the day before? I have no idea.

"Nina? Is that you?"

It's Suzanne. I straighten up, backing away from Millie's car. She is standing on the sidewalk, tilting her head quizzically at me. The last time I saw her, she looked downright skeletal, but it seems like she's lost even more weight.

"Is everything okay, Nina?" Suzanne asks.

I plaster a smile on my lips. "Yes. Of course. Why wouldn't it be?"

"We were supposed to have lunch the other day and you never showed. So I popped over to check on you."

Right. My weekly lunches with Suzanne. If there's one thing I won't miss about this life, it's that. "Sorry. I guess I forgot."

Suzanne purses her lips. I'll never forget the way she nodded sympathetically at me while I confessed everything Andy had done to me, then turned around and ratted me out. She chose to believe him over me. You don't forget that sort of betrayal.

"I heard a terrible rumor," she says. "I heard you moved out. That you left Andy. Or that he..."

"That he dumped me for the *maid*?" I catch the expression on Suzanne's face and I know I've hit the nail on the head. Everybody in town is talking about us. "I'm afraid it isn't true. The rumor mill has it wrong yet again. I was just picking Cece up at her camp, that's all."

"Oh." There's a flash of disappointment on Suzanne's face. She was hoping for a bit of juicy gossip. "Well, I'm happy to hear that. I was worried about you."

"Absolutely nothing to worry about." My cheeks are starting to hurt from smiling. "Now I've had a long trip, so if you'll excuse me..."

Suzanne follows me with her eyes as I head down the walkway to my front door. I'm sure she has a lot of questions whirling around her head. For example, if I went to pick up Cecelia at camp, where is she? And why didn't I park in the garage instead of on the street? But I don't have time to explain myself to this terrible woman.

I have to figure out what happened with Millie and Andy.

The first floor of my house is dark. Since the last time I was here, Andy told me to get out of his house, I start by ringing the doorbell instead of bounding inside. And then I wait for somebody to let me in.

After two minutes, I'm still standing there.

Finally, I take my key ring out of my purse. I've done this motion so many times before. Grab the keys, find the copper one with the letter A etched on it, fit it in the lock. The door to my former home swings open.

Unsurprisingly, it's dark inside the house. I don't hear a sound.

"Andy?" I call out.

No answer.

I walk over to the door to our garage. I push it open and Andy's BMW is sitting there. Of course, that doesn't rule out the fact that Andy and Millie took a trip together. They could've taken a taxi to LaGuardia. That's what Andy usually does. I bet they decided to take a spontaneous vacation together.

Except in my heart, I know they didn't.

"Andy?" I call out, louder this time. "Millie?"

Nothing.

I walk over to the stairwell. I peer up to the second floor, trying to detect any movement. I don't see anything. Yet it feels like someone is in here.

I start to climb the stairs. My legs are shaking underneath me and there is a real possibility they might give out, but I keep walking. I keep going until I get to the second floor.

"Andy?" I swallow a lump in my throat. "Please... If anyone is here, just answer me..."

When I don't get a response, I start checking the rooms. The master bedroom—empty. The guest room—empty. Cece's room—empty. The theater—also empty.

There's only one more place to look.

The door to the stairwell of the attic is open. The lighting has always been horrible in that stairwell. I grip the banister and look up to the top of the stairs. Someone is out there. I'm sure of it.

Millie must be locked in there. Andy must have done it to her.

But where is Andy then? Why is his car here if he isn't?

My legs barely support me as I climb the fourteen steps to the attic landing. At the end of the hallway is the room where I spent so many horrible days throughout my marriage. There's a light on in the room. It's coming from under the door.

"Don't worry, Millie," I murmur. "I'm going to help you."

Enzo was right. I should never have left her here. I thought she was stronger than me, but I was wrong. And now anything that happens to her is on my conscience. I hope she's okay. I'm going to get her out of here.

I dig the key to the attic door out of my purse. I fit the key into the lock and let the door swing open.

FIFTY-NINE

NINA

"Oh God," I whisper.

The light is on in the attic, like I thought. Those two lightbulbs are flickering on the ceiling. The bulbs need to be changed, but there's enough light to see Andy.

What used to be Andy, that is.

For a solid sixty seconds, all I can do is stare. Then I lean forward and retch. Good thing I was too nervous to eat any breakfast this morning.

"Hello, Nina."

I nearly have a heart attack at the sound of the voice coming from behind me. I was so sickened by the sight in front of me, I didn't even hear the footsteps on the stairs to the attic. I whirl around and there she is. Millie. Holding up a bottle of pepper spray, pointed at my face.

"Millie," I gasp.

Her hands are shaking and her face is very pale. It's like looking into a mirror. But her eyes are filled with fire.

"Put the pepper spray down," I say as calmly as I can. She doesn't comply. "I'm not going to hurt you—I promise." I glance over at the body on the floor then back at Millie. "How long has he been here?"

"Five days?" Her voice has a blank quality. "Six? I've lost count."

"He's dead." I say it as a statement, but it comes out more like a question. "How long has he been dead?"

Millie keeps the pepper spray trained on me and I'm scared to make any quick movements. I know what this girl is capable of. "Do you think he's definitely dead?" she asks.

"I can check? If you want?"

She hesitates, then nods.

I make slow movements because I don't want to get sprayed—I know all too well what it's like to get doused with pepper spray. I bend down beside my husband's body on the floor. He does not look alive. His eyes are cracked open, his cheeks are sunken, and his lips are parted. His chest isn't moving. But the worst part is all the dried blood around his mouth and on his white shirt. His lips are parted and several of his teeth are gone. I suppress the urge to gag.

Even so, when I reach out to check his pulse on his neck, I expect him to grab my wrist. But he doesn't. He is completely still. When I press on his pulse, I feel nothing.

"He's gone," I say.

Millie stares at me a moment, then lowers the pepper spray. She sinks onto the cot and buries her face in her hands. It's like she's just realized the enormity of what's happened. What she's done. "Oh God. Oh no..."

"Millie..."

"You know what this means." She lifts her bloodshot eyes to look at me. The rage is gone and all that's left is fear. "That's it. I'm going back to prison for the rest of my life."

Tears run down her cheeks and her shoulders shake silently —it's the same way Cece cries when she doesn't want anyone to know. Millie looks painfully young all of a sudden. She's just a girl.

And that's when I make up my mind.

I sit beside her on the cot and put my arm gingerly around her shoulders. "No, you're not going to prison."

"What are you talking about, Nina?" She raises her tear-streaked face. "I killed him! I let him die locked in this room for a week! How does that *not* mean I'm going to jail?"

"Because," I say, "you weren't even here."

She wipes her eyes with the back of her hand. "What are you talking about?"

My darling, Cece, please forgive me for what I'm about to do. "You're going to leave here. I'll tell the police I was here all week. I'll say I gave you the week off."

"But—"

"It's the only way," I say sharply. "I have a chance. You don't. I... I've already been hospitalized for mental health issues. Worse comes to worst..." I take a deep breath. "I'll go back to the psychiatric hospital."

Millie frowns, her nose pink. "You were the one who left me the pepper spray, weren't you?"

I nod.

"You were hoping I would kill him."

I nod again.

"So why didn't you just kill him yourself?"

I wish there was an easy answer to that question. I was worried about getting caught. I was worried about going to jail. I was worried about what my daughter would do without me.

But what it really comes down to is that I just *couldn't*. I didn't have it in me to take his life. And I did something terrible: I tried to trick Millie into killing him.

Which she did.

And now she could spend the rest of her life paying for it if I don't do something to help her.

"Please get out while you can, Millie." Tears prick at my eyes. "Go. Before I change my mind."

She doesn't have to be told again. She scrambles to her feet and hurries out of the room. Her footsteps disappear down the stairs. And then the front door slams shut, leaving me alone in the house—just me and Andy, who is staring up at the ceiling with his dead eyes. It's over. It's really over. And there's only one thing left to do.

I pick up my phone and call the police.

SIXTY

NINA

If I leave this house, it will be in handcuffs. I can't see any other way around it.

I remain on my leather sofa, clutching my knees, wondering if it will be the last time I sit here, while I wait for the detective to come back downstairs. My purse is sitting on the coffee table, and I grab it impulsively. I probably should just be sitting here quietly, like a good little murder suspect, but I can't help it. I pull out my phone and bring up my list of recent calls. I select the first number on the list.

"Nina? What is going on?" Enzo's voice is filled with concern. "What is happening over there?"

"The police are still here," I choke out. "I... it doesn't look good. For me. They think..."

I don't want to say the words out loud. They think I killed Andy. And I didn't kill him outright. He died of dehydration. But they think I am responsible.

I could end this. I could tell them about Millie. But I won't.

"I'll testify for you," he says. "What he did to you. I saw you locked up there."

He means it. He'll do anything he can to help me. But how

meaningful will testimony be from a man who will almost certainly be painted as my secret lover? And I can't even deny it. I did sleep with Enzo.

"Is Cece okay?" I ask.

"She's fine."

I close my eyes, trying to steady my breathing. "Is she watching TV?"

"TV? No, no, no. I teach her Italian. She is a natural."

Despite everything, I laugh. Although it's a weak sound. "Can I speak to her?"

There's a pause and Cece comes on the other line. "*Ciao, Mama*!"

I swallow. "Hello, sweetheart. How are you?"

"*Bene*. When are you coming to pick me up?"

"Soon," I lie. "Just keep working on your Italian, and I'll be there as soon as I can." I take a breath. "I... I love you."

"I love you too, Mom!"

Detective Connors is descending the stairs, his footsteps like gunshots. I shove my phone back into my purse and drop it back down on the coffee table. Apparently, he's taken a closer look at Andy's body. And I'm sure he has a whole new set of questions. I can see it all over his face as he sits down again across from me.

"So," he says. "Do you know anything about the bruising on your husband's body?"

"Bruising?" I ask, genuinely confused. I know about the missing teeth, but I didn't press Millie for further details about what happened in that attic room.

"There are deep purple bruises all over his lower belly," Connors says. "And all over his... genitals. They're almost black."

"Oh..."

"How do you think they got there?"

I raise my eyebrows. "Do you think I beat him up?" The

idea is laughable. Andy was taller than me by quite a bit, and his body was solid muscle. Mine is not.

"I have no idea what happened up there." His eyes meet mine, and I try not to look away. "Your story is that your husband must have gotten locked in the attic accidentally, and you somehow didn't realize he was gone. Is that right?"

"I thought he was on a business trip," I say. "He usually takes a taxi to the airport."

"And there were no text messages or calls between the two of you during this time, but that didn't concern you," he points out. "Furthermore, in talking to his parents, it sounds like he had asked you to move out last week."

I can't deny that part. "Yes, that's right. That's why we didn't talk."

"And what about this Wilhelmina Calloway?" He pulls a small pad of paper out of his pocket and consults his note. "She was working for you, wasn't she?"

I lift a shoulder. "I gave her the week off. My daughter was off at camp, so I felt like we didn't need her. I haven't seen her all week."

I'm sure they're going to try to contact Millie, but I'm trying to take her off the suspect list as best I can. It's the least I can do after what I did to her.

"So you're telling me that a grown man managed to get himself locked in a room in the attic—without his phone—even though the room only locks from the outside?" Connors' eyebrows inch up to his hairline. "And while he was in the room, he randomly decided to pull out four of his teeth?"

When he says it that way...

"Mrs. Winchester," the detective says. "Do you really believe your husband is the sort of man who would do something like that?"

I lean back against the sofa, trying not to let on how much my body is trembling. "Maybe. You didn't know him."

"Actually," he says, "that isn't entirely true."

I look up sharply. "Excuse me?"

Oh God. This just gets worse and worse. The detective with his graying hair is the right age to be another of Andy's father's golfing buddies. Or some other recipient of the family's amazing generosity. My wrists start to tingle, anticipating the handcuffs being snapped around them.

"I never knew him personally," Connors says. "But my daughter did."

"Your... daughter?"

He nods. "Her name is Kathleen Connors. Actually, small world—she and your husband were engaged a long time ago."

I blink at him. Kathleen. The fiancée who Andy broke up with before the two of us got together. The one I tried to find so many times, but kept coming up empty-handed. Kathleen is this man's daughter. But what does that mean?

He lowers his voice several notches until I have to strain to hear. "The breakup was rough on her. She wouldn't talk about it. Still won't. She moved far away after that and she even changed her name. She hasn't been out on a date with a man since."

My heart speeds up. "Oh. I..."

"I always wondered what exactly Andrew Winchester did to my daughter." He presses his lips together until they form a straight line. "So when I transferred out here about a year ago and started poking around, I thought it was interesting that you claimed he had been locking you up in the attic, but nobody could verify your story was real. Although truthfully, it looks like nobody did very much to try. The Winchesters used to have a lot of pull out here before they moved down to Florida, especially with some of the cops." He pauses. "But not me."

My mouth is too dry to get any words out. I just stare at him, my jaw hanging open.

"If you ask me," he says, "that attic is a hazard. Seems like it's far too easy to get locked up there." He leans back again, his voice returning to a normal volume. "It's a shame that happened to your husband. I'm sure my buddy in the coroner's office will also agree. It'll have to be a cautionary tale, won't it?"

"Yes," I finally manage. "A cautionary tale."

Detective Connors gives me one last long look. And then he goes back upstairs to join his colleagues. And I realize something incredible.

I'm not going to walk out of here in handcuffs after all.

SIXTY-ONE

NINA

I never thought I would be attending Andy's wake.

Of all the ways I thought this would end, I never truly believed it would end with Andy being dead. I knew in my heart I didn't have the nerve to kill him, and even if I tried, he seemed immortal. He seemed like one of those people who would just never die. Even now, as I look down at his handsome face in the open maple wood casket, his lips pressed closed to hide the four missing teeth Millie forced him to pull from his gums, I'm certain that his eyes will pop open as he comes back to life for one final scare.

You really thought I was dead? Well, surprise, surprise—I'm not! Up to the attic you go, Nina.

No. I won't. Never again.

Never again.

"Nina." A hand drops onto my shoulder. "How are you doing?"

I lift my eyes. It's Suzanne. My former best friend. The woman who delivered me right back to Andy, when I told her what a monster he was.

"I'm hanging in there," I say. I clutch the tissues in my right hand, which are mainly just for show. I've only squeezed out a single tear the entire day, and that was when I saw Cecelia dressed in a simple black dress I bought her for the funeral. She's sitting beside me in that same dress, her blond hair mussed. Andy would have hated it.

"It was such a shock." Suzanne scoops my hand into her own, and it takes a lot of self-restraint not to pull away. "Such a terrible accident."

There is sympathy and pity in her eyes. She's glad it was my husband and not her own. *Poor, Nina, what bad luck she has.* She has no idea.

"Terrible," I murmur.

Suzanne gives Andy one last look, then she moves on. From the casket and with her life. I suspect that the funeral tomorrow might be one of the last times I ever see her. And it doesn't make me even the slightest bit sad.

I stare down at my simple black pumps, drinking in the quiet of the viewing room. I hate talking to mourners, accepting their sympathy, pretending I'm devastated that this monster is dead. I can't wait for this to be over so I can move on with my life. Tomorrow will be the last time I'll have to play the part of the sad widow.

I look up at the sounds of footsteps at the door. Enzo casts a long shadow through the doorway, and his steps sound like gunshots in the quiet funeral parlor. He's wearing a dark suit, and as handsome as he was working in my yard, he looks about a hundred times better in the suit. His dark, moist eyes meet mine.

"I'm so sorry," he says quietly. "I can't."

My heart sinks. He isn't telling me he's sorry because of Andy. Neither of us are sorry about that. He's sorry because yesterday I asked him if when this is all over, he might come with me to live across the country on the west coast—far away from here. I never expected him to say yes, but his decline of my offer still makes me sad. This man helped save my life—he's my hero. Him and Millie.

"You will have fresh start." A small crease forms between his eyebrows. "Better this way."

"Yes," I say.

He's right. There are too many terrible memories between the two of us. It's better to start fresh. But that doesn't mean I won't miss him. And I will never, ever forget what he did for me.

"Keep an eye on Millie, okay?" I say.

He nods. "I will. I promise."

He reaches out to touch my hand one last time. Like Suzanne, I'll probably never see him again. I've already put the house Andy and I shared on the market. Cece and I have been staying at a hotel because I can't bear to walk into that place. I'm about eighty percent sure our old house is haunted.

I look over at Cecelia, who is squirming in a seat a few feet away from me. We slept in the hotel room last night, sharing a queen-size bed, her skinny body pressed against mine. I could've gotten an extra bed for the room, but she wants to be close to me. She still doesn't quite understand what happened to the man she called her father and she hasn't asked. She's just relieved he's gone.

"Enzo," I say, "would you take Cece? She's been here a long time and she's probably hungry. Maybe take her to get some food."

He nods and holds out a hand to my daughter. "Come, Cece. We get chicken nuggets and milkshakes."

Cecelia hops out of her seat instantly—she doesn't need to be asked twice. She's been good about sitting with me here, but she's still a young girl. I should handle this by myself.

A few minutes after Enzo leaves with Cece, the doors to the funeral parlor swing open once again. I instinctively take a step back when I see who is standing at the door.

It's the Winchesters.

I hold my breath as Evelyn and Robert Winchester enter the room. It's the first time I've seen them since Andy's death, but I knew this moment was coming. They had come back from Florida for the summer only a few weeks earlier, but Evelyn hadn't stopped by yet. I spoke to her only once when she called me to ask if I needed help organizing the funeral. I told her I didn't.

Except the real truth was I wasn't excited to talk to her after being responsible for the death of her only son.

Detective Connors made good on all his promises. Andy's death was ruled an accident, and neither I nor Millie was ever investigated. The story was that Andy accidentally got locked in the attic while I was away and died from dehydration. None of that explains the bruises and the missing teeth though. Detective Connors had friends in the coroner's office, but the Winchesters are one of the most powerful and influential families in the state.

Do they know? Do they have any idea I'm responsible for his death?

Evelyn and Robert stride across the room, in the direction of the casket. I hardly know Robert, who is handsome like his son and wearing a dark suit today. Evelyn is also dressed in black, which contrasts sharply with the white of her hair, and also her white pumps. Robert's eyes are puffy, but Evelyn looks immaculate, like she just had a spa treatment.

I drop my eyes as they approach me. I only look up when Robert clears his throat. "Nina," he says in his deep, scratchy voice.

I swallow. "Robert..."

"Nina." He clears his throat. "I want you to know..."

We know you killed our son. We know what you did, Nina. And we won't rest until you spend the rest of your life rotting in prison.

"I want you to know that Evelyn and I are always there for you," he says. "We know you're all alone, and anything you need—you and Cecelia—you just have to ask."

"Thank you, Robert." My eyes well up just a little bit. Robert was always a nice enough man, if not the greatest father of all time. From what Andy told me about him, he wasn't around that much when he was a kid. Mostly worked while Evelyn raised him. "I appreciate that."

Robert reaches out and gently touches his son's shoulder. I wonder if he had any idea what a monster Andy was. He had to have some idea. Or maybe Andy was just that good at hiding it. After all, I had no idea until I was scraping my fingernails against the wood of the attic door.

Robert claps a hand over his mouth. He shakes his head and grunts "Excuse me" to his wife, then he hurries out of the room. Leaving me alone with Evelyn.

Of all the people I wouldn't want to be alone with today, Evelyn tops the list. Evelyn isn't dumb. She must have known the problems I had in my marriage. Like Robert, she might not have known what he did to me, but she must have sensed the friction between us.

She must have sensed how I really felt about him.

"Nina," she says drily.

"Evelyn," I say.

She looks down at Andy's face. I try to read her expression, but it's hard. I don't know if it's all the Botox or if she always looked that way.

"You know," she says, "I spoke to an old friend at the police station about Andy."

My stomach clenches. According to Detective Connors, the case is closed. Andy always taunted me about an alleged letter to the station police that would be sent over in case of his death, but no letter ever materialized. I was never sure if it was because there never was a letter or if the detective got rid of it.

"Oh?" is all I can manage.

"Yes," she murmurs. "They told me how he looked when they found him." Her shrewd eyes bore into me. "They told me about his missing teeth."

Oh God. She knows.

She definitely knows. Anyone aware of the state of Andy's mouth when the police found him had to know that his death was not accidental. Nobody yanks their own teeth out with pliers. Not willingly.

It's all over. When I walk out of this funeral home, the police will probably be waiting for me. They will snap handcuffs on my wrists and read me my rights. And then I'll spend the rest of my life in prison.

I won't tell anyone about Millie though. She doesn't deserve to be dragged down too. She gave me a chance to be free. I'm going to leave her out of it.

"Evelyn," I choke out. "I… I don't…"

Her eyes drift back to her son's face, at his long eyelashes, closed forever. She purses her lips. "I always told him," she says, "how important dental hygiene is. I told him he had to brush every night, and when he didn't, there would be a punishment. There's always a punishment when you break the rules."

What? What is she saying?

"Evelyn…"

"If you don't take care of your teeth," she continues, "then you lose the privilege to *have* teeth."

"Evelyn?"

"Andy knew that. He knew that was my rule." She lifts her eyes. "When I pulled out one of his baby teeth with pliers, I thought he understood."

I stare at her, too afraid to speak. Too afraid of the next words that will leave her mouth. And when they finally come, it takes my breath away:

"It's such a shame," she says, "that he never really learned. I'm glad you stepped up and taught him a lesson."

My jaw is hanging open as Evelyn makes one last adjustment to her son's white shirt collar. Then she walks out of the funeral home, leaving me behind.

EPILOGUE

MILLIE

"Tell me about yourself, Millie."

I lean against the marble kitchen counter across from Lisa Killeffer. Lisa herself is immaculate this morning, her black hair shiny and pulled into an elaborate French knot behind her head, the buttons on her cream-colored short-sleeved blouse glimmering in the skylights of what appears to be a newly renovated kitchen.

If I get this job, it will be my first in nearly a year. I've had a few odd jobs here and there since what happened at the Winchester house, but I've been living off the deposit of a year's salary that Nina made to my bank account shortly after Andrew's death was ruled accidental.

I still don't quite understand how she managed that one.

Well..." I begin. "I grew up in Brooklyn. I've had a lot of jobs doing housework for people, as you can see from my resume. And I love children."

"Wonderful!"

Lisa's lips spread into a smile. Her enthusiasm since the moment I walked in here has been surprising, given she must have had dozens of candidates applying for this housekeeper job. I didn't even apply for this one. It was Lisa who contacted me on the website where I placed an ad offering my cleaning and nannying services.

The salary is great, which isn't surprising, because this house reeks of wealth. The kitchen boasts all the newest appliances, and I'm fairly sure the stove can cook dinner itself from scratch without any intervention. I really want this job, and I'm trying to project confidence. I try to think of the text message from Enzo that I received this morning:

Good luck, Millie. Remember they will be lucky to have you.

And then:

See you tonight after you get the job.

"What are you looking for exactly?" I ask her.

"Oh, the usual." Lisa leans against the kitchen counter next to me and tugs at the collar of her blouse. "Somebody to keep the house clean. Laundry. Some light cooking."

"I can do that," I say, although my situation hasn't changed much from a year ago. I still have my background check issue. My prison record will never disappear.

Lisa's hands absently go to the block of knives on the kitchen counter. Her fingers toy with the handle of one of the knives, and she lifts it out just enough for the blade to glint in the overhead lights. I shift between my feet, suddenly uncomfortable. Finally, she says, "Nina Winchester recommended you very highly."

My mouth drops open. That's the last thing I expected her to say. I haven't heard from Nina in a long time. She moved to California with Cecelia soon after everything wrapped up with Andrew's death. She's not on social media, but a few months ago she texted me a selfie of her and Cecelia at the beach together, looking tanned and happy, along with a few words:

Thank you for this.

So I guess her other way of thanking me is to recommend me for housekeeping jobs. I'm feeling decidedly more optimistic that Lisa will hire me.

"I'm so glad to hear that," I say. "Nina was... wonderful to work for."

Lisa nods, her fingers still toying with that knife. "I agree. She *is* wonderful."

She smiles again, but there's something off about her face. She tugs at the collar of her blouse again with her free hand, and as the material shifts, that's when I see it.

A dark purple bruise on her upper arm.

In the shape of somebody's fingers.

I look over her shoulder at the refrigerator. There's a magnet on there, featuring a photograph of Lisa with a tall, stocky man, whose eyes are locked with the camera. I imagine that man's fingers wrapping around Lisa's skinny arm, digging in hard enough to leave those deep purple marks.

My heart pounds enough that I feel dizzy. And now I finally get it. I understand why Nina recommended me so highly to this woman. She knows me. Maybe even better than I know myself.

"So"—Lisa slides the knife back into the wooden block and straightens up, her blue eyes wide and anxious—"can you help me, Millie?"

"Yes," I say. "I believe I can."

A LETTER FROM FREIDA

Dear readers,

I want to say a huge thank you for choosing to read *The Housemaid*. If you did enjoy it, and want to keep up to date with all my latest releases, just sign up at the following link. Your email address will never be shared and you can unsubscribe at any time.

freidamcfadden.com

I hope you loved *The Housemaid* and if you did, I would be very grateful if you could write a review. I'd love to hear what you think, and it makes such a difference helping new readers to discover one of my books for the first time.

Thanks!

Freida

KEEP IN TOUCH WITH FREIDA

facebook.com/freidamcfaddenauthor
x.com/Freida_McFadden
instagram.com/fizzziatrist
goodreads.com/freidamcfadden
amazon.com/Freida-McFadden/e/B00ELQLN2I
bookbub.com/authors/freida-mcfadden

ACKNOWLEDGMENTS

I want to thank Bookouture for taking a chance on my manuscript and introducing my work to your audience. A special thanks to my editor, Ellen Gleeson, who has an amazing insight into my books! Thank you also to my beta readers, Kate and Nelle. Thank you to Zack for the excellent advice. And as always, thank you to my incredibly supportive readers—I'm doing this for you! And thanks to Val for your eagle eye. I'm also very appreciative to Daniel for assistance with book discussion questions and promotion!